PRESSURE

A LEXI MILLS THRILLER

BRIAN SHEA
STACY LYNN MILLER

SEVERN RIVER
PUBLISHING

PRESSURE

Severn River Publishing
www.SevernRiverBooks.com

This is a work of fiction. Names, characters, businesses, places, events and incidents are either the products of the author's imagination or used in a fictitious manner. Any resemblance to actual persons, living or dead, or actual events is purely coincidental.

ISBN: 978-1-64875-317-6 (Paperback)

ALSO BY THE AUTHORS

Lexi Mills Thrillers
Fuze
Proximity
Impact
Pressure
Remote
Flashpoint

BY BRIAN SHEA
Boston Crime Thrillers
The Nick Lawrence Series
Sterling Gray FBI Profiler Series

Never miss a new release!
To find out more about the authors and their books, visit

severnriverbooks.com/series/lexi-mills

1

The writing was on the wall. Unless Milo Tilton produced another game plan, the empire he'd built over the last twelve years would crumble soon. He stepped to his office window, sipping on his daily late afternoon dose of Dr. Pepper. The carbonation had lost its pop, and the ice had melted, with only pebble-sized cubes remaining. The drink was a metaphor for the state of his life's work—flat and unsatisfying.

Adjusting his stare from the recreational yard, Milo focused on the transportation gate of the Harrington Regional Detention Center and watched it roll open. The return of only one prison bus symbolized the untenable sea change since the election. Last June, at least six buses with three hundred sixty prisoners would have driven through the gate at the end of the workday. Everyone had profited, from the farmers and ranchers who paid for the cheap prison workers to the deputies, guards, county officials, and one amicable district judge paid to look the other way. But the election had swept in a new sheriff and district attorney on top of a newly appointed judge, changing everything. The local gold mine of cheap labor was drying up, and he was losing money at this point. Milo needed to do something drastic soon.

He downed the rest of his flat soda, put on his suit jacket, and snatched up his leather briefcase before leaving his warden's office. Going home wasn't his favorite part of the day since things had gone south, but tomorrow was payday for his business partners. If he didn't distribute the money in his satchel on time, the entire venture would unravel quicker than a stripper's costume.

The housekeeper's car was gone when Milo pulled into his circular driveway. With any luck, his nag of a wife would be passed out so he could pour himself a scotch and assemble the envelopes in peace. But the absence of music or the television blaring after opening the front door was a much better scenario. Perhaps Nichole wasn't home. Perhaps she'd taken up the new golf pro on his offer for private lessons atop his office desk. What did he care? Milo had his own distractions and stayed in the marriage for self-preservation. He was losing money and couldn't afford a hefty off-the-book settlement. As long as he kept Nichole in the lifestyle she'd become accustomed to, she'd keep her mouth shut. At least that was the agreement.

He stepped inside, discovering the kitchen and living room unoccupied and the electronics turned off. All were good signs. Twenty years ago, when the marriage was fresh, Milo would have searched the house and yard until he found his bride and kissed her on the lips. But he couldn't remember the last time he'd kissed his wife, let alone wanted to. Making money had occupied his day from sunrise to sunset for the last dozen years and spending it had dominated hers.

Confident a confrontation was unlikely, he headed to his home office. Halfway down the hallway, light spilling through the open door warned him he'd found his wife, and another argument might be on the evening's agenda. If Milo didn't need the ledger in his wall safe, he'd turn on his heel, pour himself a stiff drink, and hit the hot tub.

He took a deep, calming breath and stepped inside. The safe was open, the ledger was on the desk, and Nichole was pouring through it with a cocktail glass in her hand. The once competent bookkeeper looked perplexed, but that wasn't his greatest concern. Flipping the page, Nichole looked like she was about to blow.

"I can explain." Milo hoped to defuse the argument before it started.

Nichole popped her head up. Her eyes were fiery. "When were you going to tell me about the drop in business?"

"When I thought I couldn't turn the tide." *Or never,* he thought.

"You're a fool to think Sheriff Jessup or that hussy D.A. Charlene Ford will come around."

"Everyone has a price, Nichole. I just haven't found theirs yet."

"And what if they can't be bought?"

"Then I leverage their weak spot."

"And what if they don't have one? We're already losing money." Negative Nichole had a doom's day scenario to counter every hopeful game plan. It was her nature to contradict everything Milo said or did unless the money kept flowing.

And who was this *we* stuff? He'd come up with the idea of using the sheriff and his deputies to scare off the migrants, making the local ranchers and farmers desperate for laborers. He'd come up with the idea of using detainees as cheap labor and charging the ranchers and farmers a third of their typical cost. He'd come up with the idea of cooking the official books while paying the detainees the standard federal prison wage while incarcerated—a fraction of what he took in. Even after paying everyone to turn a blind eye, the profits were insane. He'd come up with the idea of Nichole running an all-cash nail salon to launder the cash. Now he was in the red.

"I'm painfully aware we have a negative cash flow. I'm using my reserves to cover the difference until I fix things." Milo placed his briefcase atop the corner of his desk and removed the first bundle of twenties.

"You're depleting *our* reserves. Imagine my surprise when I opened the safe for the monthly salon deposit, and it wasn't there." Nichole tapped her perfectly manicured index finger against the ledger. "And this tells me we'll have to dig into our personal account within months unless you fix this."

"I know that, Nichole." He removed the remaining cash, a fraction of the typical haul before the election. When the new sheriff had visited the ranches and farms, demanding to see the contract with the prison, most of Milo's customers had gotten cold feet. They'd hired migrant workers who had reappeared in the county since local law enforcement had stopped scaring them away.

Nichole eyed the stacks of money. "It looks like things are looking up. That's not bad for a day's take."

"This is for the week." He poured himself a double of his finest scotch, downing it in two gulps. The burn didn't faze him. It stung a lot less than the reality biting at his heels.

"For Christ's sake, Milo." Nichole rose from his high-back leather desk chair, flapping her arms, prepared for one of her money rants. Her taste for designer and luxury everything was at the root of every lecture since he'd started the labor scheme. No matter how much he brought in, it was never enough. She couldn't let people see her in last year's Prada, let alone a three-year-old Mercedes. Everything had to be new with a hefty price tag.

Milo tuned her out and poured a second and another until he'd emptied the bottle. Amazingly, Nichole hadn't stopped and had barely taken a breath between insults. When the wave of alcohol-induced euphoria hit, he bent at the waist to search the lower cabinet of the built-in bar, but a firm grip on the back of his collar pulled him up.

"What the hell, Nichole?" He threw off her hold with a flip of his arm and continued his search for more scotch. Bingo! An unopened bottle of Johnnie Walker Blue.

"Don't you have anything to say for yourself?" She yanked his arm with the force of a tornado, sending Johnnie to the hardwood floor. A two-hundred-dollar bottle of his finest scotch lay in a puddle among broken shards of glass because his wife couldn't wait for a damn answer. "Well?" She balled her hands, placing them on her hips, her arms akimbo.

He detested her smug, superior expression. Without a single word, it said he could do nothing right. He was a disappointment in every respect because respect was the one thing she had never had for him. The pressure she put on him to live up to unrealistic expectations was too much, and something had to give.

He turned to walk away and address this when they were both sober, but Nichole spun him around again with the same look of disdain and unleashed another verbal beating. The third time was the charm. One more word would send him over the edge.

"Well?" she said again.

That was it. He'd had all he could take. Milo towered over her by eight inches and outweighed her by seventy-five pounds, but the disparity didn't stop him. He wrapped his sweaty hand around her skinny neck to make her shut up. She did. But the gasps wouldn't stop. He needed her to be quiet. He needed the room silent to think about how to handle the sheriff and the new district attorney. If he squeezed a little tighter, the noise should stop.

Milo pressed harder until Nichole's eyes bulged like a cartoon character. Her face turned an unnatural shade of purple. He smirked. He'd resented every arrogant expression directed at him over the last few years, but this one was his favorite. A few seconds longer, and he would never endure another verbal and visual offensive again.

The noise went silent.

Nichole's face stopped twitching. Her body went limp, becoming dead weight in his grip. Milo let go, letting her drop to the wood floor in a dull thud. Her legs lay awkwardly, one straight and one bent. One arm lay beneath her torso while the other curled lifelessly over her face. She remained still. Not even her chest moved to the involuntary rhythm of breathing. She was dead.

Reality struck him over the head. His nightmarish marriage was over, but now he faced the consequences of his outburst without a friendly sheriff at the helm. "Think, you idiot." The old sheriff would make this go away with little effort. Milo's only hope was to make it look like a burglar had killed Nichole during a home invasion robbery gone wrong.

He'd have until the housekeeper returned in the morning to create a believable scene, but he needed to get to work. The place needed to look like the burglar had rifled through the rooms and knocked Milo out when he came home. He started by transferring the cash, business ledger, and critical files to a floor safe in his office that Nichole never knew about, leaving the wall safe open to mislead the cops into thinking it was the only safe in the house. He then went from room to room upstairs, tearing apart drawers and closets and gathering a handful of valuable watches and jewelry he thought a burglar might take. Stowing them in the floor safe to keep them from the police was the ideal hiding place.

Satisfied that the upstairs looked like a whirlwind had ripped through the rooms, Milo descended the stairs to stage the main floor. Before starting, he remembered the home security system needed erasing. Walking down the hallway, he heard a noise. "What the hell?" If Nichole could, she would come back to life out of spite just to get in the last word. Or did Milo only render her unconscious? He'd had five minutes to savor the idea of a life without her nagging and thirst for spending, and it was the best future he could have imagined. The thought of that disappearing was more disappointing than his failed side business.

He took a disheartened breath but turned the corner to a shocking sight. He jerked to a stop as if he'd hit a wall, realizing his plans had to change. The trembling woman locked eyes with Milo. "Marta? You shouldn't be here."

"Do you know what happened? I found Mrs. Tilton dead," she said in a thick Hispanic accent.

He had to think fast. "Someone was here. I chased him off."

Marta squinted. "I didn't see anyone when I went out the side door to wait for my ride after hearing you two arguing."

"I wish you hadn't said that, Marta." Milo couldn't let a witness walk out of the house alive. His only weapon was the pillowcase in his hand containing the valuables he'd collected. He tipped the case upside down, emptying the contents onto the floor. Marta followed the items with her eyes before locking stares with him again. Milo wrapped one end of the case around a fist and then the other before taking a step toward Marta. Her eyes grew extra wide with fear.

Marta held up a cell phone in her right hand. "I've already called the police. They're on their way." She moved backward, and Milo followed her step for step until her bottom hit the edge of his wooden desk.

"I don't think so." He raised the pillowcase toward his chin, readying it to slip over her neck. Marta raised her arms high to block him. Her hands shook like a baby fresh out of the womb. In Milo's job as the warden, he'd incarcerated several detainees and prisoners accused of murder. He'd often wondered if he would quake in terror like Marta if faced with his impending death. Or would he confront it like a man and remain stoic?

Milo narrowed his eyes, summoning the courage for one more kill. Choking the life out of Nichole stemmed from years of needling and pent-up anger. But doing the same to Marta would be out of desperation. If she talked to the new sheriff, Milo would face a mountain of resistance in sweeping this under the rug. Killing her was necessary, but he had to make it believable. A burglar could conceivably surprise and choke one woman in the same room but not two. He would have to rough her up first to make it appear he'd knocked her out.

Milo took the final step forward.

A loud crash sounded at the front of the house. A voice shouted, "Police."

Marta yelled, "Help! In the office."

Milo's chest rose and fell to the realization the sheriff and Marta had him cornered and drained of options. He moved backward, concluding he'd have to take his chance on the Harrington justice system and his old friend Judge Powell. *Clem will get me out of this*, he thought. He had to.

2

Lexi finished the final leg of her three-mile walk, ending at the south end of the Civic Garden, and waited for the distinctive yellow and white Dallas metro bus to pass before darting across the street. The north-facing art deco Santa Fe building cast long afternoon shadows. If she had completed her traditional two-mile run, she would have welcomed the respite from the warm fall temperature, but the walk had her barely breaking a sweat. The effort hardly seemed worth her time, she thought, before glancing at the heart rate app on her smartwatch. One hundred twenty beats per minute was a decent workout, but it still didn't convince her that walking was a suitable exercise for her. It might cost her precious speed in a footrace.

When Nita had suggested walking as an alternative to running to stave off early-onset knee arthritis in her amputated leg, she'd left out one crucial point. The slower pace provided Lexi with time to think. Too much time. Thinking surfaced baggage-filled memories, and remembering made her doubt her choices. If she had known the pressure of leading Task Force Zero Impact would take an unbearable emotional toll, she might not have accepted FBI Deputy Director Maxwell Keene's challenge. Maybe she should stick to a workout requiring less thinking and more counting, like lifting weights, until she settled into fieldwork with the ATF.

Entering the building, Lexi ascended the stairs to the third floor, foregoing a shower since it was late in the workday. A spray or two of Febreze would keep her cubicle neighbors from searching for a late afternoon soda break until she went home. Before heading to her desk, Lexi strode past the equipment closet and stuck her head in her favorite supply clerk's cubicle. "Any word?"

Ronald spun on his rolling chair with a grin so devilish that Lexi thought he'd won the lottery. "It's in. I just finished adding it to our inventory."

"And which lucky explosives expert gets the new blast suit?" After working with Ronald for two years, one as the administrative chief, Lexi already knew the answer, but she wanted to make him think he'd kept her guessing. They had a friendship beyond the traditional officemate dynamic. When Lexi had first arrived at the Dallas office to rehab after becoming an amputee, she and Ronald were the only two on the floor who didn't do fieldwork, putting them in an exclusive club. They couldn't help developing a unique bond.

"My pod buddy, of course."

The new blast suit was fifteen pounds lighter than the older model in their inventory but provided a third more protection against shrapnel. And the demister fan in the helmet was virtually silent. The ATF had 195 explosive experts on staff but had purchased only 100 new suits. Every field office around the country would soon have explosives experts elbowing each other for a chance at the suit. And Ronald made sure headquarters sent one of the few smalls to their office.

"Thank you, pod buddy. You're the best." They really were two peas in a pod.

"It was a no-brainer. You're ATF royalty."

"I appreciate the suit,"—Lexi gave Ronald a two-finger salute—"but you can keep the crown." After losing three prisoners and two good federal officers in a single explosion on FBI property to the Raven, Lexi felt more like a failure than royalty. She'd let her guard down, thinking the threat to the task force had passed once she'd cut off the Gatekeepers' head. That mistake cost a good friend her life, showcasing the horrendous weight of leadership.

"Whatever you say, Lexi. I'll have the suit in your gear locker by tomorrow morning." Before she turned to leave, Ronald stared at her with curiosity. "It's good having you back, but you could have any assignment in the country. Why did you come back here?"

"To forget." But it didn't work.

Lexi continued through the maze of cubicles tall enough to camouflage her comings and goings, making her the stealthiest one on the floor. Entering her forty-eight square feet of usable space, she plopped down in her chair. After returning from the task force, her seating assignment was cruel not for its size but for its former occupant. No one wanted to backfill a desk of someone killed in the line of duty, but Lexi took it as the price of returning to her roots in a post-Tony Belcher world.

Her circumstance might have been palatable if Lexi didn't blame herself for Kris Faust's death. As her last official act as the task force leader, she'd tapped Kris to escort their last prisoners to Beaumont as a reward. She had thought being there in person to see their former boss begin his twenty-year sentence would be a gift after he'd duped Kris into giving him the intel that had kept Belcher one step ahead of them. But it had turned into the ultimate, irreversible punishment.

Lexi had intentionally not personalized the desk. The only non-governmental items in her cubicle were her backpack, gym bag, a box of tissues for hay fever season, and one souvenir. Lexi didn't intend to spend much time at her desk after returning to fieldwork, so bringing anything more would be meaningless.

Since leaving the task force fourteen days ago, awaiting her first ATF assignment, she'd completed the required recertifications from weapons qualifications and bomb suit wear on the range to sexual harassment training. The litany of annual explosive disposal tests online was pro forma. Lexi could describe any explosive inside and out and how to render it safe forward and backward by memory. But she enjoyed getting back to her roots, where her primary worry was establishing a big enough cordon to protect the rest of the agents and officers on the scene.

On one side of her desk sat two unlabeled folders, the only sign of official work aside from the laptop. She opened the folder that was two inches thick with papers of all shapes, sizes, and colors stuffed inside. Lexi had neatly organized everything she'd assembled on the Gatekeepers dating back to the first load of stolen nitro in Kansas City, documenting the breadth and depth of Tony Belcher's crimes and influence. The collection represented three years of work and a trail of lives cut short, starting with Trent Darby and ending with Kris Faust. Both were ATF explosives experts performing their duties, during which Lexi had a hand in their demise.

Lexi closed the Gatekeepers' folder and placed it in her bottom desk drawer, finally closing the book on Belcher. It was time to move on. But, as with Trent, Lexi wouldn't rest until the person responsible for killing Kris was dead or captured.

Her cell phone vibrated in her cargo pants' pocket. The unique ringtone told her who was calling, giving birth to a broad smile. While swiping the screen, Lexi opened the other folder. "Hey, sexy."

"Hey to you, too." Nita added a low, seductive tone to her voice.

"You looked extra delicious this morning in bed." Lexi closed her eyes briefly, recalling the show Nita had put on for her benefit, lingering longer than necessary while rummaging through the bottom dresser drawer. The absence of sleep shorts ultimately made her fifteen minutes late to work.

"And you *were* delicious this morning." Nita changed her voice from sexy to business-like on a dime. "But that's not why I'm calling."

"Well, that's disappointing."

"Sex isn't off the table tonight, but I called to say I picked up your black suit at the dry cleaners on the way home from work to save you the trip."

The back of Lexi's throat grew thick at the reason for her procrastination. She turned her tone solemn. "Thank you, Nita." Kris' funeral was tomorrow, and Lexi dreaded facing her parents. Whatever she said to the loved ones of the woman she'd ordered to her death, it wouldn't be enough.

Lexi focused on the one thing that would give Kris' sacrifice meaning. She scanned the few papers in the folder she'd assembled on the Raven, the arms dealer who built the dirty bomb that nearly killed her and Noah and might have left the Vegas Strip uninhabitable for years. She first learned about him through the Red Spades' second in command while he was in her custody, and her gut told her he was responsible for Kris' death.

Her eyes turned to the desk's interior corner where she kept her only souvenir from the task force. Without fingerprints or human DNA, it held no evidentiary value. But Lexi didn't need the FBI lab to tell her the black feather was from a raven. Nor did she need Kaplan Shaw, her intel specialist, to say it was likely from *the* Raven. When she had discovered it in the parking lot across the street from the prisoner transport explosion, she knew it was the Raven's calling card.

"Will you be home on time?" Nita asked. "I was thinking takeout tonight."

"Chinese?"

"What else?"

Lexi's office phone rang. "Hey, I gotta go. I have another call. I'll pick up dinner and see you around six. Love you." She hung up, glancing at the caller ID on the desk unit. It read U.S. Government, not the four-digit extension of the caller. That meant the call originated from outside the building. Lexi could count on one hand the people to whom she'd given her office number, which limited the pool to one source. The realization instantly raised her curiosity. "This is Agent Mills."

"Special Agent Mills, this is Theo Gold from the Dallas FBI Crime Lab. You asked us to call if we found anything interesting from the bomb you rendered inert in Las Vegas."

"And?"

"Once we peeled the layers back, we found a bird feather embedded between the plutonium pit and the Semtex."

"What breed?"

"The Common Raven."

In Lexi's mind, Theo's findings proved the Raven had blown up the prisoner transport van that killed Kris Faust and the U.S. Marshal escort. Picking up the feather from the desk corner, she envisioned the Raven dropping it out of his SUV moments after triggering the armed drone. He likely had a smug smile, thinking he'd cleaned up every loose end by killing the prisoners, the only three people in the world who could have linked him to the failed Las Vegas dirty bomb. But he didn't factor in Lexi's determination, because her old friend, Crew Chief Gavin, had it right. Lexi didn't know when to quit.

After hanging up the phone, Lexi dug through the top desk drawer and located two thumbtacks. She rummaged through the folder on her desktop until she found the piece of paper she wanted—a sketch of the Raven based on the description Jamie Porter and Rick Ferrario had provided before their deaths. She then tacked it up on her cubicle wall and studied it. The Raven was tall, thin, and dressed in only black, a stark contrast against his pale skin. He kept his dark stringy hair chin length and had a small scar below his left eye. But his more remarkable characteristic was his bloodred contact lenses, completing the image of a demonic raven. He'd created a persona most people would fear, but not Lexi. The Raven had met his match, and Lexi had him in her crosshairs.

The muscles in her jaw tensed with resolve. "I'm coming for you, Raven."

3

The irony of spending the night in a jail cell stripped of his belt, everything from his pockets, and the laces on his shoes hit Milo Tilton like a ten-ton truck. For twelve years, he'd overseen the incarceration of thousands of male detainees pending deportation and pretrial confinement prisoners facing federal felony charges at the detention facility north of town. Today, he was just like them.

While losing his freedom was distasteful, the sixty-year-old Harrington County Jail accommodations weren't disagreeable, merely dated and mildly dirty. They'd gone underused for decades and didn't justify an upgrade. Though recent years had seen an uptick in crime in Harrington, the county residents had yet to see a reason to build a modern facility. At least he didn't have a cellmate, and the mattress and shower facility were new.

Milo settled into the lower bunk and placed the breakfast tray on his lap, which a deputy had delivered minutes before. He snickered. The familiar bologna and cheese sandwich, canned pears, and creamed oatmeal made up the same meal the guests at his detention facility would receive today. The county must have contracted with the same provider. Taking one bite of stale bread and greasy lunch meat, he understood why the detainees nearly rioted last month over the food.

"Hey, Mr. Tilton." A deputy appeared at his cell, inserted the key into the lock, and slid the door open with a loud clank. "Your lawyer is here."

Thank goodness, he thought. Within a few hours, Jackson Price would have all the right skids greased, and Milo would be at the Cattlemen's, digging into his favorite steak dinner. He placed the lunch tray on the scratchy wool bunk blanket and approached the door. "Thanks, Rusty. Can you pick up a Spanish omelet from Tillie's if it's not too much trouble? You'll find an extra hundred in your envelope next month for the effort."

"I would, Mr. Tilton, but the new sheriff gave strict orders. You are not to receive special treatment." Rusty Ross turned his head left and right, checking the corridor. "And there are some around here who support him."

Milo patted him on the shoulder. "I understand, Rusty. I should be home by dinner, anyway."

Rusty removed the handcuffs from the pouch at the back of his Sam Browne belt. "Sorry, Mr. Tilton, but the rules say I have to cuff you."

"You're just doing your job." Milo placed his hands behind his back with a smile. Until he got out of here, he'd need a friend, and Rusty was one of a handful he could count on.

Rusty led him into the interview room where the overpriced lawyer he'd plucked from Midland years ago sat, sipping on a Starbucks cup. He flicked a crumb of his scone from his Armani navy blue tie. The money Milo paid him over the years to keep his side business running smoothly likely paid for the tie and every designer suit in his closet.

Jackson Price finally looked up when Rusty removed the cuffs and left. "You've gotten yourself into a pickle this time, Milo. Choking your wife to death and threatening the only witness won't be easy to sweep under the rug."

"It's not like I planned to kill her. She wouldn't shut up about the election and how it was the end of the world. I couldn't hear her screech for one more minute." Milo adjusted his gaze to the wall behind his lawyer. His suit, shirt, and tie hanging from a hook there gave him hope. He cast his chin toward the clothes. "Does this mean I'm being released?"

"No." Price reached below the table and plopped a pair of Milo's wingtips on top of it. "Your arraignment is in fifteen minutes, and I don't have high hopes."

"What do you mean? Clem will set bail. I pay him well to look the other way."

"You didn't draw Judge Powell. The district attorney stepped in and had him disqualified as biased. Judge Cook is hearing your case."

Milo deflated like a tire stabbed with a buck knife. His detractors had stacked the deck against him in a blink of an eye. The newly elected sheriff was quick to throw on the cuffs, and the new goody-two-shoes district attorney ensured Milo drew the one judge in the county he couldn't buy.

"How much will it take to get a new judge?"

"That boat has sailed for the hearing. I'll move to disqualify Cook as biased based on his history with you for the trial." Price spun his hundred-dollar ballpoint pen between his fingers.

"That's not good enough. Solomon Cook is squeaky clean, which is why I had the county board give the old governor Clem Powell's name to replace him years ago. All that talk about shooting corruption between the eyes. I didn't trust him when he was on the bench before, and I don't trust him now. If we don't get him off the case, we'll need to take care of everyone in my way. The judge. The sheriff. The new district attorney. I know someone who can make it happen."

"We're not there yet, Milo. Let's see how high he sets bail." Price stood and retrieved the suit from the wall hook. "Let's get you dressed for court."

⸻

Stepping into the county courtroom shackled was like stepping into a time machine. Milo hadn't been there since he was twenty, pleading guilty to Judge Cook on public intoxication and vandalism charges—spray painting a Stedman Ranch cow purple. Aside from a fresh coat of white paint on the walls and hand railings and shellac on the wood benches, tables, and floor, nothing had changed since then or when it had opened for business in 1928. Even the brass wall sconces were the same.

Locals and a handful of fresh faces had filled the gallery to capacity. Media, Milo guessed. The haters were all present to see the great Milo Tilton get his just due. When Rusty escorted him through the room, the hum of conversation came to a slow hush. There was a tug on Milo's arm when he made the wrong turn to what he thought was the defendant's table, making his handcuffs dig into the skin around his wrists. It was a tactile reminder of his untenable circumstance. Rusty removed the cuffs, but Milo couldn't shake the choking feeling they would come right back on after the bail hearing.

Price sat beside him, placing a legal-sized manila folder, a writing pad, and his fancy pen atop the table between them. "Let me do all the talking. If you have a question or want to tell me something, write it down. This judge will hit you with contempt of court in a heartbeat."

"If I don't go home today, there's not enough money in the world that can protect Cook."

Price leaned in and lowered his voice. "Save that talk for outside the courtroom."

"All rise," the bailiff bellowed. Everyone stood. The opening announcement ended with "the Honorable Solomon Cook presiding."

People in the gallery returned to their seats when the judge entered. He sat smugly atop his bench like it was Mount Olympus and he was Zeus, looking down upon the people on earth as if they were his toys to play with.

The bailiff read the court docket and the charges. Milo had seen enough police shows on TV to expect Cook to ask, "How does the defendant plead?" But he locked stares with Milo. It was cold and self-righteous, riling up every negative emotion Milo had ever felt. If he had to label their emotional states, he would say they were both spitting mad.

"Mr. Tilton, you must think you're pretty smart, having avoided coming into my courtroom since your youthful indiscretion."

Milo opened his mouth to give Cook an honest answer, but Price placed a hand over his arm. "Jackson Price for the defense, Your Honor. My client pleads not guilty to all charges."

Cook shot his stare at Price like a spear aimed right between the eyes. "I didn't ask for a plea, Mr. Price. If you speak out of turn again, I'll hold you in contempt of court." Cook returned his attention and disdain to Milo. "Looking at the faces in the gallery, I think it's safe to assume every person in this courtroom doesn't like you, Mr. Tilton. You've ruined many lives in this town. But none of that has bearing on today's proceedings. I must decide whether you pose a threat to the community based on the charges and your criminal history."

The slight upturn at the corner of his mouth clarified Cook was enjoying this. The Medal of Honor hanging in a glass case behind his bench likely made him think he was always right. That hero status made him untouchable to most, but not Milo. He was a man who was about to push an adversary too far.

Cook turned to Price and asked, "How does your client plead, Mr. Price?"

"Not guilty, Your Honor."

Cook turned to the prosecutor. "What does the state ask for bail?"

"Considering the horrific nature of the crime and the defendant's wealth, the state asks for remand." The new district attorney looked smugger than the judge in her tailored skirt and jacket. She had thrown down the gauntlet in her first big profile case. Milo expected nothing less. The stack against him was growing higher and higher by the minute. At least she was easy on the eyes.

"Mr. Price?"

"Your honor, my client has had no criminal convictions since his youthful indiscretion thirty-five years ago in this same court. He has been a valued member of the community for decades. We offer his passport and two hundred thousand dollars."

"Valued member of the community is questionable, Mr. Price. Knowing Mr. Tilton, I believe he poses an ongoing threat to the people of Harrington." Judge Cook shifted his steely stare to Milo. "I hereby remand you to the custody of the Harrington County Jail until your trial begins in"—he reviewed several papers on his bench—"three weeks." The judge hit his gavel. "We're adjourned."

The courtroom burst out in gasps and chatter.

Milo snapped his stare toward Price while a deputy handcuffed his hands behind his back. "You better fix this, dammit." He leaned in so only Price could hear. "The man's name and number are in a floor safe in my office. The combination is your birth date. Tell him I'm calling in my favor." At the time, he'd questioned the wisdom of getting mixed up with an arms dealer with a reputation for brutality, but now he realized it was the best decision he'd ever made.

"I will, Milo. I promise."

"You better."

The deputy whisked Milo away, but not before the walls closed in. The only way out depended on one man taking Price's call.

4

Never again would Lexi pride herself on being a people person. She'd worked with Kris Faust for six weeks yet had no idea she was born and raised in College Station, where her parents had taught mathematics at the Texas A&M main campus, until the preacher had stood over her casket in the chapel and given her eulogy. She didn't know Kris was the youngest of five children with four older brothers. Lexi had never taken the time to get to know Kris like the others, viewing her as the temp who kept Sergeant Mel Thompson's seat warm on the task force.

The entire network of Faust kinfolk, aged eight months to eighty-eight years, had gathered in the veterans' hall on the outskirts of College Station to remember their fallen daughter, sister, aunt, and cousin. They'd laid out a spread of Kris' favorite foods, marking each dish with a note card, explaining its importance in her life. The nachos made from microwaved American cheese slices were an after-school staple when she was a latchkey kid, while the pasta salad was her go-to side dish to bring to family events.

Lexi grabbed two plates of strawberry shortcake, Kris' favorite dessert, and navigated her way through the three dozen kids, all under twelve, balancing M&M candies on their noses. According to the sign on the table, they were Kris' not-so-secret chocolate indulgence, and the game was a childhood challenge from her brothers that had followed her into adulthood.

Lexi spotted Nita next to Maxwell Keene and his wife, Amanda. Other former members of the task force were nearby. Texas Governor Chief of Security Simon Winslow and ATF Intelligence Specialist Kaplan Shaw watched the M&M contest. FBI Agents Coby Vasquez and Lathan Sinclair were devouring plates of fried chicken drumsticks. Mel Thompson also had flown in the night before to pay her respects to the agent who had taken her place on the line. Noah Black was the only one missing.

Nita accepted the dessert plate. "Thanks. It looks delicious." She winked, signaling her plan to redeem the rain check Lexi had asked for last night sometime soon. But if today affected her as much as she expected, Lexi would need holding, not sex.

"Kris certainly had an eclectic taste in food." Amanda nibbled on a bite of spiral pasta salad. She pointed her fork at her plate. "This is very good. I understand it's her recipe."

"I wouldn't know, and I should have. Kris was my responsibility." Lexi would never repeat the same mistake with someone who vowed to risk their life alongside her.

"Kris showed only the parts of herself she wanted us to see," Simon said.

"Other than her explosives expertise, she was a stranger to all of us." Kaplan shook her head.

Mel rolled her neck and closed her eyes in apparent frustration. "I can't help but think if I hadn't shot that suspect, she might still be alive."

"It was my fault," Maxwell said. "I'd rushed the shooting board after Coby shot and killed the first Red Spades suspect. After the second shooting incident, they wanted to cross every T and dot every I before clearing you for duty again."

"Doubting ourselves does no one any good," Lathan said. "We were all there to do a job. We accomplished everything we set out to do. When you consider the type of people we were chasing, it was a miracle more of us didn't pay the ultimate price." He turned his attention to Lexi. "And we have you to thank for that. Because you put our safety above everything else, my daughter won't grow up without her father."

Lexi's eyes misted at the thought of how many other children, spouses, siblings, and parents would not have their loved ones if she hadn't been diligent. But the notion provided little solace today. Kris was dead because Lexi hadn't seen the Raven's potential threat, and every family member in this room was lesser because of it.

"Lathan is right," Maxwell said. "If Noah Black were here, he'd tell you the same thing."

Noah, she thought. Besides serving as an invaluable second in command, he had become her most trusted partner and friend. She understood why he put the task force behind him after shooting Tony Belcher unarmed before Lexi could. Taking that kill shot served justice in everyone's eyes but the law's, and that was a secret Lexi would carry to her grave.

"How is Noah?" Amanda asked. "I haven't heard from him since he returned to Nogales."

"He's undercover on a narco case, which is why he couldn't be here today. He sends his best to everyone." Lexi dug into her dessert as a form of procrastination, but once finished, she knew she'd dawdled long enough and whispered into Nita's ear. "Come with me while I talk to the family?"

"Of course." Nita grabbed their plates, placed them on a nearby cart, and held Lexi's hand tight. "Ready?"

"As much as I could be." Lexi gave her hand a tight squeeze and led the way to the immediate family tables, stopping at the one with Kris' parents and three of her brothers. Lexi waited politely for the table conversation to reach a lull before stepping closer to Kris' parents. The mother appeared heartbroken, so Lexi maneuvered closer to the father. "Mr. and Mrs. Faust, I'm Lexi Mills."

The look of recognition filled their eyes. "It's good to meet you," Mr. Faust said, extending his hand. Lexi accepted his handshake. "Kris spoke of you before she came to work for you."

"Really? I didn't realize that."

"Kris idolized you after you lost your leg. She thought anyone in her line of work who could come back from such a devastating injury was superhero material. She was positively giddy the day her boss tapped her to work on your task force. Even if temporary, learning from the best was her dream come true."

Tears pooled at the magnified guilt and trailed down her cheeks. Her voice cracked. "I'm so sorry I sent her on that transport."

The mother pushed back her chair, approached Lexi with her arms wide, and took her into a tight embrace. "Our daughter said working for you was the opportunity of a lifetime and wouldn't have traded it for anything. Thank you for trusting her and taking her under your wing. But I want you to make me a promise."

"Anything, Mrs. Faust."

"Promise you'll get the people who killed our Krissy." Kris may have been collateral damage, but the pain and sorrow in her mother's eyes made no distinction. Her daughter was dead, and she'd asked Lexi to give her death meaning.

"I promise." Lexi excused herself and took Nita by the hand. Weaving her way through the sea of Faust children and fighting a wave of guilt, she went to the restroom and pulled Nita into a stall. The dam of emotion broke when she wrapped her arms around Nita's torso. Regret swept her downstream, and shame threatened to pull her under. Thinking about her lack of vigilance and the precautions she should have taken for the prisoner transport, Lexi barely sucked in enough air to keep from passing out.

"Just breathe, Lexi." Nita held her tighter when her knees buckled, keeping her head above water. Soon her breathing steadied and strength returned.

Lexi buried her head in the crook of Nita's neck and whispered, "I'm going after the Raven."

"You wouldn't be the Lexi Mills I fell in love with if you didn't." Nita caressed Lexi's back until she could stand on her own. "Let's wash your face and head home."

"I'd like that." Lexi opened the stall door and stepped out with Nita on her heels.

Kaplan was at the bank of sinks washing up. Locking stares with Lexi, her mouth fell agape. "Wedding sex is cliché and sizzling hot, but funeral sex?" She grimaced as if she'd thrown up a little in her mouth.

Lexi sidled up to the sink beside her and splashed water on her face. "That would be wrong and require way too much bravado. I needed an emotional timeout."

"And you didn't come to your best woman? How am I supposed to keep you sane before the wedding if you don't talk to me?" When Lexi sighed, Kaplan gently rubbed her upper arms. "We're all in your corner, Lexi. Call us if you need anything, and we'll all come running."

"Thank you, Kaplan. I really appreciate the support." Lexi took a calming breath to shake off the lingering regret. "There is something you can do for me."

"Name it."

"The FBI lab called me yesterday. They found a raven's feather embedded in the Vegas bomb, so my instincts were right about the feather I found. I need you to keep your eyes and ears open for anything that might link to the Raven."

A coy smile sprouted on Kaplan. "I'm way ahead of you. The day after Kris died, I set up alerts on every national and state law enforcement database about the Raven and his MO. Since it's Friday, I'll start scouring the dark web when I get home tonight. If there's anything out there, I'll find it."

"Thank you, Kaplan. I trust you will." Lexi shifted her attention to Nita. "Let's get your purse and go home."

"Fair warning," Kaplan said. "The ATF director arrived and is talking to Agent Keene. That's why I'm hiding in here."

"Why are you hiding from him?"

"Not him. His security escort is an ex. It didn't end well. If you're heading back to our group, can you grab my purse, too? I'd rather avoid an awkward reunion."

"We have you covered, Kaplan." Nita caressed her forearm. "We'll be right back, then we can leave together."

Lexi led Nita across the main floor. She got an idea when she was halfway to her group and saw the director talking to Maxwell Keene and a woman she didn't recognize. Lexi had been on the director's radar since the attack on the governor's mansion in Spicewood earlier in the year. He'd encouraged the public relations circus she and Noah were on for months. Lexi was relieved when he didn't suggest the same during her meeting with him the previous week after the failed Las Vegas bombing. If there was ever a time to take advantage of her celebrity, this was it.

She positioned herself next to Keene and waited to make eye contact with Director Hanlon. She shook his hand. "Glad you could make it, director. I'm sure the Faust family appreciates the support."

"It's nice seeing you again, Agent Mills. I understand you're almost ready to return to fieldwork and your position on the special response team."

"About that, sir. At our last meeting, I said I'd like to return to SRT and my explosives roots in Dallas, but I've given my next assignment more thought. Does your offer still stand?"

"Of course it does." Director Hanlon overfilled his chest with overt pride in Lexi. "You've earned any job of your choosing anywhere in the country."

"Yesterday, the FBI lab discovered evidence linking the bomb in Las Vegas to the one that killed Agent Faust. I want to investigate the person we think built both bombs."

"I already have a man who has been on the Raven's trail for two years," the woman next to the director said.

Lexi shifted her attention to her. The woman, dressed in a pricey, tailored dark suit and sensible low heels, towered over Lexi by six inches. Gray strands peppered her collar-length dark blond hair. But her most compelling feature was how she carried herself. She was a woman in charge. "I'm sorry. And you are?"

"Your new supervisor." Her voice contained the unmistakable sharpness of animosity and distrust.

"Lexi Mills," Director Hanlon said. "Meet Willie Lange. She's transferring to Dallas from the Houston field office on Monday, taking Jack Carlson's position."

"SRT commander, too? It's a pleasure." Lexi extended her hand, eager to greet the first woman to command an ATF special response team. But Lange's stiff grip signaled the pleasure was not mutual.

"This could work out," the director said. "Agent Lange, how quickly can you get your man to Dallas to turn over the investigation?"

"Sir, I hate to differ, but this is Agent Croft's case. He has single-handedly compiled a profile on the Raven and feels he's getting closer." Lange glanced at Lexi, giving her the side eye of disapproval. "He doesn't deserve to have it taken away."

"Then pair him up with Mills. She's earned her assignment of choice, including the location." He glanced at Lexi. "Considering your parents' injuries at the hands of the Gatekeepers, I assume you want to remain in Dallas. Am I correct?" Lexi replied with a silent nod, holding back a smile.

"I'd hate to uproot him for a personal vendetta," Lange said.

After the feud she'd had with Tony Belcher, Lexi couldn't blame Lange for labeling her quest to hunt down the Raven as a vendetta, but attributing only that motivation to her work was insulting. Lexi's track record on Task Force Zero Impact showed she was capable of patience and the ability to focus on a broader mission.

"Then you have a decision to make, Agent Lange," Director Hanlon said. "Either relocate Agent Croft to Dallas and team him with Agent Mills, or he turns over everything on the Raven to her. Either way, this is Lexi's show starting Monday. How it happens is up to you."

5

Stopping at the perimeter of Milo's property, Jackson Price realized getting into the house might be more complicated than he'd expected. The forensics team had completed their investigation, and the sheriff had left a deputy guarding the building. He couldn't make out the deputy's face to determine if he was on Milo's payroll, so asking to go inside was out of the question. The deputy would have to escort Jackson around the crime scene, which was the last thing he wanted. His only option was to enter through the back undetected.

It had been years since Jackson had to tap into his agility and even longer since he'd had to scale a wall, but going over a six-foot-tall privacy fence was the only way into Milo's house. Golfing eighteen holes weekly might have provided a decent foundation for physical fitness if he walked the course. But he was fifty-five, lazy, and spoiled. A cart was necessary to hold his beer and portable fan with a built-in mister. Nevertheless, he gripped the top of the boards, placed his right foot high on the panel, and pulled with all his might. Once he was down on the other side, with a ripped pant leg, he swore to never do this again and to find another way out of Milo's house.

Using his key, Jackson eased open the back door and stepped inside. As he suspected, the security system was off since the sheriff's department didn't have the passcode. He couldn't explain his reasoning, but Jackson tiptoed down the hallway toward the crime scene in Milo's office. Being quiet seemed like a prerequisite to breaking into a room sealed off until the trial.

Jackson lowered to his knees, feeling the lack of wisdom in climbing a fence with every movement. He lifted the rug at the foot of the built-in wet bar. Unless someone knew Milo had hidden a safe below the floorboards, they would have missed it. The slat seams perfectly camouflaged the outline of the hidden door. Slipping the house key into a small cutout in the wood floor, he pried up the door and exposed the safe. After entering his eight-digit birthday in the panel, the lock mechanism sounded, and the electronic readout changed from "Locked" to "Open." He pulled the door up. Cash, the business ledger, and a collection of files were inside.

"Police. Stop."

Jackson flinched at the sound of the male voice at his back. His heart thumped harder, making it difficult to think clearly. He raised his hands slowly, and when he turned to face the officer, relief washed through him instantly, seeing the recognizable curls. "You scared the crap out of me."

"I thought that was you climbing over the fence." The deputy lowered the service weapon he'd aimed at Jackson's chest but remained vigilant. "What the hell are you doing here?"

A version of the truth, but never its whole, was always best. Jackson pulled the cash from the floor safe. "It's payday. Would you like your share now or in a few days after I do the accounting?"

The deputy slouched, erasing the immediate threat of an arrest for trespassing on an official crime scene. "Now would be good."

"A thousand for the month, right?" At his affirmative nod, Jackson counted out the correct amount. He pretended to enter a note into his phone, acting as if the business would continue as usual. "Let's not tell the others I paid you before them."

The deputy snorted, stuffing the money into his front pocket. "They'll never hear it from me."

If Jackson were honest, which he most definitely wasn't, he'd say he did not know when the others would get their share. The safe should have had ten times the cash to make the monthly payroll. Their operation would fall apart quickly unless Jackson found the name of Milo's contact.

"Well, then. I should get going." Jackson stuffed everything from the safe into a recyclable grocery sack he'd brought. After closing the safe and replacing the wood cutout and rug, sharp pain in both knees punctuated his clumsy rise from the floor, convincing him he was getting too old for this type of activity. From now on, he would limit himself to couches and chairs.

The deputy snickered. "You should probably use the front door."

"I was hoping you'd say that."

What in the hell have you gotten me into, Milo? Jackson Price was a lawyer who had worked on the fringes of the law for a decade managing Milo's affairs. Cleaning up his messes had become as regular as his monthly mortgage payment. But never had a simple phone call sent chills down his spine. The name alone of Milo's contact had him conjuring up a Steven King-like creation. And why a sunset meeting in Carlsbad? Was the contact a cave hound? Or did he have a fascination with bats?

Jackson arrived at the Carlsbad Cavern National Park ten minutes before sunset. The visitor's center bustled with tourists browsing souvenirs of the majestic caverns and nightly bat migration. He squeezed through the crowd to get through the exit with the sign directing visitors to the bat program amphitheater.

Descending the winding trail, replete with signs marking the native foliage every thirty yards, Jackson wondered which of these hundred people had given him the creeps over the phone. Each looked like a tourist there to see the spectacle, not to take on a hit.

At the bottom of the trail, Jackson stood at the top of the outdoor theater, scanning the eastern sky. Thousands of Brazilian bats streamed from the brush-covered cave, forming a black ribbon in the darkening sky as they escaped for their night feeding.

His phone buzzed in his black leather designer jacket. The caller ID was blocked, but the timing of it wasn't coincidental. It had to be Milo's contact. He swiped the screen. "Hello."

"Look in your left pocket." The male voice wasn't the same one that had sent shivers down his spine yesterday, but it was just as mysterious. "Leave now. Meet us in five minutes." The call went dead.

Jackson stuck his left hand into his coat pocket and felt a piece of folded paper he didn't remember being there before. He opened it. *Picnic area #13 on south trail.* "I better make it home alive, Milo," he whispered before following the signs down the dark path. Of course, picnic area thirteen was in the most remote part of the tourist area. He went to the bench and waited, hoping he didn't get a stiletto knife in the kidney for making that call.

"Right on time, Mr. Price." The deep voice made Jackson's toes tingle in his shoes. It was *the* voice from yesterday. Jackson turned toward it but couldn't distinguish the man's features in the darkness. But when the man stepped from the shadows, the moonlight shimmered off his eyes. Jackson couldn't take his gaze off them. They were blood red.

"You must be the Raven."

"You said Mr. Tilton needs to call in his favor. I can provide him with any weapon for any purpose at no cost, but once I do, this clears my slate with him. What does Milo need?" A second shadowy figure appeared behind the Raven, signaling they weren't alone, outnumbering Jackson.

"Police arrested him for murdering his wife. We need a more friendly judge to hear his case."

The Raven tilted his head as if sizing up Jackson for a casket. "I get the sense this is bigger than one man."

"You're right. Milo wants to clear the town of his enemies."

"Jessup and Ford. What do you have in mind?"

"You've done your homework. I was hoping you could advise us."

"You should take out all three simultaneously, but if you need three weapons, they will come with a price tag."

"How much?"

"If you have to ask, you can't afford it."

"Then what do you recommend?"

"Get them in the same place at the same time."

"That will be impossible until the trial."

"Then I have a solution, but you'll have to find someone to take a fall and clean up their mess if they fail."

"If they do, we will need your help."

"I can assist, but you won't like how I mop up. I will eliminate anyone who knows my name, including you, so I suggest you clean up yourself."

A hard lump formed at the back of Jackson's throat. His first impression of the Raven was spot on. He was ruthless. And his first question about this situation stood: *What in the hell have you gotten me into, Milo?*

6

Lexi climbed the stairs of the Santa Fe Building with an extra pep in her step. Today, she would officially begin the hunt for the Raven. Her new boss didn't hint at the funeral whether she would work alone or with Agent Croft, but the stony stare she received suggested either scenario was a thorn in Lange's side. Lexi had found herself in a quagmire, but after talking to Kris' mother, she would pay nearly any price to have a shot at the man who killed her daughter.

Once at her desk, Lexi dug into her backpack and pulled out a folder containing a single photo she'd printed the night before. The day before the prisoner transport, when her team was packing up to dismantle the task force, Maxwell Keene had lined up everyone for a group picture. She focused on the woman at the end. Last week, when she'd first cried over the photo, Lexi had thought Kris' broad smile was about what they'd accomplished, but she was only partially correct. According to her mother, Kris was living the dream by working for Lexi. That was the last time Lexi saw her smile.

She tacked the photo on the soft wall panel next to the sketch of the Raven. Focusing on his unhuman red eyes, she sensed she would come face to face with him soon. Returning her attention to Kris in the photo, she whispered, "I'll get him. I promise."

"Mills."

Lexi turned toward the voice at the opening of her cubicle, discovering her new boss dressed in a similar suit she'd worn at the funeral with a black leather backpack over her right shoulder and a cardboard moving box in both hands. Lexi was clearly her first stop, which didn't bode well for starting off on the right foot.

"Yes, Agent Lange."

"My office in fifteen minutes."

"I'll be there."

The cold order reminded her of when Gavin had called her into the garage bay after she'd repaired an axle on a backup race car. He had raised the car on the rack and told her to look at her work and tell him what she'd done wrong. Her inspection had confirmed she'd completed the repairs correctly, so Gavin's suggestion perplexed her.

He'd said, "*Look at it again.*"

When she did, she'd gone over every instruction Gavin had given her in her head. Then she remembered him saying to wipe everything spotless as her last step. She had discovered a small spot on the outer bearing cone of the hub plate. "*There's a grease smudge on the cone.*"

"*And what would that tell a mechanic who didn't work on the axle?*"

"*There's a leak somewhere.*"

"*Which would waste precious time diagnosing a problem during a race. We have to trust that everyone does their job right. Otherwise, we'll never win.*"

The lesson taught Lexi to be thorough in every task and to never skip a step when others depended on her. The one time she failed to follow Gavin's example, Trent Darby lost his life. Lexi got the impression she was about to get a similar lecture.

When Lange turned on her heel and continued down the passageway, Lexi peeked her head around her cubicle wall. Lange had turned toward Jack Carlson's old office, leaving Lexi enough time to conduct a little recon before reporting in.

She climbed one more flight of stairs to the fourth floor and walked down the main hallway to the third door on the right. "Did you find anything?"

Kaplan Shaw waved her in. "Close the door." One benefit of having a friend in intelligence was a private office for conversations others shouldn't hear. "Your text this morning didn't give me much time."

"There had better be a but. I thought I'd have more time, but I meet with her in ten minutes." Lexi wouldn't make the same mistake with Lange as she did with Jack Carlson. She'd started working for him without knowing his background and might have seen he was a Gatekeeper mole months earlier if she'd done her homework. Lexi wanted to walk into her new boss's office with wide-open eyes this time.

"A small but. I did the best I could in ten minutes. When you mentioned Lange was from the Houston field office, that gave me an idea. I still have access to Kris Faust's personnel records from our task force days. Lange was Kris' trainer in the explosives training school. Her name was on several training reports. Lange had high hopes for Kris and noted she was technically more capable than any of her classmates. Kris just needed to get out of her shell."

"That sounds like Kris." Lexi concentrated on Lange's familiar name, wondering where she'd heard it before. If Lange taught explosive disposal techniques, then she was once a certified specialist. That was it. Lexi snapped her fingers. "I remember Lange. She was in the first explosives class accepting women but quit explosives after a few years."

"Do you know why she stopped?"

"If memory serves correctly, she retrained into firearms after her K-9 partner died during a clearing operation. She must have gone into teaching later."

"That's sad."

"It was," Lexi said. "Thanks, Kaplan. Keep digging. I want to know everything about her and the Raven." Lexi returned to the third floor and knocked on her boss's door precisely fifteen minutes after her summons. Someone had removed Jack Carlson's belongings from the office, right down to his potted cactus. The walls and bookshelves were empty. The only thing on the desk was a picture frame Lange had pulled from the box and placed on the corner.

"You wanted to see me," Lexi said.

"Have a seat." Lange removed more items from the box, including a laptop.

While waiting for Lange to break the ice, Lexi sat and gripped the chair arms and ran her hands down their length. She had occupied this same guest chair when Jack Carlson called her in to give her her first SRT assignment after becoming an amputee. She would never forget that day. It was one year to the day after losing her leg that she'd returned to special duty. It had been a long year of challenges and setbacks, but she'd met the goal she'd set for herself in the hospital after looking at her missing foot for the first time. That day should have been the proudest of her life, but the memory of Jack Carlson tainted it.

The framed picture on Lange's desk came into view. It was an ATF explosives school class photo from five years ago with Lange at the end and Kris Faust in the center of her classmates. *Interesting*, Lexi thought. Was the picture to honor Kris, or was there something more to their relationship beyond student-teacher?

"The director might consider you the ATF golden child, but you'll get no special treatment from me," Lange said.

"I expect none. All I want is to investigate the Raven and work SRT taskings."

"Let's get this straight. Your primary job is fieldwork, investigating cases I give you. If I see fit to send you on an SRT assignment, I will. When you're not doing either, you can work the case you stole from Agent Croft. Is that clear?"

"Crystal."

"Did I miss the fun?" A male voice came from the doorway. Lexi turned her head toward it. She didn't recognize the balding muscular man, but the paddle holster and badge clipped to his belt said he was an ATF agent.

"I'm surprised you made it." Lange gestured toward the other guest chair. "Any problem at security?"

He retrieved the federal smart card from his button-down shirt breast pocket dangling from a lanyard around his neck. "Nope. All programmed for the building." He sat.

Lange redirected her attention to Lexi. "Mills, meet Special Agent Nathan Croft. He's your new partner." *Also interesting*, Lexi thought. He was not here to hand over the case. He was here to work it. And Lange had transferred him to the Dallas field office in three days but didn't see fit to give her a heads-up. The playing field had become abundantly clear. They'd drawn alliances, but Lexi was still on the sidelines.

Croft leaned toward Lexi and shook her hand without a word, only a half-cocked smile and a wink. She expected their tension to be thicker, but he acted jovial.

"Croft is a veteran agent with sixteen years of experience. He's the best firearms expert I've had the pleasure of working with in my twenty years with the ATF. The director made you the lead on the Raven case, but Croft is the senior agent in everything else."

"I have no problem with that." If Lexi were honest, she'd say she welcomed the opportunity to take second chair for a while. Briefing Lange regularly on her cases seemed like punishment. The less time she spent in this office, the better.

"Good." Lange turned to Croft. "Take the cubicle next to Mills. It should be vacant by lunch."

"You got it. Besides my files, I didn't bring much in the car. The rest of my stuff will follow with my household goods after I find a place to live."

"Until then, my couch is yours," Lange said.

"My ex thanks you. She gets testy when the alimony payments are late," Croft chuckled.

"Don't I know it."

"If that's it"—Croft pushed himself from his chair—"I'll get Mills up to speed. Then I hit the apartment listings."

"Are you looking for a one-bedroom or a two?" Lexi asked.

"Two. My teenager might come up on my weekends with him."

"One opened up in my apartment building. It's reasonably priced and is only twenty-five minutes to the office."

"I'll check it out. Living in the same building might make the transfer smoother." Croft led the way from Lange's office to Lexi's cubicle. A cardboard file box was on her desk, and a bulky backpack was on the floor near the trashcan. "Hope you don't mind, but I asked which desk was yours and dropped off my stuff."

"No, it's fine." Lexi didn't know what to think of Croft's politeness. She'd poached his case, yet he didn't seem the least bit cross. Lange, however, had that base covered. She was pissed off enough for them both.

Once Lexi and Croft were at her desk, a loud thud came from the next cubicle. She raised an index finger straight. "I'll be right back." She swung around the corner to the next opening, discovering her neighbor emptying his desk drawer and tossing the items into a box. She couldn't determine what he was mumbling, but she was sure they were curse words.

"Hey, Munsey. I'm sorry about the relocation, but the new supervisor wanted to put the new guy next to me."

He leveled his stare at her. His expression was flat. "I don't blame you, Mills. It's just that I've been in this cubicle for six years."

Last week, the other agents on the floor gave her a warm welcome with a round of applause and pats on the backs. Changing that dynamic was the last thing she wanted, and she knew the right person who could help her. "Stop what you're doing. I have an idea that will make both of us happy."

Lexi returned to her workstation. "Grab your stuff. We're relocating." She gathered her files, tissue box, pictures tacked to the wall, and the Raven's feather. Items in hand, she weaved through the cubicles and went past the equipment closet, landing at her favorite supply clerk's desk. "Hey, Ronald, this is my new partner, Nathan Croft."

Ronald eyed Croft up and down like a father vetting the boyfriend picking up his daughter for prom. "Hi."

"I have a favor to ask."

"Anything for you, Lexi."

She craned her neck around the partition separating his office space from the one she occupied for her first year in the building. They'd converted the storage area into a large workspace for her. The modular desk and chair were still there, and Ronald had stacked several boxes in the corner, presumably the new blast suit. The area was spacious enough for two people, but she'd have to scrounge more furniture to make it work.

"How would you like it if I moved back in here?"

The Cheshire Cat grin, exposing Ronald's perfectly straight teeth, said he'd turn the building upside down for the right things to make it happen. Within five minutes, he'd moved the boxes to his cube and arranged for a desk, chair, and small worktable to be brought down from the fifth floor before the end of the day.

After giving Munsey the good news, Lexi left Kris's workstation for the last time and whispered to herself, "Goodbye, Kris. This doesn't change a thing." She returned to her new office, finding Ronald at his desk.

"I put extra thumbtacks in your top drawer," Ronald said. "I remember how you like to put things on the walls."

"Thanks, pod buddy." She rubbed his arm as she passed. Croft had tacked pictures of a half-dozen firearms and explosives on the wall and stacked folders below each photo. "Is this all from the Raven?"

"These are the ones I can confirm from his calling card."

Lexi picked up the feather atop her folders, discerning every vane and barb. "You mean this."

"You're a quick learner. I've been following the Raven's work for two years. He's not just an arms dealer. He's an arms maker who creates unique weapons for specific situations to a very exclusive client list, from what I can glean."

"So uniqueness captures your attention?" Lexi asked.

"Uniqueness is only one aspect of his work. He leaves his mark in every weapon."

"Yes, in them, not on. Lab techs found traces of raven feathers in the dirty bomb I disarmed in Las Vegas." She twirled the feather once between her fingers. "I found this at the explosion scene, where my prisoners, a marshal, and Agent Kris Faust were killed."

"And that's why you're in charge of my case."

Lexi sighed. "I only wanted on the case, not to be in charge."

"But you didn't turn it down."

"No, I didn't." Lexi finally felt the tension she expected and needed to defuse it. "I appreciate and respect everything you've done on this case, but this is personal. The Raven killed someone under my command."

"And Kris was a good friend. I worked with her for four years."

And there it was. A shared history with Kris Faust was the bond between Croft and Lange. "I'm sorry for your loss. I'd only known her for a few weeks. She was a good agent and knew her way around explosives. I was lucky to have her on my team."

Croft locked stares for a moment before saying, "Yes, you were."

"Then we have something we can agree on."

The look in Croft's eyes said he didn't trust Lexi yet, and the feeling was mutual. Hopefully, that would come in time. Until then, she'd have to keep her eye on his special relationship with Lange.

7

Three weeks later

The two-year-old school photo Derek held in his hand didn't do his son justice these days. Junior's shoulders were broader, and the prominent Culter family chin had finally made an appearance during his growth spurt the previous year. Maybe if he'd been a better father or bothered to marry his mother, he'd have his son's current sophomore photo to look at on what might be his last day on earth instead of the one his son's mother dug out of a desk drawer last week.

Derek kissed the photo before stowing it in a place of honor in his shirt breast pocket. "This is for you, Junior." He dug out the frayed, grease-stained backpack that hadn't seen the light of day in years and crammed a change of clothes, a water bottle, a bottle opener, and the mini-flashlight Scooter gave him yesterday into the main compartment. He then threw on his bulkiest jacket and stuffed the unique gun Scooter had given him into the interior pocket.

He drove downtown, parking a block from the courthouse for an easy getaway. Snatching his backpack and patting his jacket to make sure the gun hadn't fallen out, Derek walked his route, noting the street-side dining, bike racks, and postal box that might impede him during a mad dash to his car.

He paused at the base of the courthouse steps, remembering the last time he was there. Judge Cook had thrown the book at him for drug possession with intent to distribute. It didn't matter that the oxy he'd bought minutes earlier was for personal use. He was one pill over the limit and earned a twenty-year sentence. He was out in eight with good behavior, but those were years he'd never get back with his son. Getting life-changing money to put a bullet in that asshole was a dream come true. But his first obstacle was getting through security.

A line had formed inside the main entrance hours before Milo Tilton's manslaughter trial. Half the people in Harrington wanted to see Milo put away for decades, so Derek arrived early to get a seat in the gallery. He queued up. When it was his turn, he placed the backpack on the x-ray machine conveyor belt, hoping the keys and bottle opener would mask the flashlight containing the three bullets he needed to pull off this job.

"Next." A deputy seated on a stool inside the secure area gestured for Derek to come through the metal detector.

He stepped through, holding his breath and watching his pack enter the machine. No alarms went off—the first sign whoever came up with this job actually knew what they were doing. His bag appeared on the other side of the machine but backed up and reentered. Derek's pulse picked up. The longer the guards took, the more he wondered if he'd put too much faith in Scooter and whoever was pulling the strings. His stomach churned the breath mint he'd accidentally swallowed with the bitter coffee, creating a dangerous combination. He waited patiently at the end of the conveyor belt, holding back the brewing volcano without asking questions.

A moment later, the pack reappeared. The guards diverted their attention to the next bag and person in line, so Derek grabbed his bag and walked away, remembering to take calm, steady strides to not attract scrutiny. He went directly to the restroom, entering the first available stall. The moment he set eyes on porcelain, the volcano blew, bringing up the mint whole.

"You can do this," he told himself. Before Derek had gone to prison, no amount of money could have convinced him to accept this job. He was a petty criminal with an oxy addiction but drew the line on certain things and killing was one. But eight years in the roughest prison in west Texas had made him more amenable, and Scooter had attached the right price tag to the right son of a bitch. Still, he wouldn't have taken the job if he didn't think he could do it and walk away alive. The sharpshooter ribbon somewhere in his shoebox of military memorabilia said he could. But being willing to shoot the man who had stolen eight years of his life, twelve fewer than he'd expected with good behavior, didn't equate to a willingness to go back behind bars. If he didn't escape today, dying in a shootout might be more palatable than being captured.

Derek reached up to flush, but an object on the linoleum floor caught his attention. *Shit!* The plastic gun. He snatched it up and stuffed it inside his jacket, praying no one saw it. After spitting out the lingering nasty taste in his mouth and flushing, he sat on the seat. He fished through his backpack, located Scooter's flashlight, and unscrewed the battery compartment. Tipping the stem upside down, three battery shells fell into his hand. He popped open each fake top and pulled out three bullets. After returning the flashlight to his pack, he carefully loaded the plastic gun and returned it to his jacket. He was set. Now, he had to get a seat in the gallery and wait.

Within an hour, deputies opened the courtroom doors, and Derek sat in the third row near the center on the defendant's side. The position offered a clear view of the judge's bench, the prosecutor's table, and the nearby strap hangar seats for the arresting officers. The gallery filled quickly. The courtroom regulars broke out their puzzle books, nibbled secretly on snacks, and sipped sparingly on water. Leaving for the bathroom didn't guarantee their seat would still be available when they returned.

Meanwhile, Derek sat silently, refusing to engage his neighbor on either side. Both had tried to spark a casual conversation about their opinion on Milo Tilton's chances, but he'd waved them off, feigning a sore throat.

Soon, a side door opened. Milo Tilton appeared at the threshold with Derek's same numb expression when he'd stepped through the same door eight years ago. He'd hoped to get a fair trial by the judge but walked out blindsided at the realization he was about to lose the next two decades of his life.

The deputy escorted Tilton to the defendant's table where his lawyer was waiting. They whispered back and forth, not realizing that today's proceeding wouldn't end as expected.

Minutes later, the prosecutor and sheriff walked in and took their positions. The district attorney unpacked her briefcase and laid out several folders and a legal notepad. She then turned around and talked to the sheriff for several minutes. Their confident nods and occasional smiles suggested they expected a slam dunk.

The bailiff let the jury in. It was an equal mix of men and women but was predominantly Hispanic, an accurate reflection of the community.

The bailiff approached the front of the judge's bench and announced, "All rise." The back door opened. Once Judge Solomon Cook appeared, Derek didn't hear another word the bailiff said. He let his seething hatred for the man take over and focused on his smug face and ridiculous long mustache. If he could, Derek would rip that thing off his upper lip and stuff it down his throat before shooting him between the eyes.

Someone tugged his coat sleeve, bringing him out of his rage-fueled trance. "Take your seat," the woman whispered. Derek looked around. Realizing he was the only one standing, he quickly sat on his patch of hardwood bench.

The son of a bitch sat behind his tall desk, looking like he was king of the mountain, while he addressed both counselors with some legal mumbo jumbo.

"This damn thing had better work," he whispered to himself. The bailiff would kill or capture him within seconds if it didn't. Finding a way out during the pandemonium was his only chance of survival. If he failed, at least he'd set up Junior for college. He'd taken the deal on one condition—half of the one hundred thousand for the job upfront. If he died, the lawyer he'd hired and given the money to would deliver ten thousand to his son the following day and give him ten thousand each year for college.

Motion behind the district attorney caught Derek's attention. The sheriff read something on his phone, grabbed his Stetson, and departed through the main doors. "Dammit," he whispered. One of his three targets had left, but there was no going back. Scooter was clear. The job had to be done today, or Scooter's employer would come after him.

Think, dammit, think, he told himself. He thought of the bright side: His odds of escaping alive had gone up. With the sheriff leaving, the bailiff held the only other gun in the courtroom. Derek could now shoot him first with the bullet meant for the sheriff. But speed was of the essence. He'd have only seconds to take out the judge and prosecutor, assuming no one in the gallery tried to stop him. That gave Derek an idea.

Derek took three calming breaths and counted down from five in his head. On zero, he stood, excused himself to the neighbor on his right, and shimmied out of his row. Reaching the aisle, emotion left him. It had to. Otherwise, he might balk at the critical moment.

He lowered the zipper on his jacket and reached his right hand inside, wrapping his palm around the plastic pistol grip. He turned toward the front of the courtroom and placed his finger on the trigger. Derek drew his pistol and stepped up to the crotch-high gate separating the gallery from the official part of the courtroom.

The bailiff had his stare fixed on him and went for his service weapon with his right hand, but Derek was too quick. Leveling his gun, he was confident of his aim and pulled the trigger. His shot was accurate, hitting his target center mass. Shrieks filled the courtroom when the bailiff tumbled to the floor in a spray of blood.

Derek pivoted toward Judge Cook, resisting the urge to pull the trigger without saying his piece. "This is for eight years of my life, you son of a bitch." The coward flinched, raising his hands in defense, but Derek fired, making his fantasy come true. The bullet struck Cook between the eyes. Blood spatter fanned out behind his head, speckling the wall-mounted seal of the great State of Texas. Derek had avenged the stain of his sentence.

He spun to his right, setting his aim at the spot where the district attorney had been making her speech, but she was no longer there and wasn't in sight. The jurors and people in the gallery were scrambling, fighting to get through an exit. It was impossible to discern which one was his final target. He had no other choice but to run.

Deputies would come in through the main entrance, so Derek ran toward the door leading to the judge's chambers. Once inside, he locked the door. He scanned the room, discovering a gambler-style cowboy hat and light jacket on a coat rack. After ditching his bulky jacket, he put on Judge Cook's hat and coat, hiding the gun inside the jacket.

The clock in Derek's head counted down. He had little time to escape before deputies searched this area of the building. The room had two other doors. He cracked one open, discovering it led to an outer office where two people had huddled against the wall. He closed the door and went to the other one. Easing it open, he found it was a private entrance leading to the employee parking lot.

Derek whispered thanks and darted outside. His heart pounded so hard he thought it might burst. This was his one chance to get away alive.

Several people were running through the lot with terrified expressions. He joined a group traveling in the direction where he'd parked his car. When they reached the street corner, he peeled off and dashed to his waiting sedan. He stabbed his hand in his front pants pocket, but his car keys weren't there. "You idiot." He'd left them in the backpack he'd forgotten in the courtroom.

Derek checked up and down the street for police but saw only civilian pedestrians. However, the police would soon figure out who he was from facial recognition, which meant he couldn't go home or to anyone he knew. His best chance was to steal a car, but from where? He didn't know how to hot-wire a car, so he'd have to find one with the keys inside it.

"Think, stupid, think." Then it came to him. "The oil fields." He'd worked there for years before going to prison. The maintenance yard had a dozen trucks, and the supervisor kept the keys in a shack with a flimsy door. If he could remain undetected until dark, he could break in, steal a truck, and be two states away before sunrise.

8

The turn leading to the access road of Lexi's childhood home came into sight, cueing another round of apologies. The first she'd made was coming home three hours early this afternoon to make up for yesterday's absence. Lexi reached across the middle console of her SUV and brought Nita's hand to her mouth, placing a long sensual kiss on the back of it. "I'm sorry I made us miss yesterday's cookout with my parents."

"As long as you make it to our wedding, all is forgiven."

"Wild horses couldn't keep me from marrying you on Saturday." Lexi kissed her hand again before letting it go to make the turn. She silently lectured herself to keep her damn promise. *Work. Will. Not. Get. In. The. Way.* Pulling behind the main house, Lexi parked beneath the old shade tree near the back porch. The left bay door to the four-car garage was open. "It looks like Dad is in the garage. Do you mind if I tinker with him while you help Mom?"

"Of course not." Nita squeezed her hand. "You need more time together."

Lexi unbuckled and pulled Nita's head closer by the chin. The slow, methodical kiss explored every curve of her lips and crevice of her tongue before pulling back. "Thank you."

Passing each other on the way to their destinations, Nita swatted Lexi on the butt. "Have fun with your dad."

"Have fun rolling wedding silverware." Lexi entered the open bay, turning toward the source of the country music at the back of the extra-long garage. Her dad was under the hood of the '65 Shelby, and his cane was against the driver's side fender.

"Hey, Dad."

He popped his head in her direction and snatched a well-used shop cloth from the back pocket of his blue pinstriped mechanic's coveralls. "I didn't know you were coming this early. Otherwise, I would have had the grill going."

"I took some vacation time to make up for yesterday. I'm sorry I was called in." It was no coincidence the first SRT tasking Lange had sent her on was over the weekend and stretched over two days.

"I'm assuming it went well."

"Piece of cake." Not telling him she had to defuse an IED after an FBI sniper took out a little girl's father after he'd taken her hostage was probably for the best. He and her mom would only worry if she told him the girl had nearly tripped the trigger, running to her while they were in the kill zone.

"I'm sure it was." His puffy harrumph suggested he clearly suspected she was holding back.

"I thought we could get in a few hours on the Shelby before dinner." Lexi grabbed her coveralls from the wall hook, regret tugging at her heart. When she'd brought her dad home from the hospital last month, she'd volunteered to take Gavin's place, rebuilding her father's wedding gift. She'd hoped to spend the time also rebuilding their relationship. But Lexi didn't count on Kris Faust's death throwing her into a tailspin, followed by losing herself in work to take her mind off the guilt.

"I'd like that. I've done everything I can." He patted his left leg, the one he'd hurt years ago on the racetrack and the one Jamie Porter had shot during Nita's kidnapping last month. "This thing stiffens up when I stand on it too long, which limits my time out here."

Lexi put on her grease catcher over her casual street clothes and zipped it up. "That's why I'm here." Lexi lowered the hood and raised the Shelby on the rack. "What should we work on first? The suspension or trans-mission?"

Three hours later, the four-speed manual transmission was working smooth as butter. Grease covered Lexi's hands, and her father was sitting in the camping chair near the radio, admiring their work. "We did good, Dad." She wiped her hands with a fresh rag. "If I'd come more often, we might have had her done for the wedding this weekend."

"It's all right, Peanut. I know you have a lot on your mind."

"I do but being preoccupied doesn't excuse not keeping my word."

"You've been like this most of your life, losing yourself in work to avoid your troubles. I think you got that from me." Her father was right. She remembered him spending more time in the garage after his accident. Then she recalled something her mother told her after she left home.

"Is that why you practically lived out here after I came out and moved away?"

"Those were troubling times for me."

"And now?"

"If Gavin were still with us, I could say not as much."

Lexi placed a hand on his shoulder. "I miss him too, Dad. How about we head inside and help Mom and Nita with the wedding prep?"

He grinned. "I'd almost rather stay out here."

"I can't disagree, but my fiancée might have me sleeping on the couch until the wedding if I don't help." Lexi and her dad washed up at the garage sink and walked across the yard in the shadows of the late afternoon sun.

"I feel like the little kid on Thanksgiving being forced to spend time with the adults," he chuckled. Her dad's limp was a little less noticeable today with the aid of his cane. And if she weren't mistaken, he was walking better than he had in years.

When Lexi held the door open for her father, the soft sound of the Temptations floated past. Walking inside, she discovered the heart-melting scene of a lifetime. Nita and her mother were behind the kitchen island, swaying to the music while preparing the side dishes for their one-day-late cookout.

"I never knew cooking could be so fun." Lexi settled behind Nita, wrap-ping her arms around her waist. Though her father had become more accepting of her relationship with Nita, Lexi showed her respect by limiting her kiss to a peck on the cheek.

"That's because you don't do it enough." Nita craned her neck, returning Lexi's kiss on the cheek. "You'd rather do takeout or nuke something in the microwave."

"Guilty as charged." Lexi released her hold, went to the cabinet for a plastic water glass, and turned around again.

"Just like your father," her mother said.

Nita looked left and right. "Where's your steam pot? I should get the carrots going."

"I'll get it." Jessie moved aside and bent to open a lower cabinet at the kitchen island. She swayed, placing a hand on the granite countertop to steady herself. "Whoa." But then she fell to the floor, landing on her bottom.

"Mom!" Lexi dropped the cup and rushed to her mother. She supported her upper torso to prevent her from hitting her head on the tile. "Mom, are you okay?"

Lexi's father rushed around the island, and Nita knelt beside her mother, checking her pupils. "Jessie, can you follow my finger?" Nita dragged an index finger left and right and up and down. "Do you know what day it is?"

The confused, dazed look on her mother's face was terrifying. "Sunday. No, Monday."

"Do you have any other symptoms? Headache? Nausea?" Nita pressed. Lexi recalled Nita asking the same questions when she fell on the treadmill while rehabbing with her new prosthetic two years ago. She was well-trained at triaging patients under her care for head and other injuries.

"No, I'm just a little weak."

"You're pushing yourself too hard again, Jessie." Worry cut through her father's voice.

"Again?" Lexi snapped her head toward her mother. "Has this happened before, Mom?"

"I'm feeling better. Can you help me up to a chair?" Lexi and Nita each lifted her mother by the arm and guided her to the kitchen table. "Thank you, it was just a fainting spell."

"How many spells have you had?" Nita asked.

"This makes three. I saw my doctor on Friday. He took some blood and scheduled an MRI next week after the wedding."

"Good," Nita said. "Many things can cause dizziness, but I'm concerned about something lingering from your head injury. I wouldn't wait until next week for the MRI. I'd go to the Emergency Room and have one done today."

"Emergency Room?" Her mother perked up. "There's no need for that, but I will call Doc McCormick in the morning and see if he can get me in sooner." She looked about the room, focusing on the countertops. "We still have to get dinner ready."

"You need to rest, Mom," Lexi said. "Let's get you to your easy chair. The rest of us can handle dinner. We'll make it a family room night."

When her mom didn't object, Lexi knew her condition was more serious than she had let on. But she also knew nothing could convince her to get to the root cause tonight, so she settled her into her recliner and had her dad stay to watch her.

Nita's worried expression when they returned to the kitchen was concerning. However, talking about it would only drive Lexi crazy, so they concentrated on fixing the burgers and veggies.

While plating the food, Lexi's phone vibrated in her pocket. The generic tone meant it wasn't from anyone in her inner circle of family and friends. She dug out her phone and read the screen. Nathan Croft was calling. "Dammit." He had the worst timing. Croft only called her cell for work, and as the junior agent on their team, Lexi had to answer it. She glanced at Nita. "It's work. Let me see what Croft wants."

Nita's eye rolling didn't bode well for Lexi if she failed to handle this quickly. The couch might still be in her future.

Kissing Nita's forehead, Lexi answered the call. "This is Mills."

"Mills, have you been watching the news?" Croft asked.

"No, why?"

"Turn on any station. The national networks have picked up the shooting of a judge in Harrington."

"I saw the alert a few hours ago." Lexi whispered to Nita to bring up a national news streaming feed on her phone, so she could continue the call. "I'm bringing it up now. What's changed?"

"There's been a twist. Just watch the courtroom video."

A newly released video showed the shooter in the middle of the courtroom gallery pulling a gun from beneath his jacket, rising to his feet, and pointing it at the judge. The video stopped when he readied to fire, likely because of the graphic nature of the killing. "I see it. How did he get the gun past security?"

"I asked the same question, so I had Kaplan Shaw enhance the video and get me a closeup of the gun. It appears to be made of plastic."

"That's pretty unique. You think it has to do with the Raven."

"I do. I called the sheriff's department handling the case. They didn't release it to the press but confirmed the shooter had gone through a metal detector. That means the gun was already in the courthouse or made of something other than metal."

"What about the shooter? The news said he'd escaped and a manhunt was underway."

"The deputy I talked to said they've brought out the dogs and are onto his scent. It's only a matter of time before they catch him. I want to be there when they bring him in. We should leave tonight."

Lexi ran her free hand across her face. This was their first solid lead on the Raven since the director handed her the case, but she had a family to think about. The old Lexi would have dropped everything, said her good-byes, and hopped in the car to meet Croft without thinking twice. But nearly losing her entire family at the hands of Tony Belcher's people had taught her perspective. Family took priority unless a ticking clock and lives hung in the balance. Croft had brought her neither.

"I hear you, and I agree this needs further investigation. But this can wait until morning."

"Dammit, Mills. If the FBI beats us there and turns this into a federal case, we'll have to fight to get it thrown our way."

"The gun angle automatically makes it an ATF case."

The heavy breathing through the line said she hadn't convinced Croft. "I'm not used to sitting on my hands. The FBI could have us waiting for weeks before they turn it over. By then, the trail might be cold."

"And if they balk, I'll call my ace in the hole." Lexi had made some valuable friends in high places while investigating the Gatekeepers and Red Spades, and she knew precisely which one could help. Maybe a preemptive strike was called for. "Tell you what. I'll call my contact tonight and make sure the FBI isn't anywhere near Harrington."

"All right, but I don't like this."

"I get that, Nathan, but I'm done with putting the job ahead of family. Have Ronald make the travel arrangements for late morning and send me the itinerary." Lexi finished the call, returned her phone to her pocket, and turned her attention to Nita. "Let's have dinner."

Nita's smile and alluring gaze said Lexi had racked up a stack of brownie points. The couch would be empty tonight.

9

Yesterday, Thomas Perez had passed his six-month mark out of the academy. Becoming a cop had been his dream since the first time he'd held a cap gun. Unfortunately, he had yet to label his time with the Harrington County Sheriff's Department as enjoyable. His first week had started with hushed conversations among the "good old boy" network spanning a good portion of the department, which the other deputies had not asked him to join. He'd dubbed them the Rat Pack. However, keeping his eyes and ears open had allowed him to piece together a few things. Most importantly, he'd learned the mystery centered on the prison north of town. Two months after the local election ushered in a new sheriff, the Rat Pack was in upheaval.

Until today, the dispatcher had sent Thomas primarily on calls involving traffic accidents, drug dealing, assaults, and domestic disturbances. But the assassination of a district judge and his bailiff had the entire department called in and buzzing. Some tried to hide it, but Thomas could tell deputies in the Rat Pack viewed the murders as a fortunate turn of events. Considering the new governor had appointed the judge after taking office, their perspective made morbid sense. Corruption touched the entire apparatus of county government offices, and the citizenry was systematically replacing the bad apples.

Thomas entered the briefing room stuffed with forty officers from the city and county, waiting to find out the details of tonight's manhunt. Many of the people didn't look familiar. Most of the new ones belonged to the city police, but a few were deputies from his own department he had yet to meet. Maybe if he'd worked something other than the night shift he would have known more of the men and women who wore the same badge he did.

"Listen up," the sheriff called everyone's attention. "Our suspect is Derek Culter, a recent parolee. The judge he killed had sentenced him in his drug case eight years ago. He's likely gone off the deep end. But most importantly, he killed one of our brothers. I want this done by the book so when we catch the son of a bitch, the state will put a needle in his arm. He's been on the loose for nine hours. An hour ago, the oil field maintenance yard reported an audible alarm. The bloodhounds picked up Culter's scent and tracked him to the oil fields south of town."

The sheriff pointed to a map of the Harrington River on the wall behind him. "We think he's going south along the brush on the river's west bank. I want twenty deputies to head to the oil fields and drive him farther south. The other twenty will pick up the river at I-20 southeast of town and head north by foot. With any luck, we'll surround him before sunrise."

Following the mission briefing, Thomas loaded up on bug spray, beef jerky, and extra batteries for his flashlight after filling the bladder in his CamelBak hydration backpack. His one tour in Afghanistan while in the Army had taught him to never go on a mission like this without the essentials. He'd made the mistake once and returned to the base hungry, thirsty, and with no light to see his way to the latrine. And looking at the officers around him, he knew several were about to do the same.

He piled into a van heading to I-20. Being among a group of deputies he called the outsiders—the ones not in the Rat Pack—put him at ease. Each gave him the impression they would have his back, not looking for a reason to distrust him. A deputy sergeant took charge at the drop-off location, assigning teams and grids. "Perez, you're with me. I can't have the rookie getting lost."

"You got it, Sergeant." Thomas slung both straps of his pack over his shoulders and tightened the waist belt before checking his weapon and extra ammo. *Old habits die hard*, he thought.

The teams fanned out in the near darkness. Light from the half moon and stars outlined the cottonwood and Mexican buckeye trees but left the mix of tarbush and yuccas in shadows. Thomas and the sergeant traipsed through the short grasses with their weapons drawn and at the ready. His team was nearest to the river, with the next closest twenty yards to their left. Everyone pressed forward, not masking their movement for sound intentionally. The idea was to push the suspect into a pocket and force a peaceful surrender.

The terrain along the shoreline was irregular, requiring a jagged course. Thomas had grown up in this region and knew not to venture too close to the edge, especially at night when he couldn't be sure of his footing. The bank was rocky and steep, and the six-foot drop at this part of the Harrington River would not be pleasant. The current was dead along this stretch, so the salty water wouldn't sweep him downstream if he fell in.

Thomas divided his focus between the well-worn footpath ahead and the riverbank below. The bends were in the dark shadows, making it impossible to discern whether their suspect was hiding there. To compensate, Thomas got into a rhythm of shining his flashlight below every few yards without stopping when the footing was safe.

Movement below captured his attention. Thomas stopped and shined his light, keeping it still to discern the source. It moved again, allowing him to adjust the light. "Oh, shit." The long tail and wet, furry body meant one thing this time of night, and it wasn't good.

"What is it?" The sergeant asked in a near whisper.

"Muskrat." Thomas withdrew the light to not anger it. Those rodents were incredibly aggressive and prone to attacking humans without provocation. The diseases they carried made them particularly dangerous.

"We better steer clear," the sergeant said. "I never understood the song 'Muskrat Love.' Those things are anything but friendly."

They snickered and moved on.

The radio squawked in Thomas' ear. "This is South Two. We've got movement. My partner fell. Twisted an ankle."

The sergeant pressed the microphone clipped to a strap near his left shoulder. "This is South One Leader. On my way. Flush him east toward the bank." He glanced at Thomas. "Hold the line here. Don't let him get past you."

"Copy." The last line of defense was a familiar role. Thomas' last mission in the sandbox was a nearly botched rescue of their interpreter taken by Taliban supporters. When attackers armed with Russian-made AK-47s had overrun his platoon, Thomas' squad mates were the last ones standing. He didn't fail that night and wouldn't now.

The sergeant took off sprinting, bounding over the low brush like a mountain lion chasing its prey. Meanwhile, Thomas slowed his pace. Instinct told him to take cover, so he stopped next to a cottonwood tree near the river's ledge. The radio continued to chirp, saying the suspect was slippery and ran like a rabbit in the dark. Faint light beams wobbled in the distance to his west and north.

"Perez, suspect coming your way."

"Copy," Thomas whispered into his microphone. Hearing swooshing in the brush to his left, he clicked off the safety of his service weapon.

The rustling got closer. Darkness often played tricks on the senses, and Thomas wasn't immune. He couldn't tell whether there was one person or more, but he swore he heard two sets of footsteps. He also couldn't be sure of their distance. They could be twenty feet away or right on top of his position.

His breathing picked up speed, matching his racing pulse, when he heard a branch snap at his ten o'clock. Someone was within striking distance. It was now or never. Thomas emerged from his defensive position, training his weapon in the area where he heard the noise. He called out. "Police. Freeze!"

He saw two shadowy figures, one barreling toward him in the dark. The other was farther back with an arm extended, carrying an object in their hand, perhaps a pistol. A light cone from the west shined on their position briefly. Thomas thought he recognized the second man with the tight curls. He was wearing a police uniform, but with multiple agencies involved in tonight's manhunt, Thomas couldn't be sure who it was.

The next second, the darting figure bulldozed him. They both tumbled to the ground. Thomas rolled toward the six-foot ledge, still holding his gun and fearing another turn might launch him over the edge. He reached his free hand, blindly searching for anything to grab onto, and felt a branch. Clamping his hand like a vise, he held on for dear life. His feet continued to slide, but his upper torso remained in place. A violent jerk brought him to a sudden stop with his boots dangling over the edge.

The absence of sharp pain meant nothing was broken. Thomas scrambled to his feet without time to take a more accurate inventory. His heart beat wildly out of control, but he focused on the unfolding scene. The second man crouched and reversed, disappearing into the brush. The first man on the ground had recovered and was on his knees. He picked up an odd-looking gun from the ground with his right hand.

Thomas couldn't make out his features but smelled his desperation. "Drop your weapon."

"I won't go back." The man's voice was brittle, signaling he was on an emotional ledge.

"Don't make me shoot you." Thomas hated killing. His body count was eight in the desert, but he'd hoped to make it through a career as a deputy in rural Texas without adding to the tally.

"Shoot me, dammit. It's the only way."

"Only way for what?" Thomas had to stall for backup to arrive. He knew he'd found the judge's killer. He saw lights wobbling closer and closer, telling him they were seconds away.

"Just shoot."

A shadow appeared behind Culter, making Thomas think the deputy he'd seen a moment ago had returned. Then, a familiar electrical pop sounded. Culter's body convulsed. His legs buckled, sending him to the uneven ground again. When the gun dropped from his hand, his jerking stopped.

Thomas looked up, finding the deputy sergeant walking forward, holstering his Taser gun. "Great job, Perez."

Thomas returned his stare to Culter, writhing on the ground in pain. "Where's the other deputy? Did he tell you where to find us?"

"What deputy?"

"I'm not sure, but I thought he had on one of our uniforms."

"Everyone was accounted for. It must have been shadows." The sergeant patted Thomas on the back. "This is your collar. You get the honor of cuffing him. Do this by the book and read him his rights. The feds are already interested in this case."

"Yes, sergeant." None of this made sense. Maybe Thomas had gotten the uniform wrong, but he was confident another man was there. However, solving the mystery would have to wait. The man lying on the ground represented his first arrest. This would be one he'd never forget.

Thomas retrieved his handcuffs from the pouch on his belt at his right hip. After placing Culter's hands behind his back, he said, "You have the right to remain silent..."

After Thomas had booked the suspect, he returned to the room where every officer involved in the manhunt had gathered for the debriefing. He let a smile form. The department had captured the courtroom killer and recovered the gun within ten hours through excellent policing. And it was crazy to think Thomas, the least experienced on the manhunt, was the arresting officer of record.

Several deputies shook his hand and patted him on the back, saying this was the most momentous day the department had seen in over a decade. "You should be proud," one said. "You'll get a commendation for this. It's not every day we capture a cop killer in a manhunt."

Thomas didn't care about a medal. He scanned the room, looking for someone with short curly hair. One of them had to be the officer he'd seen moments before Culter tackled him. He focused on one head after another but found no one who looked remotely like the man at the river. He considered the "good old boy" network in the department and his suspicion that most of the city was corrupt, and then he concluded one thing. Whoever he'd seen didn't want Culter walking away alive.

10

The soft mechanical sound of a bird chirping nudged Lexi from sleep. Her eyelids stubbornly refused to cooperate because her alarm had come too early. She had maintained traditional business hours since closing the task force and had gotten soft, not rising before the sun until today. She enjoyed keeping the same hours as Nita. It meant mornings rolling around in bed together and having breakfast at the table instead of in the car.

The alarm progressively increased in volume, forcing Lexi to do something. Throwing the phone across the room came to mind, but with her luck, it would only get louder from the far corner. "Dammit." Lexi blindly reached for the nightstand, located the phone, and finally opened her eyes to the darkness. Straining to focus, she made out the correct spot on the screen to swipe and hit it on the second try.

Nita scooted closer so their torsos touched and draped a leg over Lexi's thigh. Snaking an arm under her tank top, Nita rested a warm hand on her breastbone. Its placement was very diplomatic. Anywhere else above her waist would have sent the message, *"I'm too tired."* If Nita had cupped a breast and given a gentle squeeze, she would have made an entirely different point. But she had split the hair, letting Lexi decide how to start the day and how much time she had to dedicate to a proper morning greeting.

Having set the alarm to allow for a ten-minute cushion, intimacy wasn't out of the question, but Lexi hated to rush. Each of Nita's curves and crevices needed savoring, honoring from head to toe. On the other hand, leaving their bed without a taste was impossible. It would be a crime of the highest order during the week before their wedding.

Lexi brought Nita's hand to her lips and kissed its back before turning to face her. Legs entwined. Arms curled around the other's backs. Breasts pressed together with only thin layers of cotton from their tank tops separating them. Lexi pressed their lips together in a languid kiss. Nita's were smooth, moist, and pillowy soft. They were more alluring than ice cream on a hot summer day and more comforting than a warm spring breeze.

Nita's lips parted, an invitation for Lexi to take this wherever she pleased. *Just one taste to get through the day*, she told herself. But as with so many delicacies, one lick was never enough. One turned into two. Two turned into four. And four into eight. Each stroke fanned the heat between them, threatening to combust into a blaze and make Lexi miss her flight. If she didn't apply the brakes now, she never would. But enjoying Nita's body wouldn't be the worst thing in the world. It would be heaven between the sheets.

The birds chirped again in the worst timing sort of way. Every muscle in Lexi's right hand tightened. She wanted to punch that damn thing into tomorrow.

Nita pulled back, expelling short steamy breaths. "I thought you turned it off."

"I must have hit snooze by mistake." Lexi lowered her hands around Nita's bottom, pressing it hard against herself. Her craving told her to stay, but her conscience told her it was time to go. Releasing the pressure against her core signaled her decision, but doing the right thing didn't equate to wanting to. She sighed and said, "I have to get ready."

"How long will you be away?" Nita asked.

"I'm not sure, but I'm taking my go-bag with me in case I have to spend a night or two. But with any luck, I'll be home tonight."

Lexi showered and dressed and approached the bed to kiss Nita goodbye. She'd rolled onto her side and pulled the covers over her shoulders with her long brown hair draped over her neck. Her stillness and rhythmic breathing with a breathy exhale signaled she'd fallen asleep. Nita would disagree, but Lexi thought she was more beautiful asleep. Every imperfection surfaced during the night, showing her true self. That was the Nita she'd fallen in love with. The one she wanted to spend the rest of her life with.

"I love you," Lexi whispered and walked out. Descending the stairs, she smelled bacon and saw light coming from the kitchen. That meant one thing. She turned the corner. "You should be resting."

Her mother was standing sentinel over eggs in a frying pan. She craned her neck to look over her shoulder at Lexi. "I couldn't let you go on a trip without a proper breakfast."

Lexi kissed her cheek and snatched a strip of crispy bacon from the serving plate. "Thank you. Need some help?" Her mother gestured her spatula toward the stack of toast, which meant it needed buttering. Six pieces suggested her father was up and likely tinkering in the garage. After prepping the toast, Lexi poured the orange juice. "Want me to tell Dad breakfast is ready?"

Her mom walked to the round table and plated the scrambled eggs for Lexi and herself. "We have a west wind." Meaning the breeze would carry the mix of aromas to the garage, a better alerting system for her father than the tornado siren at the street corner.

Before Lexi could pepper her eggs, the screen door opened. Her father walked through, wiping his hands on a shop rag. "Everything smells wonderful, Jess." He patted her on the butt and reached for a piece of bacon from the serving plate.

She slapped his hand. "Don't you dare. Wash up first."

"Yes, ma'am." He saluted and turned his attention to Lexi. "Morning, Peanut. Heading off to the airport?"

"Yeah. Our flight is in a few hours. I'm hoping this won't take more than a day. After I'm back, how about we work on the Shelby suspension?"

"I'd like that."

While her father washed up at the sink, Lexi's mother sat at her traditional seat nearest the stove and refrigerator. The bags under her eyes were more prominent than in recent weeks, suggesting her head injury and caring for her father after his gunshot wound had taken a toll. Her mother would appear the strong, industrious woman she'd always been to most, but Lexi could tell she'd lost a step. Her movement was a fraction slower and not as graceful as before the attack as if she was struggling for balance.

Lexi reached across the table and gave her mother's hand a brief squeeze. "Please call Doc McCormick this morning. Nita said she'll drive you if he can get you in today."

Her mother spread a paper napkin across her lap. The recognizable forced smile meant Lexi had annoyed her. "Since when did you become a worrywart?"

"Since I almost lost you two."

Peppering her eggs, her mother remained silent, but the distant look in her eyes suggested she was worried, too. After she put the shaker down, her full smile returned. "That's over with. I'd like to put that day behind us and concentrate on the wedding. You two are going to look amazing in your tux and gown. I'm glad you chose lavender as your color. Eastman's had the perfect dress for me." She leaned in, whispering so Lexi's father wouldn't hear. "Jerry picked it out. He said it would match the button-down shirt he'd found in the men's section."

Lexi glanced at her dad at the sink while he wiped his clean hands dry with a dishtowel. "I'll be damned." He was trying his best to accept Lexi for who she was and welcome Nita into the family.

Her mother smirked. "He's full of surprises these days."

Lexi's dad joined them at the table, rubbing his hands together, nearly drooling in anticipation. "I love your mother's scrambled egg mash."

Lexi checked the time on her watch and stuffed down her food so fast she barely tasted the unique blend of spices and vegetables. It was a recipe handed down by her grandmother. She had gotten it from her grand-mother and so on, dating back to the post-civil war era in Southern Missis-sippi. Lexi would have to remind herself to have her mom teach her how to make it after the wedding.

"I hate to eat and run, but I have a plane to catch." Lexi kissed each parent on the forehead. "Bye, Mom. Bye, Dad. I'll let Nita know when I'm coming home."

Before leaving, Lexi took in her father's transformation. A year ago, they were estranged with no hope of reconciling. But her near-death experiences chasing Tony Belcher changed that. Fifteen years of rejection were now solidly in the past.

Lexi imagined coming here on Sundays for NASCAR and Cowboys games with everyone pitching in to fix the family feast. She imagined adding a child to the mix in a few years and teaching them how to use a torque wrench as soon as they could reach over the fender, just like her father had done in his garage when Lexi was little. It was a future she'd never considered, nor knew she'd wanted. After all, there wasn't any sense in dreaming of something with no chance of its coming true. But with her wedding a week away, it had become a possibility, and Lexi could think of nothing sweeter.

Lexi closed the door, letting a smile remain on her lips until her phone buzzed when she was halfway to the city. The familiar ringtone announced who was calling. She swiped the screen, connecting it to the car's Bluetooth. "You're up early, Maxwell."

"I saw your text from late last night and thought I'd chance calling. So what do you need my help with?"

"Did you see the news about the judge shooting in Harrington?"

"I did. It's a shame. More and more judges are being targeted. Before you know it, every criminal court judge in the country will need a security detail."

"I don't doubt it. I hate to ask for favors, but could you use your pull to make sure the alphabet soup of federal agencies steers clear of this one? There's a chance the ghost gun used by the shooter could be the Raven's work. If that's the case, I don't want other agencies slowing us down."

"Consider it done. I can't think of anyone I'd like to investigate the killing of two federal agents more than you. I'll clear a path when I get into the office."

"Thanks, Maxwell."

Several silent moments passed before he spoke again. "Hey, Lexi."

"Yeah?"

"I can say this from experience. The weight of losing Kris will never go away, but it will become easier to carry. I promise."

"I don't think I want it to."

"Why is that?"

"Because I might forget the hard-learned lesson to never overlook safety, no matter how mundane the task."

"Which makes you a damn good leader. When you're ready, the AG and I would like you back. You'll have your pick of leading any task force you'd like."

"I don't know if I'll ever be ready for that responsibility again. I enjoy getting back to my roots with explosives."

Maxwell snorted. "Which is why you're off to investigate a ghost gun likely connected to the Raven."

"Will you stop?" She half-chuckled to keep the conversation light. *Just the Raven*, she told herself. Once she had him in custody, she would return to SRT duties full time and never look back.

"You're a natural leader, Lexi. The ATF is wasting your talents in a field office. I probably shouldn't say this, but I've heard you're on the incoming president's shortlist to replace Director Hanlon when he retires next year."

"Me? Why me? I'm just a little fish."

"Oh, please. You're already swimming in the big pond. You've earned the respect of nearly every cop and federal agent in the nation. The country needs people like you at the top holding the reins."

Lexi's head spun so fast she had to slow her speed on the highway. She never considered herself the type to sit behind mahogany desks and dress in tailored suits every day. At heart, she was a field agent who enjoyed getting her hands dirty. Becoming the ATF Director would mean dealing with other suits, budgets, and politicians, all of which she hated as much as Brussels sprouts. And that was saying something.

"Please tell whoever you have to thank you, but I'm not interested. I'm happy with my cargo pants and t-shirts. And I'm definitely not moving to Washington D.C. Can you see me playing nice with all those congresspeople?"

Maxwell laughed. "All right, Lexi, I'll pass along the word, but the offer stands about a future task force. I'd be honored to work with you again."

11

The plane came to a slow, crawling stop at the Midland Airport gate, sparking the mad rush of impatient travelers clogging the aisle and bringing Nathan's hand rubbing to an end. He unbuckled. "I'll get the rental car." The tension in Nathan's voice was more potent than last night. His stiff body language made his thoughts clear. They'd wasted too much precious time waiting for the first plane from Dallas that morning. If Croft were in charge, Lexi would have bet her last dollar they would have arrived six or seven hours ago and already interviewed the sheriff, new district attorney, and everyone in town who knew the suspect.

If they were to continue working together beyond this case, Lexi couldn't let this fester. "Nathan, I don't want the Raven case to strain our partnership."

"I don't either."

"I hear a but there."

"The Raven was like a ghost until I figured out his signature and calling card a few months ago. Now I know what to look for, so stalling when we get a hit is as unnatural as spandex."

"Spandex?" Lexi laughed.

"Considering what most people on this plane are wearing, it came to mind first." He half-smiled.

Lexi scanned the people in the crowded aisle and laughed again. His observation was spot on. "Spandex might be unnatural, but it's also practical. It provides comfort and fashion."

"It does that."

"And practical is how I approach work and family since my brush with Tony Belcher. He taught me I shouldn't sacrifice one for the other."

"I guess that's why I'm divorced and only see my son every other weekend. I never learned balance."

"I'll make you a promise, Nathan. If the trail is hot, I won't drag my feet." Lexi locked stares with him to gauge his response. "Are we good?"

His eyes were unreadable, but his nod said they were on the right track. "We're good."

Lexi checked her phone after it vibrated in her pocket. The text from Kaplan reaffirmed her decision to put family over the job. *Court-appointed lawyer at 10. Interrogation at 2pm.* "It looks like my instincts were right about not rushing. That was Shaw from Intel. Culter finally got a lawyer. We have three hours before they interrogate him."

Croft's eyes danced with excitement. "Then let's interview the family."

"I was thinking the same thing."

A faint grin formed on Nathan's lips.

Two hours later, Nathan pulled their rental car into the parking lot of the low-cost housing apartment building in the east part of Harrington. Derek Culter had listed this location as his temporary residence following his parole three months ago. Chain-link fences, weed-laden sidewalks, and a hodgepodge of graffiti on cinder block walls highlighted their route.

After checking the Texas driver's license photo Kaplan had texted Lexi, Nathan knocked on the third-floor door. Moments later, it cracked open to a woman in her late thirties or early forties dressed in a t-shirt and dark leggings. When he held up the leather case with his badge and credentials, the woman narrowed her eyes, silently screaming her distrust of law enforcement.

"June Harris, we're ATF Agents Croft and Mills. We'd like to ask you some questions."

"This isn't a good time."

Nathan stuck his foot in the closing door's path. "This won't take long."

A fire sparked in her eyes. "I'm so tired of you cops. You ripped apart my apartment without caring what you broke. My son was here, for heaven's sake. He was so scared he refused to go to school today."

Lexi needed to do what she did best—defuse things. She stepped forward, softening her expression. "I know the last twenty-four hours have been upsetting, Ms. Harris. We're concerned whoever put Derek up to the shooting is dangerous. They might come after you and your son." That was an assumption, but Lexi needed to get her talking.

"Us?" Harris relaxed her hand against the door, suggesting Lexi had gotten her attention. "We had no idea what he was up to."

"But he was living here. Did he have any visitors or receive any phone calls?"

"I let him stay on the couch until he could get a job in the oil fields again and move into company housing. I steered clear of him as much as possible. But as far as I know, he didn't get any visitors, and the only phone he had was disposable like the kind you find at Walmart."

"Thank you. That helps. Do you know where Derek might have gotten the gun?"

"I have no idea. I would have kicked him out on his ear if I'd known he'd brought a gun into the apartment."

"How about friends or acquaintances before he went to prison?" Nathan asked.

"Friends?" Harris scoffed. "He burned every bridge in town, including the one with me. I only let him stay here because of Junior."

"Derek was convicted of possessing illegal drugs," Lexi said. "Do you know who his dealer was?"

"Scooter, the town weasel. I hate that man. He gives me the creeps. Can we go back to us being in danger? What should we do?"

"Can you stay with family or find a hotel for a few days?"

Harris harrumphed. "No, and an even bigger no. I don't have money for a hotel."

"Then stay home as much as possible and keep your door locked." Lexi handed her a business card, not expecting her to keep it. "Call me if you have any trouble or can think of anything else that might help us catch these people."

Lexi eyed the limited selection in the drink vending machine at the Harrington County Sheriff's Office entrance, realizing they should have stopped on the way. "Orange or Piña Colada Fanta."

"Without rum? I'll stick with orange." Nathan had a point. Cream coconut and pineapple should only be drunk with copious amounts of rum.

"Good choice." Lexi slipped in one-dollar bills, and following a hefty shove, the machine spat out two drinks. Taking the first sip churned up a long-forgotten memory. Her father hated the drink but stocked the orange soda in every garage when he was on the NASCAR circuit because it was her mother's favorite. She'd have to remember to ask her mom why she stopped drinking it.

A flash of their badges and credentials got them buzzed inside the secure area. Deputy Thomas Perez greeted them and gestured down the hallway. "Please follow me. Sheriff Jessup is expecting you." Halfway down, Perez glanced over his shoulder at Lexi and Nathan. "I guess you two are interested in the crazy gun Culter used."

"Yes. Have you seen it?" Nathan asked.

"He pointed it directly at me last night." The look in Perez's eyes said it was an unnerving experience. "It's not like any other gun I've seen." He entered the office with the image of the distinctive five-point gold sheriff's badge painted on the door. "Sheriff, the ATF agents are here."

The sheriff rose from his chair and circled his neatly organized oak desk, extending his hand to Lexi with adoration in his eyes. "Sam Jessup. It's an honor to meet you, Agent Mills. You're a legend in these parts."

"It's a pleasure, Sheriff." She gestured to her left. "This is Special Agent Nathan Croft."

"I'm glad you two are here. Maybe you can give us some insight into the gun." Jessup shook Nathan's hand but kept his eye on Lexi, looking as if he expected her to have all the answers.

Lexi had researched ghost guns and 3D-printed weapons on the internet during the flight but had only rudimentary knowledge. She glanced at Nathan. His pinched mouth was rightly a mix of resentment and frustration. He was the expert in these things, but Lexi's celebrity had sucked up all the oxygen in the room. "Agent Croft is the ATF's foremost authority in ghost guns. Once he examines it, he'll give you a complete rundown. Then we'd like to interview Culter. Has he been arraigned yet?"

"Yes, first thing this morning. The judge denied him bail."

"What can you tell us about him?"

"Derek Culter worked in the oil fields until my department popped him for possession with intent to distribute oxy. He had a history of bar fights, assault, and public intoxication, so the judge gave him twenty, but he was out in eight." The sheriff shook his head. "The new governor is too soft on criminals if you ask me. I can't believe the parole board let him out."

Lexi kept her opinion to herself. Her friend, Governor Ken Macalister, had ruffled many feathers in Texas with his more progressive policies. If a near insurrection and assassination attempt didn't deter him, nothing would. And that had earned her profound respect.

"Unless he refuses to answer questions, my investigator will take a crack at him. Until then"—Jessup retrieved a file box from behind his chair and placed it atop his desk—"let's have you examine the gun."

Nathan put on a pair of latex gloves before handling the weapon. "I assume your techs have already processed it piece by piece."

"Yep. It didn't match any of the known blueprints, so they had a heck of a time putting it back together again."

Nathan scrutinized the off-white weapon from all sides. "That's because it's a unique design. It's a lot lighter than anything else I've come across." He smoothly disassembled it, placing each piece on the evidence bag to not scratch the desk. "Whoever designed this is a genius. It's similar to the PG22 Maverick six-shot revolver, but he's replaced the traditional metal pieces. The barrels, cylinder, spring, guide rod, and firing pin are plastic." His face lit up, reminding Lexi of herself when she keyed on some aspect of an explosive she was disarming. It was the look of unbridled amazement and curiosity. "This is spectacular because a gun made from all plastic parts couldn't have fired multiple 9mm bullets at the distance Culter shot from, let alone with any accuracy. The barrel wouldn't have provided the right rifling to spin the bullet correctly, and the spring would have broken after the first shot. I bet a chemical analysis will show this is made of 2DPA-1 plastic."

"What's that?" Lexi asked.

"It's a new plastic MIT developed this year. It's half the weight of traditional plastics and stronger than steel." Nathan narrowed his eyes while cocking his head in more profound curiosity. "The material isn't in production yet, so the designer must have some serious connections."

"A plastic stronger than steel?" Lexi considered the frightening implications on law enforcement. Anyone with a 3D printer could produce a reliable, untraceable, undetectable firearm made entirely of plastic. "This is a nightmare. The ghost gun population will explode."

"Exactly." Nathan looked more closely at the gun's frame, focusing on one spot. "Lexi, do you see that black spot? If I'm right—"

A wave of excitement warmed her. Nathan was right. "It's part of a feather."

"Care to fill me in?" the sheriff asked.

Lexi nodded at Nathan, giving him the go-ahead to explain. He'd earned the honor. "We think an arms dealer we've been tracking made this weapon." He looked directly at the sheriff. "He not only buys and sells weapons, but he also builds them."

"He built the Las Vegas dirty bomb and killed two federal agents last month," Lexi said. The back of her throat thickened, thinking about what those events had cost. Two good agents had lost their lives, and Lexi had lost her best friend. Noah Black had taken on the burden of becoming a killer by shooting an unarmed Tony Belcher so Lexi didn't have to. However, that unselfish act forever altered their friendship.

"I remember the Vegas incident. Weren't you involved, Agent Mills?"

Lexi nodded slowly. "With both attacks." The uncomfortable memory strengthened her determination to find justice for Kris Faust and Noah Black.

Nathan returned the gun to the evidence bag and placed it inside the box. "Now, about Culter's questioning."

The sheriff handed the box to Deputy Perez. "Return this to evidence, son. Bring Culter to the interrogation room when you're done since he's your collar." He then handed a business card to Lexi. "My personal number is on the back if you need to reach me while you're in town."

Lexi snickered to herself. If that was his best come on, he needed to find a better game.

Sheriff Jessup extended his arm toward the door and shifted his attention to Lexi. "Shall we? The interrogation starts in a few minutes."

12

Without a mirror, it was hard for Milo to tell whether he had tightened his tie straight, but the clock in his head told him he didn't have time to fiddle with it. He made one more adjustment, buttoned his suit coat, and faced the cell bars when the boots clomping against the concrete stopped at his door.

"Ready, Mr. Tilton?" Deputy Rusty Ross slid the bars open. His toothless grin meant things were about to go Milo's way after yesterday's courtroom fiasco. All three of his problems were supposed to be in the morgue, but two were still walking. At least the man Jackson had found hit the one target that might get Milo out of jail today.

"As I'll ever be." Milo smoothed the flaps of his suit coat and let Rusty handcuff him while thinking about what steak he'd like to order tonight. He couldn't decide between the buttery New York strip or the tender filet. *Porterhouse*, he thought. The selection provided both cuts, one on either side of the bone. A loaded baked potato and buttered asparagus spears would complete the perfect meal after more than a month of jailhouse food.

Walking down the corridor between cells, Rusty was gentle with his grip on Milo. If he didn't, his pay envelope would be light next month. He guided Milo to one side when another deputy approached from the opposite direction.

The other deputy squinted, focusing his stare on Rusty. "Were you at the river last night?"

"Not me." Rusty pushed Milo along more firmly.

The route across the parking lot connecting the jail to the courthouse took them down a business corridor. The sheriff turned the corner. The glower he gave Milo said he knew he was about to lose this round. Meanwhile, the man and woman with him gave Milo a thorough once-over but continued walking.

Except for Milo's lawyer, a new bailiff, and the district attorney who was supposed to die yesterday, the courtroom was devoid of people. There would be no repeat of yesterday's public spectacle. Milo would be released within the hour if the right judge walked through the door leading from the private chambers.

Rusty unlocked the handcuffs, giving a furtive wink when Milo turned around. "You should be home in no time, sir."

Milo rubbed his wrists and sat next to Jackson at the defendant's table, eyeing the district attorney across the aisle. She'd set her stare on him. It was unwavering and contained a fiery determination. She placed the pen she was holding on the table, scooted her chair back, and stomped to his position.

"You don't frighten me, Mr. Tilton." Charlene Ford looked down on him as if he were the lowest form of criminal on earth. That might be true, but Milo wasn't about to spend one more day behind bars. Once he was out, he would find a way to put the right people in the right positions to get himself out of this.

"This is highly irregular." Jackson rose from his chair as a buffer between him and the righteous crusader.

"So is your client, Mr. Price. I won't let him or anyone else he hires intimidate me into dropping the charges. He has bullied this town for a decade, and now the town is fighting back. I intend to let the justice system decide his fate." Ford pivoted on her heel and marched back to her table as fervently as she'd come over. Any hope of finding her price to look the other way looked impossible, leaving Milo only one option.

Milo leaned into his lawyer. "Too many mistakes. Too many loose ends. We need to fix this."

"We can discuss it later," Jackson whispered back. "There's something you should know about the judge."

"All rise," the bailiff bellowed before Jackson could finish. If the county or state appointed another judge and his old friend didn't walk through the door, Milo was screwed. Assassinating one judge and making it look like a revenge killing by a deranged defendant was believable. He couldn't pull it off a second time.

The door opened. Milo's tense muscles relaxed when Clem Powell stepped through, wearing his traditional black robe. He didn't make eye contact with Milo as he sat behind his bench. Clem was king in his courtroom, dealing out justice how he saw fit. At times like today, a stack of Benjamins steered his decisions. Was it fair? No. But that was how west Texas worked for nearly two centuries. Milo would be just one in a long line of beneficiaries.

Once the bailiff read the court docket, Judge Powell adjusted his reading glasses and fumbled with some papers on his desk. "If I understand correctly, the defense motioned for a bail hearing, citing bias when Judge Cook remanded the defendant. Am I correct, Mr. Price?"

"Yes, your honor. As you can see in my motion—"

"Yes, yes." The judge waved off Price like a pesky fly. "I see it all here in the court transcript. An appellate court might construe his comments before rendering his decision on bail as prejudicial." He lowered his glasses, turning his attention to the prosecutor. "Miss Ford, does the state have anything to add to the record before I rule on bail?"

"Your honor, the state's position hasn't changed. The defendant sits accused of killing his wife in cold blood. He has significant wealth and the means to escape justice. Remanding him to the county jail will ensure his presence at trial."

Clem twirled his glasses by a stem in his left hand, putting on a good show of weighing the testimony. "The previous judge failed to consider the defendant's criminal record. He has no history of violence. Getting drunk and painting a bullseye on a cow does not rise to the level of scrutiny when considering bail. At the same time, the charge of murder is serious and requires some assurance of his return to court. If the state had charged the defendant with capital murder, I would have no choice but to remand Mr. Tilton. However, the state charged for the lesser crime of murder, for which the maximum bail is one hundred thousand dollars. Let's split the baby down the middle. Bail is set at fifty thousand dollars. Proceedings will resume in one week to give the trial judge enough time to get up to speed on the details. We are adjourned." Clem swung his gavel twice, thumping it against its base. The show he'd put on had also split the baby. He remained loyal to his old friend while following the law and neutering the D.A. from grandstanding in the media.

When everyone stood for Clem to retire to his chambers, he finally locked gazes with Milo. The barely there nod acknowledged he'd earned his pay this month, and if this all went away, he would see a giant bonus in his next envelope.

The district attorney slammed her portfolio shut when the bailiff followed the judge into the chambers. The noise echoed in the empty courtroom like a slap across the face during study hour at the library. She glared at Milo. "Don't celebrate yet, Mr. Tilton. Your grip on this town is slipping. You may have won this round, but I'm in this for the long haul. You may have bought your way out of pretrial confinement, but no amount of money will erase the evidence I've amassed against you. I suggest you settle your affairs quickly because you're not walking this time."

"Sweetheart, you lost me after celebrate," Milo snorted. "I'm popping the champagne as soon as I scrape up the pocket change for my bail."

When Rusty returned to take Milo back to his cell, Jackson asked for a moment alone with his client. Rusty remained by the main entrance. "Milo, I need to tell you about the message Clem sent me last night."

"What did old Clem say? I'll have to send him a bottle of my finest scotch when this is all over."

"Hold that thought." Jackson's serious tone was concerning following the win they just had in court. "Clem said the amount he set as bail would be his fee, payable before the trial started."

Milo would have bet his last dollar that steam was pouring from his ears. His head pounded so hard he wouldn't hear a jackhammer if it were right next to him. "Why, that greedy little cuss. After all I've done for him.

Virtually every official in this town has gotten rich off me, and now he wants to soak me for more money."

Jackson glanced in Rusty's direction. "Quiet down, Milo. We have a week to get the money. I'll go to Luther's and have him post the bond. You should be out of here within an hour."

"Good. Then I want to meet the cleanup man at my house. He needs to explain how this went to shit faster than a pig pen after feeding time."

13

Lexi passed a familiar-looking prisoner under escort in the hallway, but he had walked by so fast she couldn't be sure of his identity. She took longer strides to get beside Sheriff Jessup and keep pace with him. "Was that Milo Tilton, the defendant in yesterday's trial?"

"That was him." The sheriff's dismissive tone suggested he wasn't a fan.

"What's his story?"

"He's on trial for strangling his wife."

"Is there a connection between him and Culter?"

"Those two? Not a chance. Tilton runs the detention center north of town. Culter was new to Harrington. He was an oil field drifter, going from county to county after he wore out his welcome."

"How long did he live here?"

"About a year before going to jail for his drug conviction. Tilton would never associate with a man like Culter. He only consorted with people who could make him money. And that wasn't Culter." The sheriff sounded certain, but Lexi didn't believe in coincidence regarding murder. Every detail was suspect, deserving of scrutiny.

Arriving at the observation room, Lexi felt as if she was in a time warp and had walked onto the set of the original Dragnet series. An industrial metal desk and two matching chairs were the only pieces of furniture. No electronics to record the questioning or microphones to communicate with the interrogators. The only sign of modernization was a mid-century intercom on the wall next to the two-way mirror.

"Will you be recording the interview?" Croft asked. If he hadn't, Lexi would have. Nothing she'd seen so far gave her much confidence in the quality of their investigation.

"I know it doesn't look like much, Agent Mills." Sheriff Jessup approached the mirror, inviting Lexi to join him. He pointed toward the far wall in the interrogation room, where someone had mounted a cell phone to a rotating bracket. "The previous sheriff didn't record interviews or interrogations, but I made it mandatory. Unfortunately, the county won't spring for recording equipment until next year, so we improvise."

A detective walked into the interrogation room wearing dark slacks, a button-down white dress shirt with the long sleeves rolled to the elbow, and a loose tie. He'd attached his service weapon and handcuffs to his belt. He went to the phone on the wall, swiped the screen, and activated the camera function before sitting at the table in the middle of the room.

"Huh, I'm impressed with the ingenuity." Lexi had spent enough time on her father's NASCAR pit crew to see every which way to jury-rig an engine or body part long enough to finish a race. She appreciated creativity whenever people employed it effectively. Perhaps she had rushed to judgment. However, Croft's bitter smile was as visible as a bright neon sign on a dark street. He didn't share in her optimism.

"My predecessor was pretty lax with procedure, but I'm trying to clean things up."

Lexi got the impression cleaning up also included cleaning house. Corruption or incompetence, there was no room for either in law enforcement.

Another man in an ill-fitted off-the-rack suit entered, carrying a portfolio in his left hand and a Starbucks in his right. After placing his coffee cup down, the detective greeted him with a vigorous handshake and a lively conversation with a dash of guffaws.

The door opened. A vaguely familiar-looking woman dressed in a crisp pair of slacks and a matching blazer stepped inside, bringing the men's conversation to an abrupt stop. If Lexi remembered correctly, she was the district attorney, Charlene Ford, who was at yesterday's trial. Charlene inspected both men with a disapproving eye. "Care to take our positions?"

The detective sat on one side of the table with the woman. The suit sat on the other, bringing into focus a startling reality. The other man was the defense attorney. He and the detective were supposed to be on opposing sides, not chumming it up like they were at a high school class reunion.

Croft leaned closer to Lexi and whispered to her, "We should take over."

The display bolstered Lexi's initial assumption that Harrington had a fixed justice system, making it difficult to know who to trust. But until she and Croft had a reason to take over the case, it wasn't their place to interfere. They were there to determine if Culter's weapon was the Raven's work and follow the lead if it was, nothing more.

She whispered back, "Let's see how it goes."

Deputy Perez entered with the prisoner and sat him at the table next to his so-called defense lawyer. Unlocking the handcuffs, he stood against the wall nearest the door with a satisfied smile and crossed his arms against his chest. He looked fresh out of the academy and proud, as he should. Some police officers wear the badge for twenty years without making a felony arrest, but this young deputy had already collared a cop killer.

The detective spoke first to the defense attorney. "Thanks for coming, Jake. We have your client dead to rights for killing Judge Cook and Deputy Hernandez. Before we arraign your client for two counts of murder, we have a few questions."

"My client will answer questions if you take the death penalty off the table and classify him as a level two prisoner so you can house him in Fort Stockton and have visitation with his son."

"That won't happen." The prosecutor's sharp tone was unmistakable. She held the leverage in this circumstance and wasn't about to give up her advantage. "I want to know why your client chose yesterday's trial to commit his crime. Did someone put him up to killing Judge Cook? If so, who? Was he paid? I want to know how he got the gun. Who gave it to him? When? Where? And for how much? If he comes clean, I'll settle for life in prison with no chance of parole because a killer doesn't get to walk the streets on my watch. If your client fails to provide me everything I want to know, the death penalty is back on the table. Take it or leave it."

Lexi instantly liked this prosecutor—clear, concise, and not afraid to draw a line.

"Well, aren't we bitchy today, Charlene?" The defense lawyer closed his portfolio. "Then my client chooses to remain silent. We'll take our chances at trial, using a duress defense. Hell, when we finish putting on our case, my client might end up walking out of the courtroom a free man."

"Duress?" Ford cocked her head back. The prisoner's dazed look suggested the defense was a surprise to him, too. "From whom?"

"You'll figure that out when I submit our witness list. We'll see you at arraignment at three."

When the defense lawyer pushed his chair back, Croft slammed his palm against the button on the wall-mounted intercom. "Wait. Federal agents from the ATF have some questions. We'll be right in."

"What the hell are you doing?" The sheriff looked at Croft with confusion in his eyes. "His lawyer shut things down. The man isn't talking."

If Croft hadn't acted, Lexi would have. The defense lawyer was a farce. Any good counsel would have continued to negotiate a softer deal considering the public spectacle of the defendant's crime. But this shyster seemed more interested in keeping his client quiet than representing his best interest.

"We need to investigate the violation of federal law," Lexi said.

"What federal law?"

"Mr. Culter is a convicted felon. It is a violation of 18 U.S.C. 922 for him to possess a firearm or ammunition. That makes the murders a federal crime."

"You can't be serious. We have him for two counts of capital murder." The sheriff's face reddened, and his brow creased. He was steaming mad.

"Dead serious, Sheriff Jessup." Lexi used a firm tone to stress her intention. "Firearm violations fall under the purview of the ATF." She softened her voice and expression. "Look, Sheriff. What's your goal? Execute the man or put him in prison for the rest of his life?"

"I'd like to see him hang, but Texas stopped that in 1923. He deserves to die, but I'd settle for seeing him rot in prison."

"Then give us a crack at him. We can offer him what he's asking for and place him in a nearby federal prison. You'll get your desired outcome, and we'll get our answers. Plus, we'll save the state the cost of prosecuting and housing him for the rest of his life."

Sheriff Jessup rubbed the back of his neck, clearly weighing his options. "I don't like this, but I have little choice."

Lexi briefly placed a hand on his shoulder. "Thank you, Sheriff. Hopefully, this won't take long."

Lexi exited the observation room first. Croft followed, closing the door behind him. "Why were you soft-pedaling him? Once we claim federal jurisdiction, that's it."

"I don't know who to trust in this town, and we might need his help." Lexi's gut told her the sheriff and district attorney were on the right side, but until she got the lay of the land, no one was above suspicion.

"I hear you. I think I trust Culter's baby mama more than anyone here. At least she was upfront about her hatred for cops."

"Oddly, I think you're right." Lexi pulled out her phone and dialed a number she had on speed dial.

"Lexi. I didn't think I would hear from you once the task force folded. But I'm glad you called."

"Hi, Delanie. I hope I caught you at a good time because I need your help."

"Name it." Delanie Scot and Lexi butted heads more times than she could count while they were on the task force that brought down Tony Belcher and the Gatekeepers, but she was a damn good prosecutor, and she had Lexi's back.

"I need an AUSA I can trust to cut a deal with the Harrington shooter."

"The Harrington shooter? How did that become a federal case?" Once Lexi explained the connection to Kris Faust's killer, Delanie said, "You had me at the Raven. What exactly do you need?"

Lexi outlined the deal she was looking for and instructed Delanie to stand by her phone for the next half hour. Returning her phone to her pocket, Lexi turned her attention to Croft. "We're all set."

"I must admit, Mills. I'm impressed. You know how to get the ball rolling."

"It's all about making connections and friends. Treat people right, and they'll return the favor." Lexi entered the interrogation room, holding up her ATF badge and credentials. "Agents Mills and Croft of the ATF. We're taking jurisdiction of this case. Derek Culter, you're under arrest for illegally possessing a firearm and murder. You have the right to remain silent."

"Whoa, whoa, whoa." The detective rose from his chair, formed fists, and leaned them against the table. His eyes narrowed as if he was ready for a tussle. "This is my case."

"It *was* your case. Now, it's not." Lexi turned her attention to the prosecutor. "I'm sorry, Ms. Ford, but AUSA Delanie Scott has taken over prosecution."

Ford stuffed her folio in her shoulder bag and handed Lexi a business card. Her stony expression suggested she was unhappy. If she was angry like the sheriff, she hid it well. "I hope you three know the quagmire you've gotten yourselves into. Have Ms. Scott call me. I'll fill her in on the details." Ford exited quietly, but the detective stormed out, slamming the door after them.

"You too, Deputy Perez," Lexi said. "I'm sorry we're poaching your collar."

Perez responded with a firm nod and left.

Ford's characterization of the case as a quagmire made Lexi think Culter was just the tip of a messy iceberg. Her eyes were wide open now. She and Croft sat across from Culter and his lawyer, and their blank stares suggested they were confused. She placed her phone center on the table and placed a second call to Delanie. "Ms. Scott, I have Derek Culter and his counsel..." Lexi looked at the lawyer with questioning eyes.

"Jake Archer," he said.

"This is Delanie Scott, Assistant United States Attorney, the Northern District of Texas," the voice said from the phone. "I'm prepared to agree to the terms you previously outlined to District Attorney Ford in exchange for you truthfully answering Agents Mills and Croft's questions. We can send you to the Federal Correctional Institution in Big Spring, two hours from Harrington. Would that be satisfactory?"

Archer avoided eye contact and cleared his throat. "I don't like this, Derek. We need to consider our options."

Culter shrugged. "What's not to like? I'm getting everything I wanted."

"And they agreed too quickly. There must be something we don't know. Until we know more, you should remain silent."

"Mr. Archer," Lexi said. "I don't know what you and the detective were laughing it up over before your client arrived, but whatever agreement you had with him is gone. This is an ATF case."

Culter snapped his head toward his lawyer. "You were chatting up the cops?"

"I was being friendly."

"It looked more than a little friendly from the other side of the mirror." Croft wagged his thumb in its direction.

Culter pressed his hands against the sides of his head. "I don't know who to trust."

"Mr. Culter," Delanie said. "We're willing to cut you a deal today and get you into a federal prison tomorrow if what you tell the agents checks out."

"That sounds good to me." Culter turned to his lawyer. "You're fired. I'll take my chances with these two." Archer shook his head as if Culter had made the worst decision of his life. Once his lawyer retrieved his items and stomped out, Culter said to Lexi, "I have one more request."

"What's that?"

"The money. It's for my son. He has nothing, so I set up a college fund. I want it left alone so he'll have the chance at life I never had."

Delanie remained silent long enough Lexi had to interject. "Delanie? If you're okay with it, I am, too, since the money is earmarked. I've met the mother and believe he has their son's interests at heart."

"This is highly irregular," Delanie paused for a few beats. "But I can agree to leave the money alone if the information checks out. Then we have a deal, Mr. Culter?"

"Yes," Culter said. "What now?"

"Start by telling us why you shot the judge and bailiff," Lexi said.

"It wasn't my idea. Scooter came to me last week."

"Scooter? He's your dealer," Lexi said.

"Right. He said some guy wanted to pay me a hundred grand to knock off Judge Cook, the new sheriff, and the new D.A. at Tilton's trial. He gave me half upfront, but I didn't expect to live long enough to collect the second half. I've never killed a person, but I got the impression if I didn't agree to do it, I would have ended up dead in an abandoned parking lot."

"So you said yes."

"I figured the money would be enough to set up Junior for college, and, frankly, if anyone deserved a bullet in the head, it was Judge Cook."

"Did Scooter say why his employer chose the Tilton trial?" Lexi asked.

"Not really. All he said was all three people would be there."

"What can you tell us about Tilton?"

"Don't know the man. I never met him."

"Tell us about the gun," Lexi said.

"Scooter gave it to me the night before, including the flashlight with the bullets. I was supposed to dump everything into the river, but the deputy spooked me before I could."

"Did Scooter say who hired him and why?"

"Not a peep, and I learned a long time ago to never ask questions. I only cared about the money and settling a score with that asshole, Cook."

"All right." Lexi leaned closer toward her phone on the table. "Delanie, I think we have enough to go on. We'll pick up Scooter and bring him and Culter back to Dallas tonight."

"Very good," Delanie said. "I'll get things rolling on my end. See you tomorrow."

Lexi disconnected the call after Culter told them where to find his dealer. "You'll have to stay in lockup until we get back with Scooter. I'll let the sheriff know what's going on."

"I'd feel much better if you took me with you."

"I would, too, but unfortunately, there are only two of us. If all goes well, we'll be back in an hour." Lexi opened the door to the hallway, discovering Deputy Perez waiting patiently against the far wall. "Deputy, I'm glad you waited. We need the prisoner returned to his cell while we track down a lead."

"I thought I heard Scooter's name thrown around in there. He'll be hard to find unless you know where to look."

"Do you know where we can find him?"

"Yes, but I'll have to show you."

"Can you draw us a map?"

"Take me with you." The look of determination filled Perez's eyes. "You owe me for poaching my collar."

Lexi was still leery about whom to trust in Harrington, but the less time they spent searching for Scooter, the better. "All right, Perez, you're in."

Once they returned the prisoner safely to the holding cell, Lexi stopped by the bathroom before their trip. Washing up at the sink, she felt her phone vibrate with an incoming text. After drying her hands, she swiped the screen and read Nita's text. *Returning to Ponder w Jessie. Will explain later.* The message was curiously vague. Nita didn't hint whether the news about the MRI scan was good or bad or something in between, but Lexi had to know. This might be her only opportunity for privacy until she and Croft got Culter and Scooter to Dallas, so she dialed.

"Nita, how is Mom?"

14

Thirty minutes earlier

Being chauffeured around like an old lady was an indignity Jessie would have to get used to someday when her eyesight had deteriorated so much she couldn't see the stop sign until she was right on top of it. But that day was years off. If she could drive herself to church and the fairgrounds on Sundays to sell pies with Shirley Beamer, then she sure as heck could have driven herself to the imaging facility in Denton for the MRI appointment Doc McCormick had snagged for her today. But she couldn't turn down her future daughter-in-law's kind offer after she took such good care of her following last night's annoying dizzy spell. Still, Jessie felt like an old biddy whose highlight of the day was watching the Price is Right in the senior home community room.

Pulling into the parking lot of the imaging facility, Nita drove toward the drop-off circle at the main entrance. "Door-to-door service, madam. Would you prefer I wait inside or out?"

"This is silly." The fall weather was cooperating, but the sun was extra bright today. Nita would bake within minutes inside the car. "I saw a spot in the second row. Let's walk in together. You can keep me company while I wait my turn."

"Happy to." Nita pulled into the tight open spot and didn't rush to the passenger side to help her. If she had, Jessie's fears that age was catching up would have magnified.

Jessie shimmied out the narrow passenger door opening, thanking herself for not indulging in too many of her pies in recent weeks. Though her tight squeeze versus Nita's easy-peasy escape was a sign that a nightly walk might be in order. She slammed the door shut, still holding onto the handle. The metal pulsed against her fingers. Strangely, when she let go, her fingers still tingled from the vibration like a wave of electricity flowing through her right hand and up the arm. Then, as quickly as the strange feeling had come on, it stopped. Jessie waggled her fingers to get the blood flowing better in them and sensed mild stiffness.

"Are you okay, Jessie?" Concern cut through Nita's voice, too much for something that seemed like nothing to Jessie.

"It's a little arthritis, I'm guessing. Too many years of using the rolling pin." Jessie joined Nita on the walkway to the main building, feeling more tired than she had in recent days. She knew what her doctor would tell her. That she needed to slow down and let her body rest, but so much had to be done before the wedding at their house. Resting would have to wait until Sunday after the cleanup.

Once inside and out of the sun, Jessie felt much better. A glance at the directory board tacked to the wall said their destination was on the first floor, down the corridor to her right, directly across from the breast screening center. She checked in at the reception desk without waiting and filled out the repetitive forms. No matter how many times she'd been to this building for her mammograms, she filled out the same forms, providing the same information over and over again.

"Nervous?" Nita asked when Jessie sat beside her.

"A little. I don't think I'm claustrophobic but staying still for forty-five minutes seems impossible."

"When I had the MRI on my shoulder, I kept my mind busy by running through my favorite workout in my head. I imagined stretching out and going through each circuit. Before I'd finished, the tech announced we were done."

"That's a great idea, but I don't work out."

"Maybe you can think about making a pie from scratch."

Jessie patted her belly. "The last thing I need is more pie."

"Jessie," a male technician announced from a doorway, holding a clipboard.

Jessie raised her hand to acknowledge the call before squeezing Nita's hand. "See you soon." She stood, sensing the tingling in her right hand had returned. It stubbornly remained while walking down the corridor to the MRI room. She shook her right arm vigorously several times, relieving the odd sensation and convincing herself she must have pinched a nerve.

After stripping from the waist up, donning a hospital gown, and confirming she had nothing metal on her body, Jessie laid on the movable bench lined with a soft cushion. David, as the technician had introduced himself, propped her knees to a comfortable position with some pillows and covered her with a warm, knit blanket. He then locked her head into a medieval-looking mask attached to the bench. The confining feeling was more unnerving than she'd expected. Her breathing shallowed at the thought of getting stuck inside that contraption.

"Deeper breaths, Jessie. You'll be fine. I do this every day."

Jessie gave him a thumb's up, taking in slow, deliberate breaths and focusing on the reason for going through with this. She would never admit it to Jerry or Lexi, but the dizzy bouts worried her. At first, she'd attributed them to overdoing it with the wedding preparation and not getting enough rest. But sleeping and slowing down had done little to abate the spells. At least this machine could provide her answers.

David pressed a button to retract the bench inside the machine, but it stopped when her shoulders reached the outer edge. He pressed another button, and she rolled to her original position. He tried again but achieved the same results. After the fifth attempt, he called it and unlocked the head cage. "I'm sorry, Jessie, but it appears this thing won't cooperate today. We'll have to reschedule."

Jessie swallowed past a growing lump in her throat. "What would have happened if I was in there and you couldn't roll me out?"

He laughed. "There's an emergency manual release. You would have been fine. But without the bench working, I can't micro-adjust your position to get the scans right. I should have this thing working tomorrow, so stop by the reception desk to reschedule. We can probably fit you in this week."

"Thanks, David." Jessie dressed and returned to the reception area, where Nita was waiting with her head buried in her phone. She walked over and touched Nita on the arm, startling her.

Nita looked up with confusion in her eyes. "What happened?"

"It broke. I have to reschedule." When Jessie returned, Nita was typing something on her phone. "All set."

"When do you come back?" Nita slipped her phone into her mini backpack tote.

"Monday. The earliest was Friday, but I have too much to do for your wedding."

"I don't think you should wait that long, Jessie. We should walk into the Emergency Room at the next building and get it done today."

"I feel fine, Nita. If my doctor thought it was serious, he wouldn't have agreed to the original appointment at the end of next week. I'm still getting in four days sooner than planned." Jessie slung her handbag farther up her shoulder. "Now, let's get home before Jerry gets grumpy."

Nita stood, pressing her lips into a fine line and shaking her head. She still hadn't convinced Jessie of the urgency. Her phone chimed in her bag, prompting her to fish it out. "Maybe Lexi can talk some sense into you." She swiped the screen and put the phone on speaker.

"Nita, how is Mom?"

"Stubborn."

Jessie gave Nita a sour but playful look. "I prefer the term practical."

"What's going on, you two?" Lexi chuckled.

"The MRI machine broke," Nita said. "So Jessie had to reschedule. They can't fit her in until Friday, but she won't go until Monday."

"You are stubborn, Mom."

"There's too much to do before the wedding." Jessie felt as if she were on trial, forced to defend herself. "There's no way I can be gone half the day on Friday."

"I offered to take her to the Emergency Room next door, but she refused."

"Mom, please let Nita take you to the ER. Get the scan. If you don't do it today, I'll throw you into the back of my SUV when I get back and take you myself, kicking and screaming if I have to." Lexi had never used a sterner and more forceful tone with Jessie, telling her she meant what she'd said.

"For heaven's sake."

"Heaven is what I'm trying to avoid for you. Now go with Nita."

"Fine. I'll go."

"Thank you, Mom. I'll let Nita know when I'm on my way back to Dallas."

Nita finished the call and returned the phone to her bag with a self-satisfied look plastered on her face.

"I don't like you two ganging up on me."

"You'll get over it."

"Let me see if Shirley can bring Jerry some dinner if we're running late."

Nita placed an arm over Jessie's shoulder. "That's my girl."

15

Jackson Price stopped his car at the apex of the circular driveway fronting Milo's house on the north side of Harrington and handed him a set of keys. "Your house key. The alarm is on, and your mail is on the kitchen counter. There's a lot to sift through." He then handed Milo his iPhone. "It's charged."

"Come in, my friend. We need to celebrate my freedom before the cleanup man arrives." Milo tossed his keys in the air a few inches and caught them, thinking about what he wanted to drink first. He'd craved his prized scotch, but his newfound freedom required a true celebration. Only champagne would do. "I'll pop open a bottle."

"I can't stay, Milo. I have to file some paperwork with Luther, putting up your house as collateral for your bond."

"I still say he smells blood in the water and is squeezing me." Milo exited Jackson's sedan and stood at the open door.

"Nevertheless, he's the only game in town. It was either have him give you the squeeze or stay in jail. We're still not out of the woods. If the governor appoints a new district judge this week, you might not draw Clem for your trial."

"Then we'll have to find out his price. See you at the Cattlemen's at eight."

Once Jackson pulled away, Milo faced the façade of his house. It had been thirty-three days since the sheriff hauled him away for choking the life out of his wife who didn't know when to shut up. *Funny*, he thought. Every time he walked through this door for as far back as he could remember, it felt like he was voluntarily walking into a prison. He was trapped with a woman he no longer loved and who hadn't satisfied him sexually in years. However, slipping his key into the slot and opening the door, he felt as free as a bird, able to take flight whenever he pleased.

He tossed the keys into a crystal bowl near the entry table, not caring if he left a scratch. Nichole had bought it during one of her spending sprees to Manhattan. It had sat on the table for years, never used and only touched by the housekeeper when she dusted. It was pretty but was a total waste of money.

Entering the kitchen, he realized Jackson wasn't kidding when he said there was a lot of mail. The stacks covered the entire granite island, but he was down to six pieces of mail once he'd sorted through it and tossed the junk and ads. Five were bills. One was a personal letter, with his name typed and no return address. He opened it first. It contained one piece of paper with eight typed words: *No loose ends. Fix this, or I will.* He turned over the envelope, inspecting the front. The envelope did not have a postmark, so the post office hadn't delivered it. However, the Carlsbad, New Mexico stamp in the upper right corner sent a chill down his spine. It had to be from the Raven.

Going into this, Milo had known the Raven's requirement about cleaning up his mess. The service would come at an outrageous price if he had to perform it. The cleanup man Jackson and the former client had found to do the shooting were disappointments. The backup guy was supposed to tie up the loose end, but he'd become one. His only way out was to finish the job he started last night. And by extension, it was Milo's and Jackson's only way out, too. Milo would have to make the direness of their circumstances abundantly clear.

Milo glanced at the oven clock. He still had a half hour before the cleanup man arrived, so he went upstairs to wash away the scent of jailhouse soap and the memory of having his freedom taken away for the last month. Lathering his personal shampoo while standing under the massaging stream of hot water, he brought his hands to his nose to inhale the blend of bourbon and vanilla. It was the aroma of freedom, the smell of winning. Milo hadn't realized until exiting the shower how the refreshing scent lingered in the air for a while. He'd taken it for granted day after day, year after year, but he never would again.

Walking into his closet, he eyed his side with a collection of suits, dress and golf shirts, casual slacks, and shoes. So many choices. He had so many beyond the weekly exchange of prison orange, he didn't know what to wear. He was in a blue mood with Derek Culter sitting in a jail cell instead of lying in the morgue, so he picked out a blue jacquard knot golf shirt, pairing it with a pair of khaki slacks.

Turning to grab a pair of his suede shoes, he settled his gaze on his wife's side of the closet stuffed with thousands of dollars' worth of dresses, shoes, and who knew what. He'd have to hire a woman to put everything up for sale and all the other luxury items she'd bought over the years. He could carry his operation for six or seven months if he got half what she'd paid for the crap.

The doorbell rang. A check of the time on his phone confirmed the man was right on time. Milo descended the stairs, considering how to approach his epic failure. He couldn't ignore it, but his side business was falling apart. He couldn't afford to alienate the few people who still supported him and would do his bidding, even if the loyalty was based solely on money.

Opening the door, he discovered a pathetic sight. The supposed cleanup man was wearing a baseball cap, a pair of sunglasses, and a jacket with the collar turned up, looking like a member of the criminal under-world. Milo snickered. "What's with the getup?"

"I don't want people to recognize me." The man craned his head toward the property gate. Milo couldn't decide whether he was paranoid or nervous about answering for his failure last night.

"If you drove that lime green Challenger of yours, everyone in town knows you're here." Milo opened the door farther. "Get your ass inside." He ushered the man down a hallway. "Come. Have a drink with me."

When he stepped inside his office and looked at his desk, the memory of choking his wife returned. His only regret was he hadn't done it before the recent election. Maybe then he wouldn't be in a legal quagmire. Opening the stocked wine fridge, he pulled out the bottle of Perrier brut— something he'd been saving for the day he turned the business around— but celebrating his freedom was a much more impressive reason to break it open.

"Would you grab two champagne glasses?" He gestured his chin toward the stemware rack above the wet bar sink while he unwrapped the bottle's foil topper. After a lot of twisting and wrenching, he popped the stubborn cork without spilling a drop and filled the two glasses. He raised his. "Here's to freedom and getting things back to how they were."

The man clinked glasses and sipped his drink, but his tense shoulders and face were signs of confusion or reluctance. Milo could quickly clear up a misunderstanding but would have an uphill battle countering unwillingness.

Milo refilled their glasses and invited him to the leather chairs near his desk. "So tell me what happened yesterday after Culter bungled the shooting. Jackson tells me he spoke to you after the dust cleared."

The man bounced a knee up and down rapidly like pistons in the sore-thumb Challenger he drove there. "That's why I went home sick."

Milo leaned back in his chair, crossing his right leg loosely over his left to pose less of a threat. "It's all right. You've done great work for us in the past. I just want to know what happened so we can figure out what to do next." But Milo really wanted to know how far he was willing to go. If he had second thoughts about tying off the loose end, Milo would have to look elsewhere to finish the job.

The man's tight shoulders dropped a fraction, hinting Milo had put him at ease. "I tried, Mr. Tilton. I wasn't assigned to the courthouse yesterday, so I couldn't stay without raising questions. Once I heard Culter had escaped, I guessed things had gone screwy. That's why I didn't rush over with the other deputies. I wanted to stay back in case you needed me."

"That was a good call." But Milo didn't know what to think about the man's hesitation. Was he slow to react? Weighing his options? Either motivation would be problematic, considering Milo's plans. "Continue."

"Things were crazy at the department, so I hid in the bathroom to avoid being tasked with an assignment. Then, Jackson called, asking for my help.

That's when I faked having intestinal problems. In the chaos, the sheriff didn't have time to ask questions, so he sent me home. Before I left, I grabbed a portable radio to monitor the manhunt."

"That was good thinking." *It really was,* Milo thought, despite not garnering the desired result.

"As soon as I heard the tracking dogs got a hit in the oil fields by the river, I took off. Considering how long it would take to put together the search team, I knew I'd have at least a half-hour head start. But Culter was a slippery little cuss in the dark. When I finally had him in my sights, Perez showed up before I could get a clean shot. I had no choice but to back off when he called it in."

Milo bit back his frustration to not overreact, but he needed answers. Retreating was the worst choice he could have made on a dark night with dozens of officers running around the area with guns. "Why didn't you reposition and take a shot? It was dark. No one would have known where it came from."

"He saw me. We'd never met, but if he recognized me, he would have told everyone I'd taken the shot. Then I would have had to explain why I was there with a stolen street gun when I was supposed to be sick at home."

Milo took in a deep breath of relief. The man's explanation made sense, which suggested he might be willing to finish the job. "I get you had no choice, but now we have a problem because he's talking."

"But didn't Price use a middleman? Culter can only finger Scooter."

"But can you be sure Scooter didn't tell Culter who hired him and where he got the gun?"

"Scooter told me he didn't."

"Is he a problem?"

"No." The man's slight delay suggested doubt.

"You're sure?"

"Positive."

"That's good, but Culter is still a problem. The arms dealer who provided the gun—"

"The Raven, right?"

Milo rocked his head back. He shouldn't have known the Raven's identity. "Who told you his name?"

"Scooter. Why?"

"It tells me Jackson has loose lips." Milo rubbed his temple, inventorying the many things needing his attention. He was under a lot of pressure and needed to hustle. "The Raven doesn't like loose ends." Milo showed the man the note he'd found earlier. "Culter is in custody. The Raven expects us to eliminate the possibility of him giving up his name. He'll know if we don't, so I need your help."

"You want me to kill him in custody, don't you?"

"Yes. And Scooter, wherever he's hiding. You'll have to get creative, but we must keep the Raven happy."

"When do you want this done?"

"Now."

16

Despite its rich history in the old wild west days, Harrington had been a pass-through town for Lexi. She'd driven through it en route to the southwestern raceways several times as a bright-eyed kid accompanying her dad's racing team and three times as a pit crew member. It had warranted exiting the freeway in town once, but she'd only gotten as far as the truck stop to fill up the tank and buy a cherry slushy.

The apartment where Derek Culter was staying near the Walmart store and the sheriff's department was the most she'd seen of Harrington until Deputy Perez gave directions, taking them through the quaint downtown streets. The city had refurbished most of the buildings to highlight their century-old feel. Even the bronze streetlamps were in keeping with the early twentieth-century look. Everything had fresh paint, and potted flowers adorned many business entrances. This area was a tourist's dream, with souvenir, art, and confectionery shops lining both sides of the main street.

They continued north out of town in their rental car, passing a fenced facility marked Harrington Regional Detention Facility. It had the telltale signs of a low-security prison, but the weeds and trash butting against the fence line suggested authorities had neglected it for years.

"Is this the facility Milo Tilton runs?" Lexi asked, feeling a little like

Miss Daisy from the backseat with Nathan at the wheel and Perez navigating from the front passenger seat.

Perez cocked his head over a shoulder and replied, "Yes, that's it."

"What can you tell us about it?"

"Only that when I started with the department six months ago under the old sheriff, he'd assigned several deputies to escort work details from there to the local farms and ranches. That practice stopped when the new sheriff took office, pissing off a lot of those deputies."

"Interesting." Lexi adjusted her stare to the windshield. There were no buildings, and the only sign of civilization was the pothole-filled road they were on. Shrubs and scraggly trees became more plentiful when they turned east on a dirt road toward the river. The shadows they created on the road signaled daylight would disappear within an hour.

"How much longer?" Croft asked.

"A few more minutes. Scooter is off the beaten path for a reason."

"Does he cook meth?"

"I'm not sure. From what I've heard, Scooter is the middleman for anything anyone wants to find on the streets, from drugs to weapons to illegal IDs."

"So he's the type to pass along a 3D-printed ghost gun, not build it?" Lexi said it as a question, not a statement.

"Scooter couldn't build a cabin out of Lincoln Logs with a diagram, but he can find anything illegal worth selling." Perez directed Croft to park near a sandpaper tree towering above a grove of desert shrubs. "We're on foot from here, so he won't hear us coming. The last time we were here, we found cameras along the access road. He knew we were coming for at least five minutes, so he had plenty of time to stash things."

Perez guided Lexi and Croft down a footpath, weaving between five-foot-tall shrubs and rocks. It reminded Lexi of the cubicle maze at the Dallas ATF office, where the partial walls camouflaged her route. At the next turn, Perez slowed, drew his service weapon, and raised an index finger to his mouth, shushing the others. "We're close."

Lexi and Croft drew their weapons and hung their ATF credentials around their necks to make their identity easily discernible. Lexi grinned when the men crouched to stay below the shrub line. *Being short has its advantages*, she thought.

Perez knelt at the edge of a clearing. Lexi and Croft did, too. A dented, rusty RV trailer with flat tires came into view. Mattresses, junk, and trash of all shapes and sizes littered the area. Ash surrounded a metal burn barrel twenty yards from the trailer. A portable gas-powered generator was outside with extension cords snaking to the trailer, but it wasn't running.

Lexi walked lightly on her foot and prosthetic, as did the others, to minimize the noise they made while approaching the trailer. She peeked into the burn barrel and placed a hand on its side. It was still warm, a sign someone was recently here. She used hand signals to convey her findings and direct the others to circle around both ends of the trailer and look for means of entry or escape.

Both returned, shaking their heads, indicating the door Lexi was guarding was the only way inside. There were two windows on this side, one on either side of the door. One was frosted with no view inside; the other was clear with crusted layers of dirt and leaf particles. Both were too high for even Perez, the tallest of the three, to peer through effectively. Lexi wagged her thumb upward, signaling for Croft and Perez to boost her higher. She grinned. *Being the lightest has its advantages*, she thought.

Lexi offered Croft her natural leg first for greater stability. She then steadied herself with her fingertips against the trailer's aluminum wall while positioning her prosthetic foot in Perez's hands. They raised her slowly until she could see inside the trash-laden living area. The window looked slightly ajar—closed but not locked into position. Dirt streaks made it challenging to make out detail, but Lexi discerned the room was unoccupied. She angled her stare toward the filthy galley and spotted a lumpy figure lying on the floor. The lighting limited seeing clearly, but she made out the outline of a human hand.

"There's a body on the floor." Inspecting the area directly across from the entryway more closely, Lexi spotted the barrel of a shotgun duct-taped to the counter and pointed toward the door. It was a crude but effective device. "Lower me, fellas." Once on the ground, Lexi added, "It looks like the door might be booby-trapped with a shotgun."

"I'll call it in," Perez said, reaching for his tactical radio. "We can have the bomb squad from Midland here in an hour."

"No need," Lexi said. "I disarm traps like this for a living—unless you'd like a shot at it, Croft?"

Croft raised his hands shoulder high in surrender. "I know everything there is to know *about* guns, but I sure as heck don't know how to undo a booby trap. This is your lane, Mills."

"All right then." Lexi turned to Perez. "Do you have a pocketknife?"

Deputy Perez reached behind his back, opened a pouch attached to his utility belt, and handed Lexi a military-style folding knife. "You're sure about this?"

Lexi didn't know what to make of Perez's question. Did he doubt her ability because she was an unknown? Or because she was a petite woman? If it was the former, his ignorance was refreshing. Lexi had become a household name in law enforcement circles since the failed attack in Spicewood. Running across a cop who didn't recognize her and fawn all over her was a delightful change of pace. If his reasoning was based on the latter, quickly disarming the trap would be the only way to change the impression she'd made on him.

"She's got this. Don't you read the papers, son?" Croft asked.

"Not really. I'm taking online classes for my degree. I don't have time to read or watch TV." The jury was still out on Perez, but Lexi opted to cut him some slack.

Lexi stowed the knife in her pants' cargo pocket and put on a pair of latex gloves to not leave fingerprints inside. "Another lift, fellas. I'm going through the window."

Once the men raised Lexi again, she tested the sliding window panel by pressing a palm hard against it and applying pressure toward her right. The window moved an inch. "It's unlocked." She continued to slide the window with some difficulty. It was warped and caught several times before the leading end reached the frame's edge.

The tricky part was getting in without breaking an arm or triggering a trap. Thankfully, a ratty cushioned bench was directly below the window. Lexi could somersault in and take her chances with the three-foot-wide section of crud-covered floor and the second bench against the far wall opposite the window.

"I can't believe I'm saying this, but give me a heave-ho on three, guys."

Croft counted off, bending and rising at the knees on each number. Lexi extended her arm inside the window like a high diver preparing to spring off the board. "One. Two. Three." On three, he and Perez launched Lexi with too much force—the downside of being the lightest—forcing her to duck and lean into the momentum more quickly than she'd expected. A forward roll was now impossible.

Lexi curled her arms against her chest, fists pressed high against the breastbone. Twisting her torso counterclockwise, she hoped her prosthetic foot didn't catch on the windowsill, allowing her to complete a side roll and the cushion to absorb some of the energy from the landing. Unfortunately, the lift from the men was so forceful she clipped the long edge of the bench and thudded on the floor among pizza boxes, dirty rags, and filthy things Lexi didn't want to know about. The motion continued to take her across the floor until she met an immovable object—the second bench.

Lexi hit hard with a bang, forcing air from her lungs. She'd experienced twenty times the pressure against her lungs from being in the blast zone when an explosive detonated a second or two earlier than expected. Nonetheless, the force hurt like the dickens and would likely leave a giant bruise on her back.

"Shit, Lexi," Croft yelled. "Are you okay?"

"Yeah," she forced out. "Give me a minute." Lexi rolled to her butt, taking inventory of the damage. An achy back but no cracked ribs. That was a good sign. She unzipped her pant leg to check her prosthetic. The ankle and pylon appeared aligned correctly, but the socket had rotated during her fall, pinching the skin on her residual limb. She would have to doff her prosthetic and don it again, the neoprene sleeve, and protective cotton socks on her limb to adjust it properly, but Lexi didn't have the time. Instead, she pressed her hands against both sides and gave it a firm twist in the proper direction. The fix wasn't ideal, but it would do until she'd cleared the RV.

While re-zipping her pant leg, Lexi noted the prevalent smell of mold and perhaps vinegar. Scooter may have used this place to cook meth at one point. She rolled to her knees and then led with her natural leg to get to her feet. She pulled her weapon from the paddle holster at her waistband and assessed her surroundings. The matching window on the other side was boarded up. Without clear windows, the interior was darker the farther back she looked. The kitchen was beyond the living area, and a sleeping area or something like it was at the far end. In between, a person lay still on the floor.

"Federal agent. Put your hands up. Are you hurt?" Lexi waited for a response but received none. She needed to check for signs of life, but the shotgun booby trap was between her and the person on the floor. Craning her head over a shoulder toward the open window, she yelled, "The person isn't moving, but I have to disarm the trap before I can check on them."

"Steady hands, Lexi." Croft's choice of words impressed her. Most people wish her luck before performing a disposal, but luck had nothing to do with her work. It had everything to do with knowledge, skill, and calm nerves, which was why people in her line of work wished the other steady hands. He either knew enough about what she did to say the right things or cared about making an impression on her. No matter the motivation, Lexi's opinion of Croft jumped a level or two.

Returning her service weapon to her holster, Lexi shined her cell phone light at the door and inspected the mechanisms used in the trap. A wire was tied to the knob and ran upward and across the ceiling through a series of eyelet screws. The wire's other end was attached to a pulley that, when activated, would retract a metal arm with a hook resting against the trigger on the shotgun duct taped to two blocks screwed to the kitchen counter. The setup was cruder than she'd expected but was essentially sound.

Using a knife to cut the taut wire required applying force but doing so might set it off. That limited her choices to disconnect it from an endpoint. To unwrap the end at the doorknob, Lexi would have to stand in the danger zone of the shotgun blast. That left the pulley, but the wire had no slack to reverse it. Her only option was to determine the last step taken by whoever had set the trap.

A closer inspection revealed it had to be the metal arm. The hook at the trigger was hinged, capable of moving up and down. The trick was moving the hook out of the way without touching the trigger. If she had to guess, whoever built this trap had likely modified the shotgun to require much less pressure on the trigger to fire it.

Lexi's fingers were small enough to do the job, but their tips might accidentally touch the trigger, not just the hook. So she pulled out Perez's pocketknife and extended the blade. Using the fine point end, she carefully placed it below the hook and lifted it until it bent at the hinge and cleared the trigger.

With the threat of the shotgun firing gone, she moved the metal arm toward the pulley, adding slack to the wire. Lexi then cut through the duct tape with the knife and unloaded the gun. After placing it safely on the floor, she cut the wire at the knob but wasn't ready to declare the RV safe for entry.

Pressing two fingers near the carotid artery on the person's neck, whom she'd now determined was a man, Lexi felt no pulse. She lifted his arm, which loosely flopped to the floor when she let go. Turning her head, she yelled. "The trap is clear. The man is dead. Stay outside until I give you the all-clear."

"Understood," Croft replied in a clear, loud voice. "Standing by."

Lexi led with her phone flashlight, checking for signs of wires, sensors, and other devices. She inspected the bathroom, bunks, and storage cabinets but found nothing but more filth. "All clear. It's safe to come in."

The door swung open, spilling in the dim light from the early evening sky. Croft ascended the rocky metal stairs wearing latex gloves, followed by Perez. Lexi shined her flashlight on the dead man's face, highlighting the surrounding blood and brain matter. "Is this Scooter?"

"That's him. Is that a gunshot wound?" Perez's grimace suggested he was unaccustomed to bloody, gruesome scenes.

The blood and hole at his temple surrounded by black dots explained a likely cause of death. "I'd say yes. The stippling around the wound tells me the killer was up close, and the lack of decomp means it happened recently."

"I need to call it in." Perez reached for his radio again, but Croft placed a hand on his arm.

"Let's think about this, Deputy," Croft said. "This could be a drug deal gone wrong, but from what you told us about Tilton and the detention center, it sounds like you suspect corruption in the department. Am I right?" Perez offered a tentative nod. "Which of them do you trust?"

"None."

"What about the new sheriff?" Lexi asked.

"I don't know. Today was the most time I've spent with him. I keep my head down and mouth shut."

"Scooter being killed today is no coincidence." The timing of Scooter's death was suspicious. Within an hour of Culter fingering him as the middleman who hired him for the contract killing, Lexi found him dead. The list of people to trust in this town just got smaller, but her gut told her the sheriff was still one of them. "Let me call the sheriff directly. Maybe he has a better take on which deputies we can trust to not destroy evidence." Lexi retrieved the business card the sheriff had handed her earlier in his office and called his private number on the back.

"Hello?" a man answered when the call picked up.

"Is this Sheriff Jessup?"

"Yes, it is."

"This is Lexi Mills. We have a problem."

17

Once Lexi explained the situation to Sheriff Jessup and completed the call, she turned to Croft. "We have twenty minutes to search the place." Perez still had his lip curled. Lexi trusted him as an officer but didn't trust him to hold his stomach. A contaminated murder scene in a confined space would be a nightmare. "Perez, would you mind standing watch and make sure we don't get any unwanted visitors of the two-legged or four-legged variety?"

"My pleasure." After Perez took a position outside, Lexi took the sleeping area and bathroom of the RV while Croft took the living area. They agreed to meet in the kitchen in the middle.

Based on her initial search for more traps, Lexi didn't expect to find anything of evidentiary value in the back. The area was tidier and was likely where Scooter slept and did most of his living. He likely used the front and kitchen to prep his drugs and other merchandise. She quickly cleared both rooms with her flashlight and stepped over Scooter's body to attack the kitchen.

"How's it going?" she asked. Croft was sifting with one hand while holding his cell phone with the flashlight on with the other.

"Lots of little boxes and bags in this storage bench. I found a stash of weed and meth. Woo-hoo. I'm about to hit the other one."

"I'll start in the kitchenette." Lexi found a weed grinder, baggies, and a cheap kitchen scale in one drawer and a collection of driver's licenses in another. The cabinet contained some cups and dishes. She glanced in Croft's direction, ready to help finish searching the front.

Croft crossed the short distance to the other bench, the one Lexi had thudded against earlier. Leaning over the bench, he removed the cushion, flipped up the hinged wood top, and pulled out a shoebox. Holding it against his chest, he opened the lid. "Whoa. I think this is dynamite. Weird. It smells like bananas."

Bells went off in Lexi's head. "Stop. Don't move." Dynamite contained nitroglycerin and sodium nitrate. Old dynamite tended to leach nitro which could become extremely sensitive to touch.

Croft froze. "What did I find?"

"Something that could blow your head off. Let me see." Lexi crossed the room and shined her light in the box. One stick of straight dynamite was inside. Discovering a smooth dark spot on the bottom of the box, she breathed relief. If the nitro had crystallized, a gentle touch could detonate the crystals. But the nitro had pooled. It was still unsafe but was far less volatile.

"The banana smell is leaking nitroglycerin. The good news is it hasn't crystallized. The bad news is it's still dangerous. Were there more boxes in there?"

"No. Just this one."

"Good, but we need to get it outside."

"Okaaay." Croft's voice had turned brittle. Lexi had the same unnerved response the first time she'd held a live explosive despite having had the benefit of wearing a blast suit. "How do we do that?" he asked.

Lexi shined her light to see his face. Sweat beads formed on his brow. "You'll be fine, Croft. You're standing, so I'd like to minimize the number of handoffs and lessen the chance of rolling it around."

"I think that's a grand idea."

"I'll clear a path, so you won't snag on a tripping hazard. I'll exit and wait at the base of the stairs. I'll shine my light on the path. Then I need you to walk it to the door. I'll take it from there."

"You better hurry, or I might pee myself."

Lexi snickered. She moved the bench cushion to the kitchen area and shoved the trash and a plastic bucket aside, creating a two-foot-wide walking path for Croft. She then descended the rickety steep stairs. Perez was ten feet away. "Deputy, I'll need you to step back about forty feet. We found some unstable dynamite."

Perez acknowledged with a firm nod and jogged to the edge of the clearing. Lexi then shined her light inside. "All right, Nathan. Walk toward me slowly and smoothly. Don't jerk."

"Not since I was in my twenties." Nathan forced a laugh before taking steady steps toward the door. His posture was stiff as if balancing an egg on his head. Two more strides would get him to the most dangerous part of the route—a ninety-degree turn past the divider guarding the bench. He cut the turn tightly, brushing his left shoe against the partition. The change in momentum made him tilt toward the right. Lexi held her breath. If he stumbled, both wouldn't survive the blast.

He recovered and let out a loud breath. "That was close." He reached the door.

Lexi accepted the shoebox with steady hands and took two steps backward. "Okay, Nathan. I need you to come down and light my path." She gestured her chin toward her right. "I'm heading to the tree. Follow, but don't get within twenty feet."

"Got it."

"Wait," Perez yelled, jogging toward Croft. "Use my flashlight. It's a lot stronger."

With the extra light power, Lexi safely walked the shoebox to the other side of the tree and placed a metal garbage can over it to dissuade curious critters. When she returned, Croft was leaning against the aluminum side of the RV, wiping his forehead with a jacket sleeve. "How do you do this every day?"

"Training and repetition. Knowing what to do because you've done it a dozen times makes it easier to swallow your fear." Lexi left out that making a mistake was always in the back of her mind, and that she struggled to keep fear in check when someone she cared about was in danger.

"No wonder Willie Lange quit doing this. It's nerve-wracking."

"Most days, I can push that aside."

"And when you can't?"

"That's when it's time to hang it up."

Five minutes later, multiple sets of headlights appeared on the access road leading to Scooter's RV. The sheriff had said he would arrive with three trusted deputies and the field technician from the county coroner's office, but Lexi and Croft remained vigilant, holding their weapons at their thighs. Scooter's death told her news traveled fast in Harrington, and she couldn't be sure if the people in the approaching cars were friendly or someone else to make sure they'd left behind no evidence.

Three vehicles stopped near the RV—two Harrington County Sheriff's SUVs and one county coroner's van. Their lights brightened the RV and the entire clearing. Lexi's tense muscles relaxed when Sheriff Jessup stepped out first. More deputies filed out and popped open the rear hatches of their SUVs. The coroner tech exited and pulled out equipment boxes.

Jessup approached Lexi, tipped back his Stetson, and shook her hand. "This is quite a mess, Agent Mills. Thanks for convincing Perez not to call it in. I'd like to keep as many people in the dark for as long as possible."

"Which is why I called your personal line. Tell me, Sheriff, was there anyone else in the observation room when we interrogated Culter?"

"Eddie Gomez, the detective you kicked out, and Charlene Ford, the district attorney."

"What's your take on Gomez? Do you trust him?"

"Yes. He's a transfer from Odessa. That's why I assigned him the case."

The deputies hauled over portable generators and lights. They strung two strands inside the RV, lighting it up like an NFL stadium. More lights brightened the perimeter around the RV.

Lexi, Croft, and Perez waited outside with the sheriff while the coroner tech performed his examination and preserved the body for evidence. Lexi predicted what he would find, but she needed him to narrow the time of death. She guessed the lack of rigor mortis meant Scooter had been dead less than two hours or more than twenty-four.

"By the way, Sheriff," Lexi said. "We found a stick of unstable dynamite inside. I moved it to the tree over there and marked it with a trash can. You'll need the disposal team from Midland to take care of it."

Sheriff Jessup shook his head in apparent amazement. "Just another day at the office for you." Minutes later, the tech and a deputy exited the RV with Scooter in a body bag. The sheriff asked, "What do we have, Harm?"

Harm stopped. "A gunshot to the temple. Based on the liver temp, I'd put the time of death in the last two hours."

"Thanks, Harm. This one is a priority. I'll need the doc to get to it tonight."

"He won't be happy after yesterday's mess."

"The county doesn't pay him to be happy. And tell him I want the autopsy report released only to me." Harm acknowledged and continued to the van. The sheriff turned to Lexi. "The deputies I brought will process the scene for fingerprints and collect other evidence. Hopefully, we'll find something to tell us who killed him."

"We found nothing linking him to the Culter case, so we need to head back to your department and pick him up. Can we borrow Perez to get us back quickly?"

"Absolutely. I'll let you know what we find."

"Thanks, Sheriff." Lexi had intended to be gone an hour to pick up Scooter, but their trip had turned into three. Wading through the brush to where they'd left their rental car, a stomach gurgle rudely reminded her she hadn't eaten since breakfast with her parents that morning.

Once on the road, Lexi considered the night ahead of her and Croft. After picking up Derek Culter, they had a six-hour drive to Dallas. She preferred not to stop on the road while transporting a prisoner. The only wildcard would be a bathroom break. "Can we stop for fast food on the way to the jail? I'm starving."

"I am, too," Croft said.

"Most places close at eight due to low staffing," Perez said. "The only place open this late is the Cattlemen's. I can call ahead and have them make a to-go order."

"That would be great." Lexi had a sinking feeling she and Croft had already been gone too long.

18

The Cattlemen's lived up to Lexi's expectations of a Texas steakhouse, at least from the outside. Cowboy boots and spurs outlined in yellow neon lights flanked the restaurant name near the top of the wood slat façade. A lasso and horse were the only things missing to complete the tourist attraction feeling.

Croft parked near the front, and all three stepped out to pay for their to-go orders. The interior didn't disappoint. The mix of aged wood and stonework gave the restaurant a rustic feel. Deer head trophies adorned the eighteen-foot-tall walls. Chandeliers with steer horn accents hung from the ceiling, washing the room in an amber glow. Rascal Flatts played over the speaker system, but none of the patrons filling three-quarters of the place were on the dance floor. Without question, she was deep in the heart of small tourist town Texas.

They approached the host station, and Perez spoke to the woman there. "Evening, Maxine. I called in three orders a bit ago."

"Evening, Thomas. They should be ready in five minutes. You can pay at the bar."

Skirting the edge of the dining room, the three headed to the bar with two big screen TVs flanking three tiers of lighted shelves filled with high-end liquor. Lexi approached first, appreciating the soft butch fixing drinks behind the counter. Her pompadour hairstyle razored on the sides and straight black tie were a dead giveaway. Perez and Croft joined her, but the bartender locked eyes with Lexi and placed a napkin in front of her atop the counter. She stared briefly, adding a slight grin before asking, "What will it be?"

The prolonged eye contact was another hint, but the faded piece of rainbow-colored yarn around her wrist confirmed Lexi's suspicion—she was gay and looking. Lexi kept it all business by rubbing a cheek with her left hand and putting her engagement ring on display. "We placed three to-go orders. Paying separately."

"Let me guess." The bartender folded her arms across her chest but dropped the seductive stare. "Bacon cheeseburger, hold the mayo with extra crispy fries."

"Spot on. We have a long drive ahead of us and don't want to stop again for food." Lexi slid thirty dollars across the bar. "Keep the change."

The bartender grabbed the cash and winked, more in solidarity than seduction. "I'll toss in some extra, cold water bottles." She collected money from Perez and Croft and disappeared through a double metal swinging door.

Lexi turned around, leaning her back against the edge of the bar. She scanned the floor, scrutinizing the customers and wondering if the person who hired Scooter to act as the middleman was among them. Whoever it was, they must have had connections to a highly skilled weapons builder. No run-of-the-mill doomsday prepper could have produced such a unique ghost gun. And Lexi's gut told her once the Dallas lab techs analyzed it, they would be hot on the trail of the Raven.

Her gaze settled on two men near the fireplace. Both looked familiar, but one stood out with his recognizable horseshoe haircut and potbelly. "Hey, Perez. Is that Milo Tilton?" She pointed an index finger in the man's direction.

The deputy adjusted his stare and squinted. "Yeah, that's him."

"I thought he was in pretrial confinement." Lexi was perplexed. How did he get a judge assigned to his case so fast? And get one to release him on bail? It seemed too coincidental.

"I did, too."

"We'll be right back." Lexi invited Croft to join her, and they weaved through the rustic tables. "We shouldn't leave without asking him some questions."

"Good idea," Croft replied.

Three steps away from the table, Lexi removed her badge and credentials case from her back pocket. Both seated men looked up when she stopped a foot away. She flashed her badge. "Good evening, Mr. Tilton. We're Special Agents Lexi Mills and Nathan Croft from the ATF. I hate to interrupt your dinner, but we have a few questions about yesterday's courthouse shooting. Do you have a minute?" He continued to carve his steak, showing little interest in speaking with her.

The other man wiped the corners of his mouth with a white cloth napkin and placed it beside his plate of half-eaten steak and baked potato. He stood, offering his right hand. Lexi shook it. "I'm Jackson Price, Mr. Tilton's attorney. May I ask why?"

"We're investigating the gun used in the shooting. This is a small town. We were wondering if Mr. Tilton knew Derek Culter before yesterday."

"I'm sorry, Agent Mills, but I've advised my client not to speak to law enforcement while his trial is ongoing."

"I understand, but this has nothing to do with his case. We're trying to piece together why the suspect chose his trial to go on a rampage."

"Again, Agent Mills—"

"It's all right, Jackson." Tilton chewed the meat in his mouth two more times and swallowed. He stared at Lexi and smiled, the type of arrogant smirk that made her want to slap it from his face. "Harrington might be a small town, but no, Agent Mills. I did not know the shooter. How could I? The paper said he was in town for less than a year, working in the oil fields before going to jail for drug possession. Our paths wouldn't have crossed unless it was in places like this. But from what I understand, he had more of a drive-thru budget."

Smug. Arrogant. Cagey. *This man is clearly hiding something.*

"I'd read you were in pretrial confinement. The judge who took over your case today must have thought differently about your fitness for bail. It seems rather convenient. Do you think the shooting had anything to do with that?"

"That's enough, Agent Mills. Unless you plan to arrest my client, I must ask you to leave."

Lexi refused to break eye contact with Tilton. There was more to a new judge allowing him out on bail. "Have a good night, Mr. Tilton. I have a feeling we'll see each other again."

The federal agents walked away, leaving Milo with a sour stomach. He pushed away his plate of porterhouse he'd only half-finished, thinking if the cleanup man didn't take care of the one person who could link him to the shooter, he'd have to act faster than he'd thought, especially after the news Jackson had dropped on him tonight.

He grabbed the arm of a passing server. "Can you wrap this up to go? I've lost my appetite."

"Of course, Mr. Tilton. I'll be right back." The server grabbed Milo's and Jackson's plates and scurried away.

Jackson didn't look confident from across the table. His repeated tie straightening made him look just the opposite—nervous as a cat.

"Pull yourself together, Jackson. They were just fishing."

"But Scooter can tie me to the shooting."

"Our man said he was taking care of everything tonight. Have you heard from him yet?"

"No, and it's making me nervous. You should be, too, considering Clem Powell might not get to hear your case if Charlene Ford gets her way. The motion she filed with the state attorney general to get a change of venue has teeth. If we don't get a trial in Harrington, you will go to prison."

"Then we need to act quickly." Milo pushed his chair back and stood. "Can you get the bill and get our leftovers? I'll meet you in the car after I make a call."

"Do I want to know who you're calling?"

"Probably not." Milo put on his jacket, grabbed his cocktail glass, and searched the dining room for the agents on his scent. He spotted them at the bar with a deputy he hadn't seen before. The bartender handed them to-go bags. When they turned to walk toward the main entrance, the short woman who had done all the talking locked stares with Milo. The look was the same fiery one Charlene Ford had given him in the courtroom earlier after his old friend had granted him bail. It brought him to a crystal-clear conclusion: Lexi Mills had him in her crosshairs.

Milo went opposite the entrance, toward the outdoor dining patio closed for remodeling. The space would provide the privacy he needed to make his call. He sat at his usual table near the fireplace when he dined outside, kicked up his feet on the neighboring chair, and sipped his scotch, considering how to start the call. He first had to show his respect before asking for more.

Pulling out his burner phone, Milo realized he had an unread message from the cleanup man. *The darn thing must have been on silent*, he thought. The text read, *Both jobs are done*. He let a broad grin grow. The Raven was no longer a threat, freeing Milo to focus on clearing the decks for a friendly trial in Harrington. He then scrolled through his contacts list until he found the number labeled "Emergency Only" and dialed it. The call connected on the third ring.

"Yes, Mr. Tilton?" The Raven's voice was as intimidating as he'd expected, bolstering Milo's impression he was the one man in the world he couldn't afford to disappoint.

"I'm calling to let you know I received your message. You have nothing to worry about. Everyone who handled your product won't talk. Ever."

"I see you're a man of action."

"I respect the conditions you require for doing business, but I need your help with another job."

"I have cleared my debt with you. Any further work will require payment."

"I understand." The last time he did business with the Raven, he'd provided him the name of two border-crossing detainees amenable to doing some questionable work and conveniently doctored their transfer to Mexican authorities. Releasing them out the front gate to a waiting Escalade had earned him one favor, which the Raven repaid by providing the ghost gun gratis.

"What do you have in mind?" the Raven asked.

"Yesterday only settled one-third of my problem. I need to address the rest quickly, but it can't be obvious."

"I have an idea but will need a day to build the product. I will text you the price and instructions for payment. Come to the same place where I met Mr. Price on Thursday at sunset."

"That will be satisfactory." Milo returned the phone to his pocket, more confident than when he'd walked into Cattlemen's and definitely more confident than his lawyer. Now, he had two days to scrape up the money. Once he did, he would solve all his problems.

19

The mixture of baked and fried aromas from three to-go meals filled the confined space of Lexi and Croft's rental car, awakening her stomach with a vengeance. So much so that she couldn't resist nibbling on the fries. *Just a few*, she told herself, but only two remained when they pulled into the Harrington County Sheriff's Department parking lot. She stuffed those two into her mouth, took a swig of water the soft butch had gifted her, and crammed the bottle into her backpack.

Leaving their food in the car, the three entered through the employee entrance at the back of the building. The door was unlocked, giving Lexi pause. Anyone could have walked in unfettered. A few steps in, she forced back a yawn, realizing Croft was likely as tired, if not more. He was a decade older and had the bejesus scared out of him earlier, as her dad would call it. They would need to alternate as drivers on the way to Dallas.

Perez led them down the empty corridors. The echo of the radio communications coming from the dispatch center was the only sign of activity. The guard on duty at the holding cells, if anyone could call what he was doing guarding, had his feet propped on the desktop, his fingers of both hands laced together draped across his chest, and was snoring up a storm. Lexi and Croft stood at the desk while Perez retrieved the cell key on a wall hook near the guard's head. A manual key was par from what Lexi had seen of the department. Technology upgrades, such as an electronic locking system, hadn't been a priority in this town for decades.

Surprisingly, except for the rise and fall of his chest and belly to the rhythm of his breathing, the man didn't move. He was unconscious or the soundest sleeper in the world, both of which gave Lexi a sinking feeling. Anyone—Culter, an accomplice, the media, or whoever killed Scooter—could have sneaked in or out with little effort.

Croft seethed through a forceful, loud breath before shoving the guard's feet from the desk. The man opened his eyes, teetered his chair, and flailed his arms to catch his balance and avoid toppling to the floor. "Shit," he said, gathering his bearings.

"You call this standing watch?" Croft curled his lip.

"Who the hell are you?"

"I'm the man whose prisoner you're supposedly guarding."

"You're the feds."

"Deductive if not reliable." Croft smirked. "We're here to retrieve our prisoner."

The guard rose from this chair. "Well, why didn't you say so before? I'll get him."

"Don't bother," Perez said, dangling the key chest high. "We'll get him."

"You might consider packing up your locker," Lexi said. "We'll have to include this in our report to Sheriff Jessup."

"Right." The guard returned to this chair, forming an arrogant grin and folding his arms across his chest. He was smug without caring that he might lose his job. Smugness was a theme tonight, and this man's brand of it made Lexi think he was part of the group of deputies unhappy with the new sheriff's way of doing things.

Perez had a head start down the center aisle of cells. He flipped on the lights from a wall switch near the entrance, illuminating all six holding cells. Reaching the middle cell on the right, he turned his head to look inside and suddenly jerked his movement. "Oh crap." He inserted the key and shoved the door open.

The bad feeling Lexi had a moment ago exploded into pure dread. She and Croft dashed toward the open cell. The chaotic scene confirmed her greatest fear about this case. Deputy Perez was frantically untying a sheet knot from around Culter's neck. Someone had tied the other end of the sheet to the cell door bar above the crossbeam, keeping it four feet above the floor. Culter was on his knees, leaning at a forty-five-degree angle, with his arms dangling lifelessly forward of his body. His face was pale.

Lexi didn't have to check for a pulse to know Culter was dead. The three hours she'd left him alone. The arrogance of Tilton and the guard. The growing feeling of a town-wide conspiracy. It all told her the truth.

Croft rushed in and helped place Culter gently on the polished concrete floor. Before he started chest compressions, Lexi had her phone out and dialed 9-1-1, trusting the dispatcher at the front of the building, more than the deputy several yards away. "This is Agent Lexi Mills. I'm in your county lockup in the back. We have an unresponsive prisoner. An apparent hanging. Send an ambulance."

Lexi hung up. Culter exhibited no change, his only movement coming with each compression Croft applied. Perez had fallen to his knees, rubbing the back of his neck while looking on with concern.

The guard appeared at the cell, stopping next to Lexi. "What the hell?"

"Did anyone come back here after Perez and Agent Croft dropped off the prisoner?" Lexi couldn't help but add an accusatory tone to her question.

"I'm not saying a word." Refusing to cooperate could mean he was covering his ass for sleeping on the job or his involvement in the killing. Either way, Lexi couldn't let him go. She took two steps back and drew her weapon.

"Hands up."

The guard turned slowly. "What the hell, lady?"

"Until we sort this out, I'm detaining you." Lexi kept her attention on the so-called guard. "Deputy Perez, would you provide cover while I frisk this asshole?"

Perez rose to his feet without saying a word, drew his semiautomatic weapon, and trained it on the only suspect they had.

Lexi holstered her weapon. "Hands on the bars."

"You've got to be kidding. He probably hung himself, thinking about a lifetime in prison." The guard was at least a foot taller and outweighed Lexi by fifty pounds. If he didn't cooperate, she would have to use the close-quarters self-defense techniques she'd learned in FLETC.

The commotion inside the cell stopped. "It's no use. He's gone," Croft said, wiping sweat from his brow with a forearm. He leaned back, touching the backs of his thighs to his heels, looking as if all the wind had left his sails.

"A man is dead, and you were the last to see him alive. Do I look like I'm kidding?" Lexi put one hand up in a stopping motion and wrapped the other around her holstered Glock's grip. "Don't add resisting arrest to the list of things I'd like to charge you with."

"I can't believe this." The guard turned toward the cell and gripped a bar with each hand.

Lexi removed the guard's service weapon and slipped it into her waistband at the small of her back. She then patted him down, discovering a cell phone, which she pocketed, and a snub-nose revolver in an ankle holster. She stowed it next to the other gun in her waistband. "Is that it?" she asked.

"Pat me down again and find out. Take your time, lady. Take your time." He chuckled.

Croft stepped closer, staring him down through the bars. "Mind your manners, or a room like this will be your home for months. The lady asked you a question."

The guard craned his head over a shoulder and snarled. "That's it."

"Does the key work the other cell doors?" Lexi asked Perez.

"Yes."

"Open the cell across from this one." Once the cell was open, Lexi guided the guard by the elbow. The door clanked when she rolled it shut, locking him inside. "You're staying put until I review the security footage."

"There is none," the guard plopped down on the cot. "Look around, Einstein. No cameras."

"Wonderful." Lexi tossed her hands in the air in frustration. The county lockup had no surveillance beyond a jailer who slept during his shift. "Then you're staying here until I get the lab techs to go over the crime scene."

Moments later, the faint sound of a siren pierced the holding cell wall, telling Lexi the fire department must have been close. She pulled out her cell phone to notify the sheriff about Culter's death but paused, recalling what he'd said in the observation room when she and Croft were about to take over the case. He'd said he would rather see Culter hang than spend the rest of his life in prison for what he'd done, and that was precisely how he'd died. Had she misjudged his trustworthiness? Or was the manner of death a coincidence? Lexi had to follow her gut: Coincidence didn't exist in a murder case. She needed more help.

"Croft, take pictures to document the body."

Lexi scrolled through her contacts list and dialed Agent Lange, expecting an ass chewing for overstepping and not updating her sooner. She could say circumstances on the ground had moved so quickly she didn't have time to call, but that wasn't the truth. Lexi had gotten sloppy. She'd become accustomed to working autonomously on the task force and back-briefing Maxwell Keene after things had calmed down. But Willie Lange wasn't Maxwell and ran a tighter ship.

The call connected on the second ring. "Agent Mills, I wasn't expecting an update until tomorrow."

"Sorry to call after hours, Agent Lange, but Croft and I have run into a snag in Harrington." Lexi explained why she took jurisdiction in the case, how Culter admitted the killing was a contract hit, and they'd found the middleman to the crime dead in his trailer. "When we returned to pick up the prisoner, we found him dead from an apparent hanging in his cell. The jail has no security cameras to see who might have come in and out, so we have little to go on. I don't trust the locals to process the scene. How quickly can you get a lab team here?"

"The El Paso field office is the closest. I'll alert their SRT leader and have them in Harrington in two hours. Let me put you on hold."

So far, so good, Lexi thought. Lange didn't blow her stack. Maybe the bitterness Lange had for her was waning. But that didn't excuse Lexi from not looping her boss in sooner. It was a flaw she would have to work on.

While Lexi waited on the phone, the paramedics rolled into the corridor with a gurney. When Lexi stepped back to give them room to assess Culter, Lange returned to the call. "Mills, the lab team will be en route in fifteen minutes. I gave them your number and asked them to text when they're thirty minutes away."

"Thank you, Agent Lange. I appreciate the help. I'll let you know what the team finds."

"Not so fast, Mills. Now that we've taken care of business, we need to address—"

"My disrespect." Lexi interrupted. "I realize I was wrong for not calling you sooner, Agent Lange. I have no excuse." She split her attention between Lange and the scene in front of her. The paramedics radioed the patient was still unresponsive and would transport immediately.

"Being the lead on a case doesn't mean you have free rein. We all have someone to answer to."

"Yes, we do." Lexi recalled using those exact words a few months ago while on the task force and realized she and Lange were alike. "I will do better."

"I'm going to hold you to it, Mills. We're on the same team and need to trust one another." Lange's tone turned softer. "I read somewhere a smart, talented law enforcement officer once said the most knowledgeable, skilled team will fail without trust in each other and its leaders."

The quote Lange referred to threw her aback. Lexi had added the line on the fly to close out her speech at the National Police Chief's Conference in Las Vegas two months ago after she'd learned her former ATF boss had betrayed her and the badge. Lexi had forgotten the conference officials had recorded her speech and posted it on their website. She got the impression bringing it up was Lange's version of a white flag.

"Whoever said it knew what they were talking about through hard-earned experience." Lexi completed the call, optimistic the animosity between her and Lange might soon end.

After Lexi told Croft about the ATF lab team's pending arrival, the paramedics loaded Culter onto the gurney and packed up their equipment. As they wheeled him out, she realized she needed to call in another favor and dialed another number.

"Well, if it isn't my personal one-legged Eliot Ness. It must be important if you're calling at this hour." The man's thick Texas accent made Lexi smile. He knew how to put a person at ease with a single turn of a phrase.

"It is, Governor. I need your help."

Croft signaled he'd be right back.

"Name it," the governor said.

Lexi explained the case and her mistrust of the local officials. "Can you have the state's medical examiner reassign the autopsies of Culter and Scooter to another coroner? I don't know how far corruption runs in this town."

"Consider it done. I'll have the bodies transported to Midland." Governor Macalister changed his tone from businesslike to playful. "Now, I'm looking forward to seeing your parents on their own turf this weekend. The last time I saw your father, he promised to let me test drive his latest pet project."

"The project is my wedding present, so you'll have to wait in line, Governor."

He laughed. "Fair enough, Lexi. I can't stay long on Saturday, but I promise not to miss the wedding."

When she hung up, Croft returned with their dinners. "We might as well eat while we can."

"Great idea."

Before Lexi stuffed down the last bite of her bacon cheeseburger, Sheriff Jessup entered the lockup area. "What the hell happened here, Agent Mills? Dispatch called me and said EMTs took the prisoner away in a rig."

Lexi wiped her mouth and hands with a paper napkin and swallowed the bite in her mouth. "My guess is whoever wanted Scooter dead wanted Culter dead, too."

"Why didn't you call me?"

"This isn't your case, Sheriff." Lexi wanted to show him the respect a sheriff deserved, but the only person in this town she could trust was Perez because he was with her and Croft when Culter died.

"But it is my jail." Jessup's voice had transitioned from surprised and disappointed to angry.

"I realize that, but Culter was in my custody. We left him here for safe-keeping. That makes it an ATF case, and the absence of video surveillance makes everyone here a suspect."

"You're saying I'm a suspect?" Jessup tapped his chest with an index finger.

"You said you wanted to see Culter hang." Lexi pointed to the sheet still tied to the cell bar. "That's exactly how he died."

"Oh, for Christ's sake, Mills." Jessup placed his hands on both hips, elbows pointed outward. Lexi had clearly offended him. "I'm the good guy here."

"I'd like to believe you, but I can't rule anyone out. The building door was unlocked." Lexi gestured to the cell across from Culter's. "And your supposed guard was sound asleep when we got here. An entire army could have rolled through the jail with tanks, and he wouldn't have woken."

"You locked him up?"

"He refused to say if anyone entered the lockup area and was the only one on scene, which makes him a primary suspect. If he didn't do it, he's either covering for who did or covering his own ass for sleeping on the job."

Sheriff Jessup walked to the cell. "Ed, tell me what happened, or I'm taking your badge tonight."

Ed stepped closer to the bars. "I don't know who came in. After Perez and the fed dropped off the prisoner, I got some coffee. I got tired, and the next thing I know, they're back, the prisoner is dead, and she's locking me up."

"It sounds like someone may have drugged you," Lexi said. "Why didn't you say so?"

"Because this isn't the first time you've fallen asleep on the job," the sheriff said. "Is it, Ed?"

"No, sir." Ed lowered his head.

"You're suspended until further notice. Now, where's the cup?" the sheriff asked.

"It should be on the desk."

"I'll have our lab techs test it." Lexi turned toward Perez. "Let him out." She then handed Jessup Ed's weapons and phone. "I found these on him."

Jessup shook his head at Ed. "A backup? I specifically said only department-issued weapons while on duty. It looks like I have a lot more cleaning up to do." He turned to Perez. "It's way past the end of your shift. Go home, get some sleep, and come back for another day shift. You've earned the move after the few days you've had."

"Thanks, Sheriff." Perez turned to Lexi and Croft and shook their hands. "I'd say it's been a pleasure working with you, but this has been my screwiest day since putting on the badge."

"You're not alone," Lexi said. "This ranks pretty high. I appreciate the help today."

After Perez departed, Lexi checked the time on the last message she'd received. She calculated the lab team wouldn't arrive for another ten minutes, so she stepped outside into the cool night air to make a private call.

Two lampposts lit the employee parking lot in a faint glow. One car pulled away, presumably Perez, and another pulled in, parking close to the building. A deputy in uniform Lexi hadn't seen before exited with his gear bag from a green Challenger and walked toward the door where she was standing nearby. His distinctive tight red curls came into focus when he walked closer and removed his baseball cap steps before the threshold.

"Evening." He kept walking. Lexi waited to dial until he slipped inside.

Nita picked up. "You're not coming home tonight, are you?" If she was disappointed, she hid it well, which Lexi needed right then. Her gut told her the Raven had supplied the ghost gun, but there was much more going on behind the scenes. She had two dead suspects as part of a massive cover-up, but she didn't know for what.

"I'm afraid not. Things got a little complicated, but I called in a favor with Ken Macalister, so I'm hoping to get answers overnight."

"If you called the governor, then it must be big."

"It is but getting home to you sooner is bigger. How's Mom? Did she get the MRI done?"

"She did. They found some swelling but no signs of bleeding. They think her symptoms are concussion related."

"That's good news, right?"

"It's not great, but it's not the worst. They put her on some medication to reduce the swelling." Nita yawned. "Hey, I'm sorry to cut this short, but I have two clients tomorrow morning."

"You're not in Ponder? Who's watching Mom and Dad?"

"Your dad is almost healed. He's perfectly capable of keeping an eye on your mother. But just in case, I snooped through your mother's address book and called Shirley Beamer. She'll swing by your parents' place in the morning."

"Thank you."

"You can thank me properly Saturday night." Nita lowered her voice, adding a seductive tone.

"That goes without question." Lexi's phone vibrated with an incoming text, so she lowered it. The message was from Governor Macalister and read, *Midland Coroner arrived in Harrington. Will conduct an autopsy tonight. Passed along your number.* Lexi formed a grin. Whenever the governor made calls, things happened at breakneck speed. When she looked up, another set of headlights entered the parking lot. The dark suburban pulled up close to the door. The federal plates on the front bumper told Lexi that Lange's team had arrived.

"I hate to cut this short, Nita, but I have to get back to work. I'll let you know when I'll be back in Dallas." Lexi slipped her phone into her back pocket when a man and a woman stepped out of the car. The credentials hanging around their necks identified them as ATF agents. "Glad you could make it so quickly. When you're done processing the scene, I have a ghost gun I need you to take back. I'll need a complete analysis."

20

Four days later

It's just a ceremony, Lexi told herself. She and Nita had been living together for nearly a year and already knew everything important about each other. A devastating injury, obsessive focus on work, and an addiction relapse had already tested them. They'd come through the other side stronger because they had each other. Lexi wanted only Nita and wanted only Nita to want her. So why was she so nervous fixing her bow tie?

Lexi's hands shook as she fumbled with the ends, failing miserably to recall the correct sequence. "It's no use. Can you help?"

A smile sprouted on her father's lips. It stretched to his eyes and made them glow brightly with boundless pride. "I'd be happy to help." Her dad unfurled the tie and leveled the two ends to start from the beginning. "I had the same problem on my wedding day, and my father had to help me."

"Are you sure you can do it? Mom says you're horrible with ties."

"I only make her think I am. I'm very good at it."

"Then why do you have her do it every time you wear a suit?"

"She enjoys helping, and I enjoy the attention. It's a win-win."

Lexi grinned. "I never knew you were such a sly dog."

"That's the secret to a solid marriage. Figure out what makes your wife happy and give it to her daily without question."

"Besides helping and cooking, what makes Mom happy?"

"Doting over the people she loves and being right, even when she's wrong." He chuckled, bobbing the ends of his long mustache up and down.

"I beg your pardon." Her mother appeared in the bedroom doorway. "You fixing your daughter's tie thirty minutes before she marries the most beautiful bride in the world is proof I'm never wrong."

"That you are, Jess." Her dad's eyes glistened with the tears of fifteen lost years between father and daughter. Fifteen years of missed birthdays, Thanksgiving dinners, and bear hugs because he couldn't accept Lexi was gay. Lexi knew what he was thinking because she had the same regret. He shook his head. "So many wasted moments."

"We're together now, Dad. The past doesn't matter." Lexi squeezed his large, wrinkled hand. It was dry and chapped from decades of car grease and harsh soaps. Everyone on his team had them, and in a way, Lexi wished she had them, too. Her dry, scaly hands would have meant the fifteen years of estrangement never happened. *But things happen for a reason*, her mother always said. Lexi needed to detour from her father's footsteps to find her calling and the love of her life. She had him to thank for finding herself and Nita, but there was no painless way to voice it, so she remained silent and gave his hand an extra squeeze.

"This is everything I've wished for." Her mother's voice cracked. "You've made me a very happy woman today, Jerry."

"That's my job." He put the finishing touches on Lexi's bow tie, pulling on both ends one more time. "There. It looks perfect."

Lexi's mom inspected her dad's handiwork and winked at her. "Almost as good as mine. He thinks I didn't know about his little tie game, but I've played along for decades. I learned that your dad likes to make sure the people in his life are happy. That's why he gives such great hugs and why it crushed him when he didn't accept you for who you are. He failed you but didn't know how to reverse a lifetime of belief."

Lexi's lips trembled.

"You should have seen him the day I told him you were being assigned to Dallas. A light went on inside him I hadn't seen in years. It was the light of hope that one day he could hug you like he used to. But he knew that day wouldn't come until something changed. He spent hours talking to his best friend. Gavin made your father see you were the same person you'd always been when you came out to us. He also made your father understand his responsibility to accept you for who you are, not the image of you he'd created in his head. Gavin had said, 'God doesn't make mistakes. Lexi is the way God made her.'"

Lexi's eyes welled. This moment marked the most profound, most revealing conversation she and her parents had shared. Ever. And it was precisely the gift she needed on her wedding day.

"Got it!" Kaplan burst inside, out of breath, holding Lexi's cell phone head high in her right hand. "You left it in the fridge when you got a soda." Her parents laughed.

"The fridge?" Lexi let out a puttering breath. "I have to pull myself together."

"You have a lot on your mind after the Harrington case fizzled," Kaplan said, handing her the phone.

"Especially since the ghost gun contained traces of raven feathers." Lexi rolled her neck to push back the disappointing memories of the lab tech and coroner's findings. "*The jail cell was a grab bag of fingerprints, but the sheet tied to Culter's neck had only his fingerprints,*" the tech had reported. "*The toxicology report was clean, and the cause of death was asphyxiation, but the bruising around the neck was inconclusive. They were consistent with a self-hanging,*" the coroner had said. She and Croft had left Harrington empty-handed the following morning without links to the Raven. That afternoon, the lab results on the ghost gun made the dead-end sting more.

"You'll find him, Lexi." Kaplan pointed to Lexi's phone. "Check your messages. There's one you might want to return before the ceremony. It might be what you need today."

Lexi thumbed the lock screen, ignored the multiple news alerts, and focused on the missed text. It brought a smile. The message from Noah Black read, *You got this. Call if you need a pep talk.* "It is. I'll be right back."

"Don't take too long, Peanut," her father said. "We start in twenty minutes."

"I won't miss this for the world."

"I'll go check on Nita," her mother said. "Her cousin should be done with her hair by now." She kissed Lexi on the cheek. "I'll see you on the aisle."

Lexi grabbed her mother's hand before she walked out of reach and squeezed it firmly. "I love you, Mom."

Pressing her lips into a puckered smile was her mom's way of forcing herself not to cry. "I love you, Peanut," she said with a thick voice before disappearing down the hallway.

Lexi descended the stairs and exited the front door to the wraparound porch, avoiding the back where the wedding guests were gathering. She sat on a chair not visible from the gravel road and dialed. The call picked up on the first ring.

"The world may think you have nerves of steel, but I know the real Lexi Mills. You're jumpy right now."

"But I shouldn't be, Noah. I've never been more sure of anything in my life. I love her with all my heart."

"Nita is the right person for you, but that's not what you're afraid of."

"Then tell me what has made me so skittish."

"You failed to protect her from Belcher, and you're afraid you'll fail her again."

Lexi hadn't realized it until now, but Noah was right. He was skilled at breaking down Lexi's façade and getting to her core. It was a gift he shared with her mother, but his insight went deeper like their friendship. He was by her side when the job pushed her to the limit and when the love of a good woman pulled her back to safety. Her mother knew what made her tick when it came to her father, but Noah understood what powered the rest of her.

"I'd never forgive myself if something else happened to her because of my job. I've thought of quitting to protect her, but I can't bring myself to do it."

"That's because you were born to do this. If you quit or took an office job, you'd grow to resent the change and why you made it."

"I'd never resent Nita."

"You say that now, but what about in five years when you're fed up with your dull, mundane job? You would feel trapped, like your life was over. No,

Lexi. Law enforcement is in your blood, and so is Nita. You wouldn't be whole without both."

"But how do I protect her?"

"By trusting your gut. It has never failed you. Chasing Belcher taught you security while working a case must extend to your family. Working with you, I learned you never make the same mistake twice. You won't fail Nita, Lexi. Now, make sure your best woman hasn't lost the ring, and go marry her."

Noah was right about security. When the dust cleared after Kris Faust's death, she installed security systems in her and Nita's apartment and her parents' house with live camera feeds. *But that wasn't enough*, she thought. Her father knew how to handle a gun, but Nita and her mother avoided them. She made a mental note to train both well enough to defend themselves.

"I miss you, Noah Black."

"I miss you, too, but returning to Nogales has been good for me. I'm doing a lot of good here. It doesn't make up for the choice I made, but it's a start."

"I wish you peace, my friend." When Lexi disconnected the call, her nerves were gone. In their place was an anxiousness to begin the rest of her life with Nita.

She darted inside and up the stairs, returning to her old bedroom and discovering Kaplan and her father sitting on the bed, chatting carefree, Kaplan with her arms flowing in the air to dramatize a point, and her father snickering so hard the ends of his long mustache moved up and down. They turned their heads when a floorboard creaked at the threshold. "What are you two sitting around for? I'm getting married in a few minutes."

Lexi tightened her arm around Nita's torso, swaying her on the dance floor in her parents' backyard and inhaling the white roses in her hair. The sweet, candy-like scent reminded her of the violets her mother used to grow in the flowerbeds at the base of the front porch. It brought her back to carefree childhood days of picking flowers for Sunday dinners, warming her heart and giving birth to a smile.

A soft turn on her heel with Nita in her arms brought the food table into view. A caterer stumbled over a wire leading to a speaker playing Tim McGraw and Faith Hill. He recovered without spilling his tray, but it brought Lexi back to her and Nita standing at the rose-covered altar an hour ago and a particular part of Nita's wedding vows. *"I will walk through life with you, brace you when you stumble, and let you lift me when I falter, because I choose you."* She remembered the extra squeeze on her hand and the resulting thickness in her throat when Nita said those words. They were Nita's promise that her battle with addiction had become theirs without argument or resistance. The sentiment, acknowledging they each had inner strength but were stronger together, meant more to Lexi than all her other words of love, respect, and patience.

Lexi drew her lips closer to Nita's ear and whispered, "You're stronger than you know."

Nita shifted until their warm breaths mixed the love and joy between them. She moved their clasped hands chest high between their pressed-together bodies, holding their promise in a cherished place. She whispered back, "I'm stronger with you."

"We both are." Lexi pressed their lips into a brief, tender kiss, sealing their pledge to make the other sturdier in moments of weakness.

"Do you know what your tux is doing to me?" Nita ran the back of her fingers down a lapel, grazing a breast and sending tingles radiating through Lexi's chest.

"Oh, I have a pretty good idea." Lexi traced the plunging edge of Nita's gown, touching more skin than fabric covering three-quarters of her breasts. "And in a few more days, we'll have an entire week in Napa to fully explore the effect we have on each other." She stopped at the midpoint when Nita shivered.

The song ended, bringing their few minutes of privacy to a close. Lexi glanced toward the tables, where Simon Winslow, Governor Ken Macalister's chief of security, gestured her over. "It looks like the governor is about to call it a night and return to Austin."

"We'll continue this later. We should say goodbye before they leave." Nita clutched Lexi's hand and steered her toward the tables.

Winslow stood several feet to the side of his protectee. They were both tall, but his unassuming, quiet presence was in stark contrast to the governor. Simon's role was to disappear into a crowd, observe, and act quickly to counter potential threats. Ken "Bear" Macalister was the polar opposite: conspicuous and friendly. He was a politician through and through who could command the attention of a room and work everyone in it within minutes. But he was also a loyal friend who came to Lexi's aid in her darkest moment when Nita was missing. If he hadn't lent her Lieutenant Sarah Briscoe's Texas Ranger team and airplane, Nita would have died, and Tony Belcher would still be on the loose.

When Lexi and Nita approached the governor, he stopped his conversation instantly and gave his full attention to them. He enveloped Nita in one of his signature bear hugs before inspecting her from head to toe. "Lexi told me you were beautiful, but she didn't warn me you were positively stunning. You stole the show, young lady."

"Thank you, Governor." Nita lowered her eyes and struggled to force back an impish smile. "I never got a chance to thank you properly for helping Lexi and lending her the tools to keep us safe. I'm very grateful."

"I was happy to help, darlin'. I'm just glad she found you in time. You married a very impressive woman. When the contractors have completed the renovations at my Spicewood home, I'd love to have you two over for an extended weekend. Your wife can finally see the old homestead in all its glory without bullets flying."

"We'd love to."

Macalister turned to Lexi. "Could you mention it to Noah? I'd like to give my personal protection team the royal treatment."

"Of course, sir. I just spoke with him today. I'll check with Simon and arrange a weekend that is convenient for all of us. It would be nice having everyone together again."

"I must say it was a wonderful ceremony, Lexi. I'm so glad to have been part of it, but I must be going."

After bidding the governor and Simon goodbye, Lexi spotted her mother giving the catering staff instructions and clearing dirty dishes from a collection table. "I'll be right back," she said to Nita before walking to the table. Her mother had stacked the plates with the collection of scraps on the top plate. "Mom, we're paying an entire staff to take care of this. You should mingle."

"I've mingled with what few friends of ours bothered to show their face at a lesbian wedding." Bitterness and sadness laced her mother's tone. "I can't believe Shirley Beamer didn't come."

"It doesn't matter." Lexi grabbed the dishes from her mother's hands and returned them to the table.

"But it does matter. I went to all three of her children's weddings, and she couldn't get over her bigotry." Her mother shook her head with the vigor of disappointment. "She never let on that she had a problem with you being gay."

"I think it has more to do with Nita and me marrying than sleeping together."

Her mother's eyes narrowed in a rare moment of anger since the days when Lexi had been a defiant child. "I thought I knew her. How your father acted when you came out nearly tore us apart. I forgave him because he was my husband, but I won't put up with it from someone who is supposed to be my friend."

"Let's not worry about her. This is my wedding day. Today should be a celebration."

"You're right. When things settle down—maybe tomorrow morning—I have something I want to give you."

"Can we make it late morning? Nita and I—"

Her mother put up a hand in a stopping motion. "No need to explain. It's your wedding night."

Lexi laughed. "All right, Mom. Let's eat this incredible food, drink champagne, and dance until our feet are sore with the people who love and accept us."

The corners of her mother's mouth inched upward into a devilish grin. "You have an unfair advantage with only one foot."

"You could say I have a leg up on everyone here." Lexi snickered. That marked the first time her mother had joked about her losing a leg, and it was beautiful. Whenever the topic had come up, pain floated in her mother's eyes, but once Lexi sifted through her disappointment in Shirley, she saw nothing but joy.

Lexi offered her mother an arm. "Let's find our spouses."

Lexi and Nita and her mother and father danced with family and friends, putting aside the ugly business of prejudice. One each of Lexi's two aunts and two uncles and three of her six cousins had come. The only members of Nita's family to attend were her cousin, Jenny, and her wife. But the absence of her mother and brother was about burning bridges when Nita was in the throes of addiction, not being gay.

Loads of friends from their workplaces had attended, including the Keenes and everyone from the task force except for Noah. Even Sarah Briscoe and half of her response team were on the dance floor. The day was a beautiful celebration of love, friends, family, and new beginnings.

21

A dead drug dealer in an RV trailer was terrible enough, but a prisoner dying while in jail would have repercussions for years. The citizens elected Sam Jessup to clean up Harrington's perceived corruption, but four days ago, it had struck right under his nose, giving the people the impression he was feckless against it. He couldn't disagree. The stacks of reports on his desk detailing complaints tied to Milo's operation not investigated or referred for prosecution proved he was just one man against an army.

After his election, Sam had expected an uphill battle, knowing Milo Tilton had his claws into the court system, the prosecutor's office, the city council, and the sheriff's department. He'd thought a new judge and the election of a district attorney would improve his chances of cleaning up the town, but it had become clear Milo wouldn't go away without a fight. First, Culter had shot the new judge—the trustworthy old one—in his courtroom in public fashion. It was bold and sent a loud and clear message. Then ATF agents found the only two people tied to the murder dead the following day, one in Sam's own jail.

He thumbed through the coroner's report on his desk for the tenth time. He knew the Midland coroner's findings were scientifically cautious, listing the bruising around the neck as inconclusive and consistent with a self-hanging, but he suspected something different. It wasn't beyond the pale to think a deputy friendly to Milo drugged his guard and killed Culter, making it look like a suicide. And other than Deputy Thomas Perez, who was with the ATF agents when Derek Culter died in his cell, he didn't know which of his deputies he could trust. He needed to root out the bad apples, and he would start by building an inner circle.

A knock drew his attention. "You wanted to see me, sir." Deputy Perez waited in the doorway. "It surprised me to see you here on a Saturday."

"Thanks for stopping by after your shift. Close the door." Once Perez sat in the guest chair, Sam continued. "I need to talk to you about Derek Culter, among other things." Thomas issued a soft nod. "What did you think of the coroner's report?"

"It's not my place to dispute his findings."

"I'm not asking you to. The report said the manner of death was inconclusive. I'm asking what you think happened." Thomas shifted in his seat, rolling his neck. He clearly wasn't comfortable with the question. "You've been in the department and town long enough to know I was elected to clean up things, including the rotten apples in this building. I don't include you among them. My gut tells me you're one of the good guys, and I can trust you."

Perez released a long, loud breath. "I was hoping you'd say that."

"Though we couldn't prove someone drugged the jailer, I think he was. I also think the same person may have done something to Culter to make it look like he hung himself. I know you weren't involved, so that leaves thirty-two other deputies as suspects."

"That was my guess. My money is on the Rat Pack."

"The Rat Pack? What's that?"

"They're the deputies I think are on Tilton's payroll."

"How many?"

"There are still a few deputies I haven't worked with, but of those I have, I'd say six."

"Can you provide names?" The names Perez provided made sense. Each had been with the department for over a decade, and all worked the day shift when Sam took office. Those six grumbled the most when he canceled the detention center assistance program, where deputies escorted and guarded the work details to and from the local farms and ranches. "Thank you, Thomas. This is a big help. If I were to show you a roster, can you point out the other ones you've worked with? That might tell me who else I can trust. And the jury will be out on the others you have yet to work with."

"Sure thing, Sheriff." Perez went through a roster in alphabetical order with the names and photographs of every deputy on staff, placing a checkmark next to the ones he'd worked with. The guard from the night Culter died in his cell was on the list, bolstering Sam's suspicion he wasn't a Rat Packer and was drugged to not leave any witnesses.

When Perez got to the last page, he pointed to a name. "He's the guy I saw at the river the night of the manhunt. I thought he was going to shoot Culter, but something spooked him, and he disappeared."

Sam looked closely at the name. "Sergeant Ross?" Sam sank farther into his chair. Rusty Ross was the senior deputy sergeant on staff and his second in command. He would be in charge if anything happened to Sam. "Thanks, Thomas. This is a big help. Now for the big ask. I'll need you to keep your eyes and ears open and report anything suspicious with the Rat Pack."

"I'd hoped to never work with them again."

"Until I can vet the others, you're the only one I can count on. That means partnering you with them so we can figure out which one killed Culter."

Perez rubbed the back of his neck. "I don't like those guys, and they don't like me. I doubt they'll show their hand."

"It's the only play I have, Thomas. I can't clean house without your help."

"All right, sir. I'll help."

"I had a gut feeling I could count on you." He retrieved the business cards Agent Mills had given him before they left Harrington and jotted down their contact information. "You already worked with Agents Mills and Croft on the case, and I want you to have their numbers. Expect to be reassigned soon."

Once Perez left, Sam gathered the files, including the coroner's report on Derek Culter, and locked them in his desk drawer. He grabbed the personnel roster, turned to the last page, and stared at the picture of

Sergeant Ross. When they'd first met, Ross had seemed relieved Sam was on board. That he wanted nothing to do with the former sheriff. Sam now realized Ross was merely acting. That was a betrayal.

The next step in cleaning house included scouring the personnel records of Ross and the Rat Pack to ferret out a deficiency that might be cause for termination. He doubted the old sheriff would have documented infractions or kept complaints, but the records were a starting point. He'd then pour through every report and ticket they issued and bounce them against the official shift log. Something might pop up that would tell him for sure which deputies were dirty, or at least put him on the right trail.

He grabbed his coat and Stetson and headed to the dispatch center to review the day's log. The rookie dispatcher was on shift. After all, it was Saturday night, and the newest person always got the crappy hours. She was young, two years out of high school, but calm under pressure and had a clear and distinct radio voice. She'd go far as a dispatcher if she wanted to make it a career.

"Evening, Julie. Anything interesting today?" He looked over her shoulder at the computer monitor with the activity log on screen.

The department didn't have a modern, high-tech dispatching system and still managed things old school with decade-old software. If they did have a modern system, Sam would receive alerts on his phone, customized to his liking. It was a handy feature at his previous department in Pecos County. It had kept him up to date on activity in his county in virtually real time.

"Not much, sir. Three traffic accidents, two shoplifting complaints, and a fist fight broke out at the little league park."

"We were called out for kids fighting on the baseball field?"

"Not the kids, the parents."

"It figures." Sam straightened and took a step back. "I'm heading home. Call me if anything interesting goes down."

"Will do." Julie gave him a two-finger salute on his way out.

Sam exited the building to the employee parking lot via the back door, which now had an automatic lock. The day after someone killed Culter, Sam paid for a handyman out of his own pocket to install a keypad lock he'd picked up at a local hardware store. He also bought an internet-based wireless security camera and mounted it in the lockup area until the county board of supervisors coughed up money for a robust system. Both solutions weren't perfect but were a dramatic improvement.

He unlocked his department SUV using the fob and tossed his Stetson onto the front passenger seat. Turning on the engine, the car radio came on. Hall and Oates were singing about a rich girl. On the department radio, Julie conducted a status check of the deputies on patrol. All six reported they were in service.

Sam reversed out of his space and drove slowly to the parking lot exit. Before turning onto the road, he rolled down the driver's window when he spotted Charlene Ford walking toward her car parked on the street near the courthouse next door. The building also housed the District Attorney's office. "Miss Ford," he shouted.

Charlene looked in his direction, waved, and walked toward his car. He waited. "Hi, Sam. Working late on a Saturday night, too? Aren't we pathetic?"

"When you have big messes to clean up, there is no such thing as a day off."

"I hear you. I don't know who to trust in my office, so I pour through records over the weekend. I'm getting a picture, and it isn't pretty."

"I do the same thing with similar results," Sam said. "Eventually, we'll get to the root of things and clean up this town."

"I hope so."

After saying good night, Sam pulled onto the street and started the route to his rental home on the outskirts of town. He'd considered buying a house when he first arrived but thought better of it when he realized the enormity of the corruption he faced. However, having a list of the Rat Pack members, thanks to Perez, buying a house seemed like a future possibility.

Sam brought his SUV up to speed when he reached the county highway. A rapid beeping sound started, reminiscent of the car alert when a passenger had undone their seat belt, but it sounded fainter than it should have. He craned his head toward the backseat, but nothing was there. He then checked the dash, but—

An explosion.

A flash of orange with searing heat.

The floor of Sam's SUV ripped open on the passenger side, sending metal flying into the cabin and through his body. The pain was unbearable, like nothing he'd ever imagined. He prayed for death to take him rather than endure one more agonizing second.

Everything turned mercifully black.

22

A noise roused Lexi awake. Her right side should have felt warm with Nita pressed against it with an arm and a leg draped over her, but cool air churned by the ceiling fan whispered on her bare skin. The scent of sweat from last night lingered in the air, sparking an involuntary smile. Lexi sent an arm toward the other side of the bed, blindly searching for Nita, but she found nothing but cold cotton. She popped her eyes open, confirming she was disappointingly alone between the sheets.

Lexi turned her head toward the nightstand to check her phone but remembered she'd forgotten it in her parents' kitchen after the wedding. Being unreachable for eighteen hours was more freeing than she'd thought possible. She'd last touched that damn thing after Noah gave her the pep talk she needed to walk down the aisle with a clear mind. Afterward, the day was about celebrating with family and friends, and the night was about making Nita feel she and Lexi were the only people in the world. She was in no rush to be reachable again, but her job required it.

The distinct sound of the shower door opening signaled Lexi had missed a golden opportunity to pick up where she and Nita had left off last night. But the silver wedding ring reminded her they would have many more chances to start the day with passion. She twisted it, replaying memories of yesterday's wedding in her head. Except for Shirley Beamer refusing to come and upsetting her mother, the day was perfect. Even the food was unadulterated bliss, especially the roast beef sliders. And having her mother walk Nita down the aisle was special, symbolizing the family they'd already become. But having her father escort her to the altar was the cherry on top. He truly loved her for who she was. She finally had her dad back in every way.

The white noise of Nita's hairdryer starting meant Nita was already in her clothes, but that didn't mean Lexi couldn't coax her out of them. She donned her prosthetic and strode confidently toward the bathroom without bothering to put on anything. Nita wore casual athletic wear. It accentuated every tantalizing curve but covered too much skin while Lexi was still in wedding night mode.

Stepping behind Nita and nuzzling her neck, Lexi wrapped her arms around her wife's torso and pressed their bodies together. The hairdryer stopped instantly to the sound of giggles. That wasn't the reaction Lexi had hoped for, but she would take it. Moving a hand closer to a breast, the giggles grew stronger and uncontrollable. Definitely not the reaction she wanted. Now she had to know what had prompted Nita's laughing fit. One look in the mirror and she knew the answer—the worst bedhead ever. It looked like Lexi had stuck her finger in a wall socket, been tossed around in a tornado, and had half of her head run over by a pickup. Her hair was crazy, even to Lexi's standards.

"Wow," Lexi laughed before tightening her embrace. "But it was so worth getting it this way."

"I'd have to agree."

"Why are you up so early the day after our wedding?"

"You left your phone at your parents' house. I know how you're attached to that thing, so I'm guessing you're feeling naked in more ways than one."

"A little more than you might think, but you're right. I need to pick it up." Lexi's stomach growled, reminding her she hadn't eaten since yesterday's reception.

"Someone sounds hungry," Nita said with a smile. "I can make us some eggs and toast."

"That's sweet, but how about we head to my parents a few hours early? We can raid the leftovers from the wedding."

"Oooohhh, and maybe snag a beef slider." Nita turned and kissed Lexi on the lips. "Deal."

Jerry fluttered his eyes open to an uncommon occurrence—the sun was up. Shifting his arms and legs, he realized he overdid things at Lexi's wedding. Everything from his back to his calves to his feet was sore, but he had the best damn reason in the world. Yesterday was perfect. He'd walked his daughter down the aisle and, despite a bum leg, danced with the three most beautiful women at the reception.

After four decades together, Jess had fit him like a glove in his arms on the dance floor. Nita was stiff at the start of his first dance with her, but by the end, he had her laughing at his corny dad jokes. Lexi was his most awkward dance partner. Clearly, she was accustomed to leading, and it took her some time to learn how to follow without stepping on his feet. It was the most fun he'd had with her in years.

He gingerly craned his neck to not aggravate his back. Jess was still asleep on her side of the bed. The numbers on her nightstand alarm clock said it was seven thirty, well beyond their typical rise and shine time. Considering Jess had done more running around yesterday than he and Lexi combined, he didn't have the heart to wake her.

His morning shower loosened the old joints and muscles enough to make going down the stairs a cinch. Nita's private physical therapy sessions had him walking better than before the gunshot to his leg. After putting on a pot of coffee, he opened the refrigerator and rubbed his hands. Since the caterer wrapped it up last night, he'd had his eye on the last of the roast beef sandwich concoctions. He'd never say it aloud, but those things beat anything his wife cooked, save her apple pies. Doing so would earn him several nights in the guest room.

After five minutes in the toaster oven, the roast beef things didn't disappoint and would tide him over until lunch when Jess was up and going. He poured a second cup of joe and went to work cleaning up the backyard from the wedding activities. The caterer had done a spectacular job and didn't leave a single piece of trash on the property after stowing their dishes, tables, and chairs. Jerry had instructed them not to bother cleaning up every stray food scrap because the rabbits or coyotes would take care of the rest overnight. He was right. The gravel and grassy area were spotless.

The only task left was prepping the garage band sound equipment the Beamer's high school senior son had brought for a fraction of the cost a rental company in Denton wanted. The young man would be over in a few minutes to pick up his things. Jerry removed the tarp he'd thrown over the speakers and control boxes the previous night to protect them from the elements, including those rabbits and coyotes. He rolled the cables and lined every item up for inspection just as he used to demand of his crew in his NASCAR garage on race day.

Soon, the sound of crunching gravel alerted Jerry to an approaching vehicle on his private access road. He stood by his row of perfectly aligned equipment and puffed his chest like a proud papa. The car appeared around the corner of the house, but it wasn't Charlie Beamer. It was someone much more welcome. He smiled, waived, and waited for them to park.

The car doors slammed shut. "Morning, Dad." Lexi clutched Nita's hand when she circled the end of the SUV and joined her. Bright expressions with a glow in their eyes, they looked genuinely happy. And so was Jerry. Accepting Lexi for who she was, instead of wishing she was something else, paved a road of possibilities. It was now possible for him to share in his daughter's life. To see her through sadness. To elate in her happiness. And if Lexi and Nita were willing, to make him and Jess grandparents.

"Morning. I thought you two weren't coming for a few more hours." Jerry recognized both women's satisfied smiles and furtive winks when they glanced at one another. He remembered his and Jess' wedding night and hoped Lexi and Nita's evening was just as memorable.

"We were up, and I realized I'd forgotten my phone here last night. I'm supposed to be on call twenty-four-seven."

"People and their damn phones."

Lexi chuckled. "I thought we could give you a hand cleaning up." Lexi scanned the pristine backyard. "But I see you have that handled." She focused on the equipment lying on the tarp. "Just like race day."

"Thank you." He gave her a flamboyant bow. "At least someone appreciates my hard work."

A second car advanced on the gravel access road. The familiar beat-up 1982 Ford pickup driven by the high school senior came into view. Charlie backed up the truck and lowered the tailgate. "Good morning, Mr. Mills. Lexi. How was the shindig?"

"It was really nice," Jerry said. "It surprised me you didn't come back after dropping off your equipment."

Charlie lowered and shook his head. "I wanted to, Mr. Mills." He shifted to look Lexi in the eye. "I'm sorry, Lexi, but my mom said I couldn't."

Lexi rested a hand on the young man's shoulder. "It's all right, Charlie. I understand. We all must bite the bullet at times to keep the peace. But I am disappointed in your mother. She doesn't have to approve of gay marriage, but she owes my mother more of an explanation than she didn't feel comfortable coming. They've been friends for thirty years, and that should mean something."

"I don't disagree, and I want you to know I think it's cool you got married."

"Thanks, Charlie. I appreciate it." Lexi gestured toward Nita. "I'd like you to meet my wife."

"It's a pleasure to meet you, ma'am." He shook Nita's hand. "I'm sorry I wasn't here for the big event."

"It's a pleasure, Charlie. Don't worry about it. You were stuck in the middle. According to your mother, we don't fit nicely into an approved box. And I'm guessing your nose ring means you don't either." She paused at his nod. "In my experience, I wasn't truly happy until I started living my truth. Once I did," Nita kissed the back of Lexi's hand, "I found this wonderful woman."

Jerry shrank inside himself. For fifteen years, he'd acted like Shirley Beamer—intolerant and bigoted—because of a stupid, outdated belief. He was ashamed, disappointed, and angry with himself. *There should be no room in this world for such arrogance and selfishness*, he thought. In contrast, Lexi and Nita stood confidently, turning the other cheek while voicing their philosophy of tolerance and respect for others. He couldn't be prouder of his daughters nor feel more love for them.

Charlie left after loading his equipment, giving Lexi and Nita hugs, and promising to let them borrow his gear again, next time for free.

"Are you two hungry?" Jerry asked. "We have a ton of leftovers from yesterday."

"Is there any roast beef left?" Lexi asked.

Jerry rubbed his belly proudly. "You're too late." Lexi's pout was a poor attempt to make him regret raiding the fridge that morning. She should have remembered the rule: unless it had your name on it, everything in the refrigerator was fair game.

He led them inside, expecting to see Jessie tinkering in the kitchen, but strangely she was nowhere in sight. Even after her most exhausting days, she never slept past eight, let alone past nine.

"Where's Mom?" Lexi asked.

"She was sleeping late. I'll tell her you're here while you two fix something to eat. Your phone is on the island." Jerry ascended the stairs with a sense of urgency. He didn't hear water running through the pipes, telling him the shower was on, nor did he hear the floor creaking, telling him Jess was getting ready for the day. She must have pushed herself beyond her limits yesterday to be sound asleep at this hour. At least that was what he told himself while her dizzy spells stirred in the back of his mind. He feared she might have fainted getting dressed and hit her head again on the way down.

Pushing the bedroom door open, he focused on the bed, releasing a sigh of relief. Jess was still under the covers, lying on her side with her back to the door, just the way he'd left her earlier. He sat on the edge of her side of the mattress and placed a hand on her hip. "Jess, Lexi and Nita are here. It's time to get up."

She didn't move, which she always did when he touched her in the morning. The stillness was breath-stopping. A terrifying chill enveloped him when his worst fear crashed to the surface: he would outlive his bride. He shook her vigorously, but her arms remained limp. "Jess! Jess! God no! Jess."

He continued to shake her and call her name, but nothing woke her. Nothing made her eyes flitter open and look at him with love stemming from four decades of marriage and friendship. Nothing made her throw an arm around his neck and draw him in for a tender kiss. "Come back to me, Jess," he pleaded, but she remained fixed. He couldn't bring himself to think of the word lifeless. She couldn't be gone. They still had too much living to do.

Footsteps pounded from somewhere in the house. "Dad?" Lexi burst through the doorway.

When he looked up, confusion and fear etched his daughter's face. He wanted to comfort her, but he was too weak from shallow breathing and the crushing reality he had yet to fully understand. "She won't wake up."

Lexi dashed inside, circling the bed.

Nita leaped on top of the mattress with a cell phone in her hand in one graceful move like a deer hurdling a barbed wire fence. "Sixty-year-old woman. Unconscious." Nita was the first to reach Jess. She rolled her to her back and placed a hand on her chest. "She's not breathing." Nita put two fingers on Jess' neck and tossed the phone on the mattress.

Lexi eased Jerry from the bed with both hands on his upper arms. "Give her some room, Dad." The brittleness in Lexi's voice was heartbreaking.

"I'm not getting a pulse. Starting chest compressions," Nita said in a calm tone.

"Paramedics are on their way," a voice reported over the phone speaker.

Nita pumped Jess's chest in a firm, rapid cadence. "Tell them she had a serious head injury almost two months ago and still has brain swelling."

The brave first responders would come. They would perform every life-saving procedure they'd trained for, but Jerry already knew the terrible truth: they were likely too late. The blank stare and tears rolling down Lexi's cheeks signaled she knew it, too.

Jerry and Lexi remained glued to the floorboards, grasping each other's hand tight, chest high. He felt helpless like he did after the accident that had him laid up for months. But he had Jess to get him through it. Losing her would break him, and he wasn't sure if he could put himself together without her. He wasn't sure if he would want to.

Nita was relentless, sweat pouring from her as if a spigot was wide open. She worked like a machine, refusing to stop after the paramedics arrived. One rested a hand on her shoulder and said, "We have her."

Nita finally stopped and slid off the bed, letting the medics do their job.

She moved to the foot of the bed and wiped the moisture from her brow before placing a hand on each hip. Her posture was limp, looking as if she'd finished a marathon.

One paramedic continued chest compressions while the other connected Jess to a monitor and placed an oxygen mask over her mouth. When the one performing the compressions stopped, the one at the monitor said, "I'm getting a heartbeat. Pressure is eighty over fifty. We need to transport now."

"She has brain swelling from a head injury almost two months ago," Nita said.

"Thank you. That's helpful," one said. The medics eased Jess onto a gurney and navigated the stairs with some doing. At the backdoors of the rig, the other said, "There's no room. We're taking her to Mercy in Denton."

"We'll follow," Nita said. After locking up the house, she took Lexi's car keys. "Sit in the back with your dad. I'll get us there."

Once they piled into the car and were on the road, Lexi's phone buzzed several times. She ignored it and held Jerry's hand. He welcomed it because he needed the extra assurance.

Nita handled the wheel like a seasoned NASCAR driver, catching up to and keeping up with the ambulance. *Thank God for Nita*, Jerry thought. She'd brought Lexi back to life after losing her leg, and today she brought her sweet Jess back. They were all lucky to have her.

23

Four hours earlier

Nathan Croft woke to a loud ring and took in a startled breath. A sound sleeper, he'd discovered over the years that turning the volume up to the maximum was the only way to ensure he didn't miss a middle-of-the-night call. His heart thumped hard as he reached blindly in the dark for the cell phone on the nightstand. First knocking over his cup of water and sending the television remote to the floor, he felt the phone teetering dangerously on the edge. He grabbed it. The generic tone meant it wasn't from anyone on his contact list, but the 432 area code caught his attention, so he answered it.

"This is Croft." Nathan remained flat on the mattress, one hand draped over his face and the other holding the phone to his ear.

"Agent Croft, this is Deputy Thomas Perez from Harrington. I tried to reach Agent Mills, but she didn't answer."

"She got married yesterday. Why are you calling?"

"Sheriff Jessup gave me your numbers just in case something happened to him. Well, something did."

Nathan sprung upright, sitting with his legs straight on the bed. "What happened?"

"He was killed in a car accident several hours ago. By the looks of the wreckage, it appears there might have been an explosion."

"Where?"

"Just outside of Harrington in the county."

Nathan bounced from bed, scrambling for the switch on the bedside lamp. His mind focused on the quickly forming dilemma. If the accident occurred under any other jurisdiction, he would be confident of the investigators' ability to process the scene and collect and preserve evidence until he could get there. "Are you at the accident scene?"

"Yes, and I know what you're going to ask. Other deputies are here, too, but they're not part of the Rat Pack."

"The what?"

"The sheriff and I believe they're connected to Milo Tilton. Any of them could have killed Culter and the sheriff."

"What's their connection to Tilton? Does it have to do with the detention center he runs?"

"Yes. The previous sheriff loaned deputies to escort work details from the center to local ranches and farms. I got the impression they were making extra money to do it. When Sheriff Jessup took over and canceled the program, the Rat Pack went nuts."

Nathan reverse-engineered everything about the judge's murder and the Raven's involvement. Judge Cook was hearing Tilton's murder trial when Culter killed him. A deputy could have drugged the jailer and killed Culter to keep him from talking. But Culter had talked. He'd said the shooting had to occur during Tilton's trial. Moments ago, Perez connected the Rat Pack deputies and Tilton. The players formed an elaborate circle of corruption, working toward keeping Tilton out of jail.

Nathan shook his head. He was dead wrong about Lexi's hunch the last time they were in Harrington. He'd disagreed that the sheriff was on the right side and was in the crosshairs of whoever had hired Culter and Scooter, but he couldn't have been more wrong. If Culter was right, the district attorney was next on Tilton's hit list. He had to warn her.

"Can you hold the vehicle until we can get there?"

"I can't, but I have a solution. The sheriff's car went off into a deep ditch and rolled. The fire department is waiting until daylight to get a crane and wrecker out here to recover it. My cousin is on the fire crew working the scene. I can have him stall for as long as possible."

"That will work. I'll keep you posted on my ETA." Nathan checked the time. It was five o'clock. If his memory was correct, the first flights to Midland started in an hour. "If I leave now, I could be there in about four hours, five at the most. Until then, can you reach District Attorney Ford and tell her to watch her back? She might be next."

"I'll do my best, but the acting sheriff will start asking questions if you take too long, and I'm not sure if I trust him."

"Do you think he's part of the Rat Pack?"

"I'm not sure. He called in sick the night I captured Culter, but I saw him there. I thought he was going to shoot Culter, but something spooked him, and he disappeared."

"Just stall, Perez. I'll get there." Nathan hung up and dialed Willie Lange, putting her on speaker while he dressed and threw a few things into a backpack. "Sorry to wake you, Willie, but I have to get to Harrington." He explained Perez's call, highlighting the dilemma with a corrupt sheriff's department and Lexi being unreachable. "If the explosive used on the sheriff's car ties back to the Raven, we'll have a good idea who hired him. And if we can leverage him, he might tell us how to find the Raven. But I'll need Lexi to inspect the wreckage. Explosives are her lane, not mine."

"Take the first flight out. I'll track down Lexi and get her out there ASAP."

"While I'm en route, can you arrange for a wrecker and a team from the El Paso office to meet me in Harrington? I want to take the vehicle where I'll know it will be in safe hands until Lexi can inspect it."

After catching the first flight to Midland and renting a car at the airport, Nathan had made good time. When he pulled onto Interstate 20, he texted Perez, telling him he was about an hour and twenty minutes out, less if he sped, which he did. Nathan had shaved off at least ten minutes when his phone rang. It was Deputy Perez.

"I'm sorry, Agent Croft, but my cousin stalled as long as he could. The wrecker is on its way to the department's evidence yard."

Nathan pressed the gas pedal on his rental car farther, increasing his speed well beyond the seventy-five miles per hour speed limit. "I'm about five minutes behind. Can you be at the yard when the wrecker arrives? That way, the Rat Pack won't have a chance to tamper with the evidence. My team from the El Paso field office should be there right behind me."

"Will do. I'll stay unless I'm dispatched on a call."

"You're a good man, Perez."

Hitting the city limits, Nathan slowed his speed. When the Harrington Sheriff's Department came into view, he saw the wrecker pulling into the lot at the back of the building, which he suspected was the evidence yard. Nathan peeled off and parked in the visitor's lot at the front of the building. He checked his phone. He'd left several messages, and so had Willie, but there was still no word from Lexi. If she was in the same shape he was the day after his wedding twenty years ago, he had a hunch the phone wouldn't register with her until dinner time.

"What a time to get married and be off the grid," he said to himself.

Nathan entered through the main entrance and approached the reception desk. It also doubled as their dispatch center. The female dispatcher rose deliberately from her chair and came to the window. "May I help you?" Her eyes were red and puffy, and her voice was gravelly and filled with sadness.

"I know this is a difficult time." Nathan showed her his badge and ATF credentials. "I'm here to speak to the next in charge about last night's incident."

"That would be Sergeant Ross. He's waiting for the wrecker to arrive with the—" She cleared her throat. "With the sheriff's vehicle from last night."

"That's why I'm here. I need to see him immediately."

"I'll try to raise him on the radio." She returned to her workstation and put on her headset. Her stiff posture and curt tone suggested either his presence wasn't welcome or her interaction with the interim sheriff wasn't pleasant. After some back and forth, she returned to the window. "The shift commander will escort you back."

"Thank you." While Nathan waited, he texted Perez asking whether he was in place. He replied with a simple *Yes*, putting Nathan at ease. He was no longer in a race against the clock. Perez was his insurance policy against the Rat Pack disposing of evidence that could make the sheriff's death look like an unfortunate accident, thereby erasing all links to the Raven.

Minutes later, the shift commander, a sergeant, arrived and shook Nathan's hand. The gesture was friendly, giving Nathan the impression he might not be part of the Rat Pack. "I understand you're here about the sheriff's accident. I'll walk you back. The wrecker just arrived."

"Thanks." Nathan followed him down the central corridor, traversing the length of the building to the back door. Once outside, the sergeant guided him toward a fenced area of the employee parking lot. Perez was standing by the open gate as he'd said he would be. Three other deputies were standing by, watching the spectacle of their former boss's death trap rolling in.

A black SUV, followed by a commercial wrecker, pulled into the parking lot. Nathan provided hand signals, directing them to wait near the entrance. Once Nathan was at the gate of the evidence yard, he saw the truck driver preparing the wrecker to lower its load onto the ground. He stepped faster, holding up his badge and credentials. "Stop. Federal agent."

All heads turned toward him. Perez grinned, signaling to Nathan he'd done his job. The evidence from the wreckage was safe. Another deputy with stripes placed his hands on his hips. His eyes grew fiery, and Nathan could have sworn steam poured from his ears. He must have been Sergeant Ross. He may have been the interim sheriff, but he wasn't the man in charge of the wreckage. "What the hell is going on?"

"I believe Sheriff Jessup's death could be related to the Derek Culter case, which puts it under the ATF's jurisdiction. I'm taking custody of this wreckage."

"You have got to be kidding." Ross flapped his hands in the air before stepping up to Nathan, toe to toe. He was so close that Nathan smelled his morning coffee on his breath. "There's no way I'm letting you take that car. The accident happened in Harrington County, so it's our case."

. . .

Obstinance never scared Nathan. He had backup and the law behind him. "If you fail to cooperate, I'll arrest you for obstruction of justice and impeding a federal officer while performing their duties."

"You and what army?"

Nathan glanced over his shoulder and waved up the ATF SUV. It zoomed toward him, parking several yards shy of Ross. Four doors opened, and five ATF agents poured out. "This one. Trust me when I say you don't want to test me."

Ross narrowed his eyes. His internal battle manifested in deep, deliberate breaths. "Fine. Take the damn car."

"Wise choice." Nathan waved up their wrecker. Within half an hour, the ATF crew transferred and secured the vehicle, and they were on the road to El Paso. All Nathan needed was an explosives expert to comb it over, but the closest one was somewhere in Dallas with her new bride.

"Where the hell are you, Lexi Mills?" Nathan pulled out his phone and dialed again.

24

Lexi had a robust dislike for hospitals and their antiseptic smell. She hated the bright lights, the tile floors, and the throng of sick and injured swarming the emergency room. Hated waiting for information that never seemed to come. But such was the nature of an overwhelmed medical system with a limited staff.

Lexi recounted her hospital stays and the number of visits in the last two years. Her amputation had made her a patient for nearly a month. Earlier this year, she'd seen Nita through a gunshot wound to the shoulder. And less than two months ago, Belcher put Nita and her parents in separate hospitals. Nita from a forced overdose of meth. Her father from a gunshot wound to the leg. And her mother from a vicious blow to the head. Now, Lexi was back because her mother barely clung to life. Hospitals meant one thing: something was horribly wrong.

She dug deep into her front hip pocket, hoping to find enough cash to buy a soda from the outdated vending machine in the hospital corridor. Her hand came out, clasping a thin fold of dollar bills. *Not enough*, she thought. Another thing she hated about hospitals. She turned around, defeated, and retraced her steps toward the waiting room to join her father for news about her mother's surgery. With each step, her legs felt like lead weights, especially her left with the prosthetic. It felt more like an anchor than an extension. It carried the heavy weight of her greatest fear: unavoidable grief.

Before reaching the waiting area, Lexi's phone buzzed in her pocket. She pulled it out. The screen said she had an incoming call from Nathan. This wasn't the time or place she wanted to talk about work, but she couldn't forget her responsibilities. She swiped the screen, answering the call. "This isn't a good time, Nathan."

"Where in the hell have you been? Lange and I have been trying to reach you for hours." His tone was sharper than she could tolerate at a time like this.

Dammit, she thought. After retrieving her phone from her parents' kitchen, she'd never got the chance to check for messages before hearing her father's pained cries upstairs. "I forgot my phone after the wedding."

"While you've been busy screwing—"

"I haven't been screwing this entire time," Lexi yelled. She wanted to explode but dug deep to calm herself. "My mother had a stroke or a brain bleed this morning and is in surgery."

"Christ, Lexi. I'm so sorry. I had no idea."

"You couldn't have known." Lexi released a long, calming breath. "Now, what's happened?"

"All hell has broken loose in Harrington." Nathan told her about Sheriff Jessup's death, the suspected explosive, and Perez's help in securing the wreckage. "I'm en route to El Paso with the vehicle."

Lexi quickly pieced together the staffing shortage plaguing the ATF. The El Paso field office didn't have an explosives expert on staff, and her counterpart at the Dallas regional office was on an SRT assignment. "And I'm the only available expert in the region."

"It's not just availability. You're the best at your job. If anyone can find a link to the Raven, it's you."

Lexi couldn't leave until she'd gotten word her mother was safely out of surgery. She released a loud, deep breath. "I should get news about my mom in another hour or so. Once she's in recovery, I'll update you and get on the next flight."

After hanging up, Lexi checked her messages. She'd missed several from Nathan and Lange. Lange was her next call. "Sorry I missed your calls, Agent Lange."

"On call means on call, Agent Mills. If you can't honor your commitment, it's time to move on."

Lexi couldn't disagree. Forgetting her phone was a lapse in judgment, but this wasn't the time for a lecture. "My mother is in the hospital having emergency surgery for a stroke or brain bleed. I didn't check my messages until Croft called a few minutes ago."

A moment of awkward silence passed before Lange responded. "Well, don't I feel like an ass."

"Croft filled me in. I should have an update on her condition in an hour. I'll hop on the first flight once I know she's in recovery."

"Tell you what, Mills. I'll head to El Paso and conduct an initial assessment. Stay with your family today and fly out tomorrow. You can double-check my work."

"Thank you, Agent Lange. That takes the pressure off." Lexi ended the call feeling a heavy weight lifting. Now she could focus on what was really important: family.

Entering the waiting area, Lexi searched the crowd over the white noise of dozens of conversations, most in soft tones and some in the loud, high-pitched whining of bored toddlers. Nita and her father were in the same stiff chairs where she'd left them, a sign the doctor had yet to show with an update, which was a good sign. It meant her mom was still alive and in surgery.

Nita had slid over one seat, filling the gap created when Lexi had gone searching for something to drink. Her backpack was on the unoccupied seat to her right, saving it for Lexi. The gesture of providing her father support was small but meaningful.

Lexi knelt between them. "There's a vending machine, but it only takes cash. I can head to the cafeteria if you'd like." Doing anything was better than sitting around a hoard of sick people, snapping her head toward a set of double doors every time they opened and hoping the doctor walked through with a smile on his face.

Nita lifted her pack, scooted to her original seat, and patted the middle one, inviting Lexi to sit. "My cousin texted. She's picking up drinks and sandwiches and will be here any time. I couldn't talk her out of it."

"Why don't we wait in the drop-off area for her?" At Nita's soft nod, Lexi turned to her father. The last time he'd looked this harried, his best driver in his best car was two seconds off the lead on the white flag lap. That was his final race as a team owner, and the driver crashed in the last turn for a DNF. It was a disappointment that took him years to get over. If her mother didn't pull through the surgery, Lexi wasn't sure if her father could get over such a profound loss, especially after losing his best friend, Gavin. "Dad, would you be okay for a few minutes alone while we wait outside for Jenny? She's bringing food for us."

"Alone," he said in a solemn tone as if alone was his future. He looked up. "Sure. Sure. I could use something to drink."

Lexi patted the back of his hand, not having the heart to remind him she'd gone to the vending machine in search of a drink after he'd said he was thirsty five minutes earlier. "We'll be outside the sliding doors if the doctor comes, okay?"

"I'm not a child, Lexi. I'll be fine." His uncharacteristic acrid tone stung. He was hurting; they both were.

If he were in the operating room and her mother was out here, Lexi would have known exactly what she needed to get through the excruciating worry. Lexi would have passed the time by talking about the undone pet projects about the house. The topic would have let her mother talk about her husband's talents or lack thereof for the repairs and upgrades she had in mind for him. Focusing on a future with him would have replaced the fear of one without him.

But her father was still a mystery to her. They'd spent fifteen years apart, and in some ways, he was not the same man she'd known before he cut her from his life. Back then, he walked through the world, sure of his capabilities. He'd rooted every decision in conviction and faith. But the man who walked her down the aisle yesterday at her gay wedding did so out of love and compassion.

Lexi grinned. Gavin's needling might have started her father on the road of transformation, but her mother's example of acceptance had likely worn him down enough to give him the courage to make the leap. Nevertheless, he'd become vulnerable, a state Lexi had never witnessed in him before yesterday. That fragility magnified when he found his wife of four decades without a pulse that morning. Did he need hand-holding like her mother did? Did he want quiet companionship, knowing Lexi was there if he needed a shoulder? Or did he want solitude like he did in Lexi's youth when he would disappear into the garage and stay out there until all hours of the night? He was hard to read, but Lexi refused to give up on him.

"It's all right, Dad." Lexi squeezed his hand, sensing he needed a little reassurance. "Nita and I won't be too long."

Lexi took Nita by the hand and exited through the automatic sliding glass doors, stopping at the first available bench along the sidewalk. The portico covering the circular driveway shielded them from the early lunch hour sun, adding a slight chill to the late fall air. The coolness nipped at Lexi's arms, reminding her she'd forgotten her light jacket in the car. She crossed her arms and rubbed them with the opposite hands to counter the emerging goosebumps.

"Aren't you cold?" Lexi glanced at Nita, but she appeared unaffected by the drop in temperature, despite wearing a light t-shirt.

Nita faced her and rubbed both arms fast enough to start a campfire on a wilderness excursion. "You're still numb from everything going on."

Lexi considered telling Nita about the calls and tomorrow's pending trip to El Paso, but the conversation would have required too much explanation when work was the last thing she wanted to discuss. Instead, she scanned the drop-off area. Three pedestrians and two vehicles with passengers were nearby, but no one looked familiar. "Which car is Jenny bringing?"

"She's a lesbian in Texas. It could be the pickup or the Subaru."

Lexi laughed. Nearly every lesbian from Dallas to Houston to El Paso drove an SUV, pickup, or some variation of a Subaru. She gave kudos to the couples that had one of each, especially to Jenny and her wife and Lexi and Nita, who fit the stereotype to a T. Nita joined in. It felt good to have the weight of her mother's condition off her shoulders. Lexi laughed so hard she snorted, which turned into another round of a full-throated belly laugh. She laughed so hard her eyes watered, putting her on the edge of peeing her pants.

Lexi bent over, placing her hands on her knees to catch her breath. And when she did, the dam broke. Every emotion in her flooded the concrete driveway. From the first skinned knee her mother treated with Bactine, a Band-Aid, and a kiss, to her mother walking Nita down the aisle in a beautiful ceremony for which her mother had done most of the planning. Every sweet, wonderful memory poured out, spilling on the ground as if they would no longer hold meaning once her mother was gone.

Reality grabbed Lexi by the shirt collar, forcing her to her knees. She knew the cold, hard truth. The odds of her escaping permanent brain and muscular damage were nearly impossible if her mother survived the catastrophic stroke, and, sadly, the doctors suspected she might not. No matter the outcome, she had already lost the mother who had raised her, loved her unconditionally, and taught her how to walk through the world proudly as a woman of color.

Nita dropped to her knees and pulled Lexi into a tight embrace, keeping her from falling deeper into the emotional quicksand threatening to pull her under. Her strength and calm were a compassionate beacon guiding her to firm ground. And when their lips touched, Lexi was sure she would be safe. Nita wouldn't let go, wouldn't let Lexi sink to the depths from which it had taken her years to claw back. She had told Lexi that losing a father she adored when she was a teenager had destroyed her. Lexi hadn't fully understood how grief could be so paralyzing until she saw her mother lying in bed without a pulse. Now she saw how easily the strongest and boldest person could succumb to its pull. The only difference between Lexi and teenage Nita was Lexi had Nita to keep her anchored.

"Have you no shame?" A woman scoffed. Lexi broke the tender kiss, watching the woman push her kindergarten-aged child past her and Nita and scurry away like a frightened rabbit. Her vocal narrow-mindedness when Lexi was at her lowest was brash and hurtful.

Typically, Lexi would ignore the insensitive comment, but in a moment of weakness, she lashed back. "It's not contagious unless you want it to be."

Nita snickered and pulled Lexi to her feet. The woman disappeared inside at lightning speed, making Lexi laugh again.

"Get a room, you two," a woman giggled. Lexi looked up, discovering Jenny had pulled up beside her and Nita in her Subaru. "Or you might offend some uptight Christian sensibility." Jenny handed Nita two plastic shopping bags of sandwiches, sodas, and bottles of water through the open passenger window. "Any word yet?"

Nita shook her head. "Not yet, but we're hopeful."

"Let me know if you need anything else." Jenny shifted her attention to Lexi. "I've cleared the decks to be your standby." A car horn behind her sounded three times. Patience clearly wasn't present in a place for patients. "I should go. Text me when you hear anything."

"Thanks for the food, Jenny." Lexi waved goodbye. "We will."

"Let's go inside. Maybe we can spread a little gayness." Nita extended her hand and had the darndest grin. It was simultaneously comforting and naughty.

Lexi laced their fingers together and pointed at Nita with the index finger of her other hand. "Right there. That's why I love you."

Stepping through the swooshing glass doors, Lexi spotted Miss Shame and her son in line at the emergency room reception desk. When the woman glanced back and locked eyes with her, Lexi made a show of bringing Nita's hand with her wedding ring to her lips, kissing the back of it and eliciting the precise reaction from the intolerant bigot as intended.

"You're bad." Nita used a playful tone.

"Just spreading a little repressed joy." Lexi continued to where she'd left her father, but he wasn't there. A het couple had taken their seats. She scanned the room's entirety, thinking he might have changed locations after returning from the bathroom, but he was nowhere in sight. She leaned in, whispering to Nita. "Stay here. I'll see if he's in the men's room."

Lexi rushed down the hallway, passing several sick-looking people and their companions. A man exited the restroom when Lexi reached the door. She pressed a palm against it, stopping it from closing. "Jerry? Are you in here?"

"I'm the only one in here," a male voice said. "And I'm not Jerry."

"Thank you. Sorry for the intrusion." Lexi retraced her steps, an uneasiness commanding her stride. Her dad wouldn't have left unless he'd gotten news about her mother. She returned to the waiting room, shaking her head when Nita looked in her direction. She pointed to the reception desk and approached it, thinking the tech could provide her with information.

Miss Shame was being helped, so Lexi waited patiently next in line. The next moment, the woman turned, gripping her son's hand. This time she had nothing to say but the scowl on her face was priceless.

Lexi stepped up to the counter. "My dad and I were waiting for news on my mother, Jessie Mills, but I can't find my dad. Can you tell me if there's been an update on her condition?"

The female tech checked her computer before looking up with an unreadable expression. "Your father is waiting for you inside." She buzzed a security door and gestured for Lexi to enter.

"Thank you. Can my wife come, too?"

"Of course."

Lexi waved Nita over, and they passed through the double doors. Several yards inside, a row of four plastic chairs lined one wall. Her father was sitting in one, leaning forward with his elbows propped on top of his upper legs and his face buried in his palms. An emptiness swept through Lexi. Positive news would have wiped him out and had him acting nervous at the prospect of more waiting until he could see his wife, but his posture reflected utter devastation.

Her pace slowed involuntarily. Whatever news had put her father in such a state had her terrified, shallowing her breathing. Her residual limb pulsed at the bottom of her prosthetic socket. Her entire body resisted the truth. The pressure on her leg and the idea of a life without her mother became unbearable.

Lexi dug deep and moved her legs, feeling the weight of dread heavy on her shoulders. She sat beside her father, matching his bent posture and dreading the answer to her next question. "The news isn't good, is it?"

He raised his head slowly, turning it enough for Lexi to see the tears in his eyes. "She's gone, Peanut."

25

The dishes in Milo's double kitchen sink had multiplied since he'd been out on bail, forming Jenga-like stacks along the bottom. He was hesitant to pull out his favorite scotch glass for fear of causing a devastating chain reaction, but he formulated a plan quickly. He braced a plate that had held his leftover porterhouse from the Cattleman's with a water glass and gingerly recovered his Charles Russell gold-etched tumbler without scratching it. "Yes!" He pumped a fist in victory. The cup was a treasured gift from the Montana Attorney General when Milo had consulted on the state's plan to vie for a federal detention center in Cascade County like the one he ran in Harrington. Milo would have been upset for weeks if it broke, so he made a mental note to hire a new housekeeper.

Milo filled his glass with three ice cubes, added two fingers of scotch, and returned to the great room. The Cowboys game was about to start, and the pizza delivery was still warm. Without a wife to nag him about money or his poor choice of food because his waistline had grown two inches since last football season, this should prove to be the most pleasant Sunday afternoon he'd spent in years. Especially after the cleanup man's coded text last night, breaking the news the sheriff was dead. He raised his glass. "Thank you, Raven."

By halftime, the Cowboys were up by two touchdowns, making Milo's first weekend out of jail much more enjoyable. He'd polished off half the pizza, two more refills of scotch, and was searching the freezer for a pint of mint chocolate chip when someone pounded on his front door. He slammed the freezer shut. "There goes a perfect day."

While Milo walked toward the front door, the crowd roared on the television when the kick receiver broke a return for sixty yards to start the second half. He kept an eye on the screen during the replay as he opened the door.

"We have a problem." The nervous tension in the man's voice forced Milo to turn his focus on him. He bounced in his uniform loafers and didn't wait to be invited inside. He pushed past the threshold and Milo, stopping in the marbled entryway.

Milo would be concerned, but the man had a history of acting skittish at the slightest wrinkle. He interpreted every misstep as a threat and wanted to go nuclear or shut things down. "Have a seat, Rusty. Kick your feet up and watch the game while I fix you a drink. Then you can tell me what has you riled up."

"Dammit, Milo. I don't want to watch a game. We have real trouble." Rusty's wide-eyed, stiff posture reminded Milo of a Catahoula dog he used to own. It would flinch whenever the air conditioner kicked on and rattled the ceiling vents. Rusty was genuinely frightened.

"All right, Rusty. At least let me get you a drink. You look like you could use it." Milo didn't wait for a response. He poured a double scotch into a paper cup that had been sitting on the coffee table for a day or two.

"Thanks." Rusty downed it in one gulp. It reduced his jittering from a scared Catahoula to a mangy cat Milo nearly ran over last night in the driveway.

"Now, tell me what's wrong. Your last message said the sheriff died in the crash. That's good. Though I was disappointed you didn't take care of the D.A. too."

"I couldn't. She parked on the street across from the bank, and the bank has cameras. But that's not the problem. The ATF swooped in and took the wreckage before I could check for explosive remnants. You'd said the Raven was very specific. The explosion might not destroy all the pieces, and we needed to be thorough and check the wreckage afterward."

Milo rolled his neck, sensing his anger starting a slow boil. "You had twelve hours. What were you waiting for?"

"The fire department babysat the scene until daylight to get a crane and wrecker to pull the car from the ditch. When it finally rolled into our evidence yard, the ATF was there and swooped it up."

Blowing up at Rusty would only worsen the situation, so Milo sat in his favorite chair to look at things logically. "Let's think this through. Did the car burn?"

"Most of it." Rusty sat in the chair next to him.

"That's good. Then it's likely whatever wasn't destroyed in the explosion burned up later. And if something survived, there's nothing to link you directly to it. You used gloves, right?"

"Yes, but I've seen on those FBI shows how they can get DNA from a fly's spit after landing on a human."

"That's bullshit, and you know it. You're worried about nothing. No one saw you plant the device, so no one can link you to it. You need to return to work and go about your business."

"What do I say to my deputies or the media?"

"Make a speech to your men about what a terrible loss the sheriff's passing is to the department. If anyone asks about the ATF involvement, say you think it's appalling the feds have stuck their nose into something so personal to the Harrington Sheriff's Department before you could fully investigate. Say it's an overreach of the greatest proportions, but you'll work with them to determine the cause of the accident."

"I'm not good at speeches, Milo." Rusty rubbed the sweat gathering on his neck. "That's your expertise."

"You'll do fine, Rusty. Just remember what's at stake. If you act suspiciously, people will start asking questions. And we don't want questions. Tomorrow, when she's at work, place the other type of explosive the Raven made for us."

Milo patted Rusty on the back several times, giving him more words of encouragement before sending him out the door. Rusty was a few slices shy of a whole pie, but he was the only man Milo could turn to for his dirty work. Milo had to trust he wouldn't crack under pressure.

26

Choking silence filled the cabin of Lexi's SUV. Her father had insisted on sitting alone in the back row for the return ride to Ponder. Lexi understood the buffer he'd erected between himself and the rest of the world. The world was now a lesser place without his wife, without Lexi's mother. Despite still having each other, Lexi felt empty, and being happy without her mother in the world seemed impossible. But losing his life partner and friend of the last forty years had served her father a devastating blow. She imagined her mother's passing had ripped from him a piece so vast and vital that living seemed impossible.

Nita pulled into the space next to the shade tree. Most of its leaves had dropped for the coming winter, revealing an intricate weave of branches. Everyone remained seated without reaching for their door handles.

Lexi closed her eyes, soaking in the energy this place emitted every time she arrived. It was home. After joining the ATF, she'd lived in several cities and apartments, one with Nita, but the Ponder house always conjured up the feeling of home. It was where she spoke her first words and took her first steps. It was where she first realized she was gay. It was where she learned to fix a car and make her mark on the world as a woman of color. Lexi and her father had changed over the years while living here, but her mother had remained the one constant. The wisdom she imparted never waned, and her love never wavered. Being here, knowing her mother's aura would never again fill this space, was gut-wrenching.

Lexi was the first to exit. Nita and her father followed seconds later. He stood, inspecting the shade tree, focusing on the exposed roots. "Your mother and I planted this tree our first fall here. She said she wanted to watch her children swinging from its branches from the kitchen window."

"I'm sorry you couldn't have any more after me. I feel like it's my fault," Lexi said. Her mother had discussed her birth only once when Lexi had asked why she and her dad never had more children. She'd said the doctors had to perform a hysterectomy after the delivery.

"Don't say that, Peanut." His voice turned strong, and he stood straighter as if standing up for his wife, who wasn't there to stand up for herself. "With her history of fibroids, your mother knew going into the pregnancy she could die in the delivery room, but she took the chance. She nearly bled to death in the delivery room, but the hysterectomy saved her life."

"I never knew." Tears rolled down Lexi's cheeks and Nita's. Lexi instinctually reached for her hand. It pulsed comfort and compassion, absorbing her pain.

"That's how much she wanted you." Her father sniffled and rubbed his nose with the back of a hand. "We should go through your mother's papers. She wrote down instructions after you lost your leg."

Lexi followed her father through the back door, absorbing the idea her mother had put her affairs in order after Lexi nearly died. He paused, seemingly to take in the room. She gripped Nita's hand tighter, feeling her mother's energy stronger. The kitchen was her happy place, where she was most alive. She filled every corner with joy and love, baking pies and cooking holiday meals. Cooking was her way of sharing herself with the people she loved. Lexi remembered the delight in her mother's eyes whenever someone smiled after biting into one of her creations for the first time. It fueled her larger-than-life presence wherever she went.

Her father cleared his throat. "Everything should be by her chair in the living room."

"I'll go with you, Dad."

"We need to eat," Nita said. "I'll fix us a late lunch from the sandwiches

Jenny dropped off and bring them out."

Lexi kissed her on the cheek, letting it linger a few moments to gather her strength before following her father to the other side of the house. He took strides much slower than his typical determined pace. Lexi noted his limp had returned.

Reaching the seating area, he sat in his wife's chair and picked up the reading glasses she'd left on the table between their matching recliners. He wept. "She has an appointment with the optometrist next week to get her eyes checked. She said her vision had gotten blurrier since the head injury."

Lexi slumped on the couch, burying her face in her hands under the crushing weight of guilt. She couldn't deny the facts. Tony Belcher had sent the man who hit her mother on the head, and Lexi had brought Belcher into their lives. Her mother was dead because of the damn dangerous job she'd tried to convince Lexi out of for years.

But Lexi was stubborn. She was good at her job. The president had labeled her the best in the business, and she knew deep down it had gone to her head and made her blind to the dangers her job posed to her loved ones. She'd taken precautions for herself and her task force without considering the possibility Belcher would go after her family. And by the time she figured out they were at risk, she was too late. The damage had been done. Tony Belcher had finally won. He'd made Lexi feel the same unbearable pain she and Noah had inflicted on him after killing his brother's woman at the Gladding missile silo.

Lexi rocked back and forth, losing the battle between collected and devastated. She needed to be the rock in the room, considering her father had looked utterly lost walking out of the hospital. He'd been on autopilot since telling Lexi the horrible news and was in no shape to deal with the mountain of tasks that came when someone died. She dug deep, remembering what her friend Gavin once told her about flipping the switch. She told herself to turn off the emotions long enough to get things done.

Lexi popped to her feet, shoved her sadness and guilt into a box, and knelt in front of the end table by her mother's chair. She thumbed through several manila folders stacked at the bottom of the cubbyhole opening below the drawer. Her mother had written "Just in Case" on one. She opened it. On top was a typed collection of papers titled "In the Event of My Death." They contained lists of people to notify and instructions with names and phone numbers of people to contact to arrange a church funeral and burial in the cemetery south of town.

"I found it, Dad." Lexi looked up. He was still rummaging through the things his wife had left on the table—a book, a selection of coupons to the local stores and restaurants, and a basket containing a nail file, nail clippers, and eye drops. She repeated, "Dad, I found it. Mom wrote everything down. I'll start making phone calls."

"Let me help." Nita appeared with a serving tray, doled out the sliced sub sandwiches and chips onto paper plates, and distributed the sodas.

Lexi's father laid the plate on his lap, turned on the television, and tuned it to the NASCAR race in its early laps. He chewed, sipped, and stared blankly at the screen while cars zoomed around the track. He didn't show one ounce of disgust that his least favorite team was in the lead.

The volume was high to accommodate her dad's tinnitus earned from years of working around loud engines as a youth without proper hearing protection. It was too loud for Lexi to make her calls. "Hey, Dad. If you're going to watch TV, Nita and I will head to the kitchen and make those calls. Do you need anything?"

"No, I'm fine." He turned his attention to Nita. "Thank you kindly for the sandwiches. The chips were Jess' favorites."

"I'm glad I picked the right ones." Nita repacked the tray with her and Lexi's food and followed Lexi into the kitchen. She laid out the food and drink at the round dining table. Before sitting, she drew Lexi's chin gently toward her using her fingertips. The love in Nita's eyes wrapped around Lexi like a warm blanket on a cold winter night. "I see you acting strong for your father, and that's a good thing. He'll need you in the coming days. I also know you're hurting. It's okay to need comfort, too. When you do, I'll be there."

Lexi pulled her into a deep embrace. If she said anything more than thank you, the volcano of heartache would erupt, but Lexi couldn't afford that happening, not until she completed what needed doing. Instead, she hugged her wife a little tighter. Since the first time Nita called her on defeatism while rehabbing her amputation, Lexi had known this was the woman for her. Nita lifted her whenever she was low and filled her heart when it seemed empty. More importantly, she gave Lexi understanding and encouragement to grieve in her own way.

"We should start those calls." Lexi kissed Nita before taking her seat. She nibbled on her sandwich while taking in her mother's instructions, then turned to Nita, handing her the second sheet. "If you call the church and funeral home, I'll call her list of family and friends."

"Sure." Nita moved to the seat directly across from Lexi so their conversations wouldn't bleed into one another.

The first name on the list was her Aunt Bev, her mother's only sibling who had accepted Lexi's sexuality and attended yesterday's wedding. "Yesterday," Lexi whispered. Twenty-four hours ago, her parents were dancing, and her mother lit the yard with her smile. Joy had marked the day, but now a dark cloud hung over them.

Lexi took a deep breath and dialed. "Hi, Aunt Bev. This is Lexi."

"Shouldn't you be on your honeymoon after such a beautiful wedding?"

"That will have to wait. I have sad news."

Over the next hour, Lexi made a dozen calls filled with shock, tears, and words of sympathy. Like her father, she was on autopilot, saying the exact words repeatedly. But placing a checkmark next to the last name on the list left Lexi drained. The last name, the one she'd skipped, made her blood boil, but Lexi would honor her mother's wishes and make the call.

Lexi took another deep breath and dialed. "Hello, Shirley. This is Lexi." Silence punctuated the tension after yesterday's slap on the face. Lexi only cared that Shirley hadn't come to her wedding because it hurt her mother deeply. "Shirley—"

"If you're calling to give me a lecture, please don't." Shirley's tone was more dismissive than apologetic, foretelling the rift between her and her mother would have continued.

"That's not it. I have some sad news. My mother passed away this morning from a brain bleed."

"No, no, no, no, no." The pain in her voice ripped another hole in Lexi's heart. Each response did, but this one contained the heavy weight of regret, of lost opportunity. Catching her breath, Shirley asked, "Was she in pain?"

"It happened in her sleep, so I don't think so."

"Dear Lord. She was such a good woman."

"Yes, she was." Lexi dug deep to not blame her for marring her mother's last day on earth with her bigoted beliefs and small-mindedness. Shirley would have to live with the guilt for the rest of her life. "We'll pass along details about her service soon, but I suspect we'll hold it within two weeks."

"Thank you, Lexi. If you need help planning or organizing things, please call. It's the least I can do for my old friend."

Hanging up, the dreadful chore had Lexi wholly spent, feeling like she'd run a marathon. She leaned back in her chair, grateful it was done, but another daunting task still loomed—El Paso. It left her torn. Leaving her father a day after losing his wife seemed selfish, but she had little choice. If she stayed home, she might never catch Kris Faust's killer. "How are things coming?"

Nita jotted down several notes during each call and had finished a while ago. "I left a message with the funeral home director, and he called back. We have an appointment Tuesday morning to go over arrangements. The pastor at the church picked up. He wanted to come over tonight, but I asked him to wait until tomorrow. I know church was your mother's thing, not your dad's."

"That's perfect. Thank you. But there's a chance I might not make the Tuesday appointment."

"I know. I called Kaplan to tell her the news. She said you're going to El Paso tomorrow."

Lexi shook her head. "Of course she knew. That woman knows everything going on in the Dallas office."

"She wouldn't be a good intel officer if she didn't. When do you leave?"

"In the morning." Lexi clutched Nita's hand, dreading leaving tomorrow. "For the first time, I don't want to go."

"Then maybe it's time to take a step back." Nita wrapped her free hand around their clasped hands. "You've been going nonstop for almost a year since Spicewood. We have a week in Napa starting this weekend. Use that time to think."

"That's our honeymoon. Trust me. I won't be thinking about work."

Nita laughed. "You are incorrigible, but whatever you decide, I'll support you."

27

Rolling her suitcase across the El Paso airport terminal, Lexi couldn't get last night from her mind. She'd let go the instant she melted into Nita's arms in their Ponder house bed. Every bit of devastation had poured from her, more than it had at the hospital entrance earlier that day. She groaned in agony so loudly Gavin likely heard her from the grave. The pain ran deep, stiffening every muscle. She couldn't breathe, couldn't move. Her stomach had turned rock hard, fighting against the misery, stealing every ounce of energy. Then as quickly as it came on, the bout stopped, and she fell asleep.

She dreamed of her childhood, skinned knees, and her mother's tender first aid. Of her raiding the fridge at midnight for her mother's pies. Of her mother giving her the birds and bees talk and adding an example of two girl birds flocking together. Lexi was only eleven, yet her mother had seen her truth and laid the seed that would shape the rest of her life. And when she woke, Lexi was stronger. She left without guilt, knowing Nita was there to tend to her father's needs.

After picking up her checked luggage from the carousel, Lexi slung the heavy fifty-five-pound bag over her shoulder and exited through the doors at the pickup area. She checked her messages. She expected Croft, but—

A horn honked three times, and a government sedan pulled up. When the front passenger window rolled down, the driver came into view. "Hop in, Mills." Agent Lange popped the trunk open.

Lexi stowed her large duffel and overnight bag and jumped into the front. "I was expecting Croft. Is something wrong?"

"He's hovering over the lab techs at the field office while they run an analysis on a remnant I flagged last night." Lange signaled and pulled into the traffic lane.

"I'm sure that's going over like a lead balloon."

"It's one of his blind spots." Lange navigated onto the airport access road. "Was that the new generation blast suit?"

"I thought we might need it."

"Good idea." After driving onto the highway, Lange glanced at Lexi with a soft, concerned expression. "How are you holding up?"

"I'm good." Last night Lexi was numb, empty, and heartbroken in Nita's arms, but today she pushed it all aside. Her head was lighter from the struggle to stay focused on her job, reminiscent of a mild hangover, but not so much to pose more than a nuisance.

"Losing a parent is never easy," Lange said. "The first is shocking but losing the second changes your anchor point in the world. The generation ahead of you is gone, making you the last link to the past. It's humbling and makes you question your life choices."

Lexi forced a swallow past her thickening throat. "How long has it been for you?"

"Eight years since my dad passed. Six since my mom."

"I'm sorry."

"I can tell you it gets easier over time, but the hole they leave never fully heals."

Lexi nodded, soaking in Lange's wisdom, but *easier* seemed a long way off. Working was her best remedy until then. "How did it go last night?"

"It's been ten years since I last sifted through debris in the field, so I was a bit rusty. However, I found one item that didn't appear native to the vehicle."

"I'm sure you were thorough. Anyone who can teach explosives disposal and investigations knows her stuff."

"Still, I agree with Croft. You have a gift. We need your keen eye on this."

"I'll do my best." Lexi's best required forgetting about her dead mother and her father sitting at home with a broken heart. It would be the toughest thing she'd done, but Croft, Lange, and Kris Faust depended on her. "If this is another Raven device, we have an idea who commissioned it and can squeeze him. Maybe then Kris will get some justice."

"She deserves it." Lange's sigh and brief pause before her reply was telling, raising Lexi's antennae.

"She meant a lot to you," Lexi said.

"She did." The strain in Lange's voice and the absence of an explanation of why Kris was special to her set off bells in Lexi's head.

Her initial impression of Lange was spot on. They were lovers, or Lange loved Kris, which explained the hostility the day they first met. Lange blamed the Raven for setting off the bomb that killed Kris and Lexi for failing to take precautions to protect her. Lexi understood that kind of anger for the person responsible for the death of a loved one. She carried it to the point of obsession for her old partner Trent Darby and Gavin before Noah killed Tony Belcher. But those two didn't have Lexi's heart like Kris may have had for Willie Lange.

"I wish I would have done things differently and asked for an armed caravan."

"Yes, you should have." Lange twisted the leather steering wheel, turning her knuckles white. "But you had no reason to suspect the Raven would go after Jamie Porter and Rick Ferrario. Maybe if the Vegas lab had completed and logged in their analysis of the dirty bomb sooner, we would have known the Raven had built it, and Croft and I could have warned you."

"I'm sorry, Agent Lange. I won't make the same mistake again. I won't let my guard down."

Lange released a heavy breath. "Let's concentrate on finding something to link us to Kris' killer."

"That I can do."

Lange weaved through the El Paso downtown area, skirting the tree-lined San Jacinto Plaza. The century-old Moore Building, home to multiple federal agency offices, including the ATF, came into view. Lange drove past it.

"We're not heading to the field office? Isn't Croft at the lab?"

"He is, but the wreckage is at the evidence yard. I told him to meet us there." Lange drove several blocks and pulled her sedan up to the guard shack protecting the parking lot with privacy fencing and barbed wire. The signage identified it as a restricted area. She displayed her badge and credentials to the armed officer who buzzed them in, retracting the security gate.

The lot contained two buildings with metal garage doors and two other fenced areas. Lange proceeded to the first building and parked. Once inside, Lexi and Lange changed into clean coveralls before entering the garage to prevent contaminating the evidence.

Lange's phone buzzed with an incoming message. She read it. "The item I flagged is a dead end. Tests showed only trace elements of tire rubber. Croft is on his way."

Lexi followed Lange inside after acknowledging her with a nod.

Lange had raised the chassis on a specially designed rack with added supports. The lift was constructed to move the vehicle back and forth on the struts easily, allowing for a quicker and more thorough examination. Three large tarps with debris were on the right of the rack on the floor. Items on one tarp appeared to have been parts of the SUV, while things on the others looked to have been scrapings from the road and accident site.

"Which tarp is from below the vehicle at the accident site?" Lexi asked.

Lange pointed to the middle one.

Lexi walked to the one closest to the garage door. "And this one? From the suspected explosion point to the impact point?" Lange confirmed with a yes. "How far back did you go last night?"

"Fifty yards from the first skid mark. That's where I found the item I'd flagged."

"Do you have a picture of it?" Lexi asked. She inspected the photo Lange brought up on her cell phone. The rulers running below and beside the concave chunk of plastic showed it was about one-by-three inches. "What drew your attention?"

"The plastic molding in the SUV was black. This piece was dark gray."

"Good eyes." Many investigators would overlook that detail, especially at night. "Okay. I'll get started."

Lange sat in a chair against the wall near the entry door without offering a rundown of her findings last night. A good investigator preferred to let the evidence speak for itself. Anything Lange offered might influence Lexi's approach.

Lexi pulled from her go-bag the Fido X4, the most advanced handheld explosive trace detector on the market and still her favorite toy in the field. It was accurate, easy to use, and fast. She meticulously tested objects on the farthest tarp, pausing when Croft entered the room. He approached Lexi, clad in the same thin red coveralls.

Briefly placing a palm on her shoulder and drawing his brows closer, he spoke gently. "I'm so sorry about your mom, Lexi. I know it was hard to leave your family, and I appreciate you coming." He softened his eyes. "Thank you."

"Working helps."

When Croft retreated, sitting next to Lange, Lexi continued her inspection. The Fido showed no significant results until she reached the tarp containing the fragments recovered from below the wreckage. A piece of metal showed trace elements of RDX, the primary component of C-4 plastic explosive, and one other element.

Lexi popped her head up, focusing on Lange. "RDX?" Lange nodded. "Lithium hydroxide?"

"No. I didn't find that." Lange pursed her lips. "So the explosive must be British PE4. That makes sense. It's cheaper and more plentiful on the underground market." She approached the tarp. "Which item did you get a hit for lithium?"

Lexi picked up a chunk of metal with her latex glove-covered hand, thinking it might be a fragment of the gas tank, and shined her flashlight on it. "See the dark smudge on the corner?" The area was only a quarter inch in diameter.

"I can't believe I missed it."

"It's easy to miss, especially if you're tired. I missed it on my first pass. I only spotted it when I used my flashlight."

"Impressive."

Lexi returned to work. The Fido identified more elements of RDX on the fragmented gas tank dangling from the undercarriage, confirming their suspicion an explosion had caused the accident. Over the next two hours, she inspected every inch of the vehicle, moving it back and forth and up and down on the rack. The damage confirmed the PE4 must have been attached to the bottom of the gas tank.

Besides the RDX and lithium, she found no traces of the explosive or the triggering device, which was odd. Based on the explosive placement, gravity, and the force of the explosion, parts of the device would have fallen to the pavement. They might not have been intact, but some pieces should have survived. But Lange had said she and Croft searched fifty yards before the first appearance of skid marks. What was she missing? Lexi stood back, rubbing the back of her neck. She was thorough and methodical, so the only answer was that Lange had missed something.

"What was the speed limit of the road Jessup was on?" Lexi asked.

"It was near the edge of the city limits, so it changed from thirty-five to sixty-five."

"If he was accelerating, fifty yards might not have been a sufficient search area." Lexi did the rough math in her head. "Assuming he was going sixty to sixty-five when the explosion happened, and it might have taken him up to two or three seconds to slam on the brakes, the first skid mark would appear about seventy to ninety yards back. If any part of the device survived, it would be there."

Lange slumped back in her chair. "Damn. We need to go back."

Lexi checked the time. "If we leave now, we should have enough daylight."

They caravanned to Harrington in Croft's rental and the sedan Lange borrowed from the ATF motor pool. Thirty minutes in, Lexi realized she'd made a horrible choice by riding with Lange. She'd become accustomed to Croft's preference for classic rock band music to pass the time, but Lange's music bordered on torture. No one in her right mind would consider Barry Manilow and Captain and Tennille road trip music.

They hit Harrington at the beginning of the rush hour. Lange pulled into a fruit stand gravel lot on the outskirts of town while Croft pulled to the shoulder of the county highway where the speed limit changed. Unfortunately, the road was well-traveled and would require patience or ingenuity to conduct a thorough search. Before Lexi had finished walking off one hundred yards from the start of the skid marks, Croft brought the creativity. He'd popped the trunk and retrieved a set of three reflective emergency roadside triangles. He assembled them and placed them in intervals three feet into the driving lane. His solution would slow and divert traffic.

"Brilliant, Nathan," Lexi shouted.

"Willie, you take the shoulder. Lexi, start from that end," Nathan shouted back. "You and I can meet in the middle. Then we can reposition the triangles on the other side. We should knock out both directions in twenty minutes."

Armed with latex gloves and a plethora of plastic evidence bags, they scanned the search area and picked up several pieces of debris without pausing to examine their finds. All the while, drivers passing by were curious and impatient. Some gawked, slowing to a crawl, and others honked and flipped the bird.

When they were close to finishing a search of the westbound lane, a sheriff's vehicle appeared. The driver turned on its overhead lights and chirped its siren behind Lexi, making her stop and turn. An officer with sergeant stripes stepped out. "What the hell are you doing on my road?"

Lexi read the name tag on his uniform. He was Sheriff Jessup's acting replacement Croft had mentioned, the one Perez had said couldn't be trusted. She displayed her badge and credentials. "Sergeant Ross, we're federal agents from the ATF conducting an investigation."

"I don't care who you are. You can't block half the highway during rush hour."

"Would you rather I shut down the entire highway? I'd be happy to speed along our investigation."

Croft stepped up behind Lexi. "Do we have a problem here, Sergeant? Or was yesterday's little beatdown not enough for you?"

Ross narrowed his eyes at Croft. The look said if Croft and Lexi didn't have badges and guns, Ross would throw them in the county lockup to meet the same fate as Derrick Culter. "Hurry it up. Before you leave town, you need to sign more paperwork to document the evidence transfer."

"I signed a bunch of forms yesterday."

"Well, you need to do it again. Otherwise, your chain of custody is for shit."

Croft rolled his eyes as if recognizing Ross' attempt at death by a thousand paper cuts. "Give us twenty minutes."

Once Ross had returned to his cruiser and driven on, Lexi turned to Croft. "That was interesting."

"You should have seen him yesterday. I couldn't tell if he was more scared than angry when I took custody of the evidence."

Another westbound car honked. "We better finish," Lexi said.

After completing their sweep, Nathan retrieved the emergency triangles. At the same time, Lexi rummaged through the see-through bags from the backseat of his rental. One item stood out with Lange's initials on the outside.

"Where did you find this, Agent Lange?"

"About eighty yards out on the edge of the shoulder. It must be the trigger."

"I think you're right." Lexi inspected the partially mangled square electronic device. It appeared intact enough to get a fingerprint. Slightly larger and thicker than a smartwatch, it resembled the new generation of portable GPS speedometers for vehicles. The better models had an over-speed alarm feature designed to go off when the car exceeded a specified speed. The Raven could have easily modified it to send an electrical impulse to trigger a blasting cap mounted to the PE4.

Croft hopped into the driver's seat and prepared to drive away.

"Wait a minute. Lange found the trigger. I want to check it out." Lexi opened the bag, pulled out the device, and closely inspected each side. The back holding in the electronic board was ajar. Lexi retrieved her pocketknife and used the screwdriver to pull the back off. "Well, well, well. What do we have here?" Sunlight was fading quickly over the horizon, but the tiny hidden object was recognizable up close.

Croft and Lange shifted higher in their seats with their necks craned in

Lexi's direction to get a better view. "What is it?" Croft asked, rushing his words.

"Someone shine a light on it." Lexi waited for Lange to activate her phone flashlight function and direct it toward the device. Lexi angled the opening in their direction. "The tip of a black feather."

"Well, I'll be damned, Lexi." Croft sprouted a half-cocked smile. "It's the Raven's work. Now we can squeeze Tilton."

"We have no proof he's the client." Lexi pointed to the twisted speedometer. "But this can get us one step closer." She turned to Lange. "How quickly can you return to El Paso and get the lab techs to process it?"

"Maybe four hours if everything goes well," Lange said.

"You should get a head start. Croft and I will wrap things up with the sheriff's department, get a hotel room, and wait for your call. With any luck, we can make an arrest before morning."

The walls were closing in on Rusty faster than he could drive away. The ATF storm troopers were back in town, poking their noses in a place that might earn Rusty a death sentence because he'd lied about using gloves when he rigged the device to Jessup's SUV. If those agents found the remnants the Raven had warned might survive the explosion, they could tie him directly to the sheriff's death. It was a possibility he couldn't chance coming to fruition. Rusty was sure about one thing. He wasn't going down alone or without a fight.

Speeding down the highway, Rusty decided the plan had to change whether Milo agreed or not. He dialed his cell phone, calling the one on-duty deputy he could rely on to rally the troops.

"Hi, boss. What's up?"

"I need every man we trust to track a vehicle off the air, especially if it leaves town. I need to know where it is at all times. Got it?"

"I'm on it, boss."

28

A deputy escorted Lexi and Croft to the administrative office deep inside the Harrington Sheriff's Department. He instructed Croft to sit at a workstation in front of a stack of forms a half-inch thick. "You signed the forms yesterday but didn't initial them, so you have to do them again."

"You've got to be kidding," Croft said with well-deserved derision in his voice.

"I don't make the rules. I just follow them."

Croft glanced at Lexi. "I'm going to be here a while."

"Then I'll step across the street." Croft acknowledged Lexi with a nod. Not knowing who to trust in the department, she'd kept her comment intentionally vague. It was nearly six o'clock, and she didn't want the district attorney leaving for the day without first giving her a heads-up about the overnight developments in Sheriff Jessup's death.

Lexi exited the building, crossing the lot shared with the courthouse and other county offices. Inside, the corridor was vacant with the notorious stillness that came at the end of a workday in government buildings. She followed the signage, passing a dozen darkened and closed offices, to the district attorney's suite. She limped slightly ascending the stairs, feeling minor swelling in her residual limb, a natural result after flying in a pressurized cabin and standing on it for hours.

A trapezoid of dim light spilled into the hallway, showing signs of the only activity on the second floor. Lexi adjusted the backpack that had slipped lower on her shoulder before walking past the threshold. The outer office was unoccupied, but the door to a secondary room was open. Lexi headed there, discovering Charlene Ford at a neatly organized desk with her face buried in a case folder.

"Working late?"

Ford popped her head up, turning her attention toward the door. Her reaction was neutral, not surprised to see someone unexpectedly and not disappointed to see it was the person who had stolen a capital murder case from her. The ability not to give away her emotions was admirable. "Agent Mills, right?"

"That's right. You should know we've been looking into Sheriff Jessup's death."

"The entire building heard how your partner swooped in yesterday."

"He does have a flair for the dramatic." Lexi snorted before turning her tone serious. "It was no accident. Someone set off an explosive, and we think you could be next."

Ford slumped back in her chair with a blank expression. "Deputy Perez had warned me. Sam and I had hoped to make some headway in cleaning up this town, but it appears Milo Tilton and his army of thugs have something else in mind."

"We have nothing linking Tilton, but we're getting close. He must be pulling the strings. Until we find out who is doing his dirty work—Jessup, Culter, and Scooter—I suggest you exercise caution. My gut tells me they're desperate now that we're investigating. They might try something quickly, maybe tonight. Is there somewhere else you can stay?"

Ford shook her head. "I haven't made too many friends in town, a byproduct of the job."

"I know what you mean. My partner and I are crashing at the Beacon. We could get you an adjoining room and keep an eye on you."

"I don't think that's necessary but thank you for the offer."

"At least let me check out your car before you leave."

Ford pushed up from her chair. "After what happened to Sam, I would appreciate it." She closed the folder that had held her interest when Lexi walked in and stuffed it into a leather satchel at the foot of her desk.

Ten minutes later, Ford led Lexi to her sedan in the official parking lot shared with the sheriff's department. Ford pulled out her key fob.

"Don't," Lexi barked, raising a hand to stop her. "Let me check first."

Ford stepped back, giving her a wide berth. Lexi used her phone flashlight to augment the little light provided by the two lampposts in the lot to examine the vehicle's exterior. She looked for wires and unusual smudges or prints that might tell her if someone had touched the car in an odd location. She then crawled on her back and checked the undercarriage from stem to stern, paying particular attention to the gas tank, brakes, and fuel line, the parts most vulnerable to sabotage.

Though Lexi had eliminated the presence of an external visual threat, the possibility of an internal one still existed. She had Ford step back to a safe distance of thirty yards away. Lexi braced for an explosion before unlocking the doors with the fob. None came, but they weren't in the clear yet. "Stay here." Lexi popped the hood, shining the light in every crevice and recess, finding no devices. After starting the engine, Ford's listening selection surprised her. Lexi listened for a moment, realizing the audiobook narrator was reading a steamy sex scene in a het romance novel, describing heaving chests and pulsating body parts in a deep sultry voice. It was well written but wasn't her cup of tea.

To be polite, Lexi turned off the stereo, exited the car, and waved Ford over. She forced back a grin, thinking she should be home in Dallas, creating her own steamy lesbian romance scene with her bride. "It's safe, but I'd feel much better if you let me clear your house before going inside. Culter was clear. You were a target at the courthouse last week."

"I don't want to put you through any trouble." Ford appeared concerned but not convinced.

"It won't be any trouble. I do this for a living. It shouldn't take more than thirty minutes, and we'll be on our way."

Ford squeezed her lower lip with her left hand. "All right, but only if you let me buy you and your partner dinner."

"Deal." Lexi would agree to nearly anything to get Ford's buy-in. She sensed whoever was behind the killings wouldn't stop until Ford was dead.

"I'll have my partner meet us there." Lexi pulled out her phone, ready to text Croft. "What's the address?"

Ford navigated through the city streets. The confident, intimidating prosecutor Lexi first met last week had disappeared. The nervous finger tapping on the steering wheel signaled growing fear. Culter had identified three targets during his courtroom shooting spree, and two were dead. It was only a matter of time before Ford was number three unless Lexi and Croft stopped whoever was behind the killings.

They arrived at a 1920s craftsman-style single-story home on a corner lot. Ford pulled onto the long driveway leading up to the carport at the house's rear, but Lexi had her stop short. The Raven designed sophisticated explosives, which might include proximity devices at the carport entrance.

Croft pulled onto the weed-laden concrete driveway, parking behind Ford's sedan. He parked and got out. "Where do you want me?"

"Grab my duffel from the trunk." Lexi wasn't taking chances after the car bombing. She turned her attention to Charlene Ford. "Stay here with my partner while I make sure it's safe to enter the house."

"Please excuse the dirty dishes. I wasn't expecting company." Ford handed Lexi her house key with an impish smile.

"Is there an alarm?"

"No. It's Harrington. Break-ins don't happen here."

"Yet." Lexi winked. "I'll be right back." With Croft's help, Lexi donned her new blast suit, the most lightweight and technically advanced suit on the market. Considering what devices she might run into, she retrieved wire snips, electrical tape, an extendable handheld mirror, a multifunction screwdriver, and a flashlight from her duffel. She then slipped them into their appropriate pockets on the suit.

Stepping toward the carport threshold, Lexi flipped on the bright lights of her helmet, noting how easy it was to maneuver in the suit. She estimated it could cut her clearing and disposal times by a quarter or a third.

She checked the interior walls for a proximity device that might trigger by breaking an invisible beam but found only yard tools and trash cans. The backdoor appeared undisturbed, with no wires or tape, so Lexi inserted and turned the key. Once she pushed the door open, her helmet lights brightened a country kitchen similar to her parents' in Ponder. A tiled floor, updated cabinets, and a granite island showed signs of a remodel in the last twenty years. The kitchen sink was brimming with dishes, but the rest of the room was spotless and organized. If that was the only thing Charlene was worried about, Lexi expected a more manageable time clearing the house than she'd projected.

Lexi considered the obvious hiding spots for an explosive. Electrical triggers might be inside wall switches, lights, electronics, appliances, or remotes. Doors, drawers, and windows could have trip wires. Area rugs, mattresses, and chairs could have pressure devices hidden underneath. Her search had to be thorough and methodical.

After clearing the kitchen, she moved into the next room, the empty living room. The only personal items were a row of potted plants by the panoramic window and a sheet hung by thumbtacks covering the glass.

Moving onto the next room, Lexi discovered an empty bedroom with file boxes stacked neatly in the closet. Ford's minimalist lifestyle painted a clear picture. She was starting over. The bathroom had a few cabinets, drawers, two rugs, one light switch, and one wall socket, which Lexi cleared quickly. Only the primary bedroom remained.

The lights from her helmet preceded her entry, bringing into focus a fully furnished, decorated room. Lexi carefully opened each dresser drawer, feeling underneath for wires. The open, sleek design of the Euro recliner in the corner made it easy to check beneath the seat cushion. Lexi had intentionally left the bed for last. It was the trickiest item to inspect because of the mattress size and weight. Typically, this would be a two-person job, but Croft wasn't trained, and they had only one blast suit.

After checking the underbelly, Lexi removed the pillows one by one and gently pulled back the bedding until it cleared the foot of the mattress. She let it fall to the wood-slat floor. If a pressure plate had been placed in the bed, it would trigger when weight heavier than the queen mattress was added, not weight taken off. Hence, she lifted one corner slowly at the foot, exposing the center point.

Nothing.

Lexi moved to the head and lifted gingerly, revealing a flat two-foot by two-foot rectangular metal sheet. Her pulse picked up when she lifted more. Wires ran from the plate connected to a portable phone charger and another to a flat block of plastic explosive embedded with a blasting cap. If she had to guess, this was the same British explosive used in Sheriff Jessup's car, and this batch was enough to take out the entire room. The suit might be enough to protect her from the fragments, but that amount of explosive would create enough pressure to rupture her lungs.

After painstakingly returning the mattress to its original position, Lexi checked the other corners, confirming the presence of only one device. The trick now would be getting it off the box spring without adding additional weight or creating too much motion, but she had a solution.

Lexi lifted the side nearest the plate six inches and slid the mattress in the opposite direction over the edge of the box spring until gravity tipped the leading side to the floor. She then circled the bed and rested the mattress on the floor. Disarming the device was now a piece of cake. She disconnected the USB cable from the power source to the pressure plate, used her snips to cut the wire from the plate to the blasting cap, and secured the ends of the wires with electrical tape. Now that the trigger was inert, she removed the detonator from the PE4.

Releasing a breath of relief, Lexi removed her gloves and helmet. Now she faced the problem of safely storing the plastic explosive and blasting cap without drawing attention while in enemy territory until they could make an arrest. She snapped a picture of the bomb with her phone and dialed Croft.

"All clear?" Croft asked.

"Just about." Lexi explained about the pressure bomb. "There was a shovel in the carport. Can you dig a hole in the backyard about eighteen inches deep?"

"I'm on it."

Minutes later, with the explosive safely buried, Lexi returned to Charlene, showing her the photo of the explosive device. "I found this between your mattress and box spring. It would have triggered the first time you laid down and it would have taken out the entire room."

Charlene's face went pale. She covered her mouth with a palm. "My God."

"You should come to the hotel for the night. You'll be safer with us."

"I think you're right."

29

"Good work, Mills," Willie Lange said over the phone. Her tone was complimentary, suggesting Lexi had successfully broken the ice with her. "How is the D.A. doing?"

Lexi stepped to the open door separating their adjoining hotel rooms and rested a shoulder against the door jamb. Charlene was sitting at the desk, eating her French fries one at a time and staring blankly into space. Lexi recognized that stare. Nearly every person she rescued from a bomb had it. She had come close to death and was coming to terms with her mortality.

"She'll be fine. She just needs a stiff drink."

Lange laughed. "I remember the type. She was lucky to have you in her corner. What did you do with the explosive?"

"I kept the blasting cap and a small sample of the PE to test later and buried the rest in the backyard for safekeeping. I don't want to bring in a disposal team yet. It might spook whoever is planting the devices when we're close to getting answers. How much longer?"

"Good planning. I'm an hour out from El Paso. Once I get the lab techs going, we should have the results in another half."

"We'll sit tight until then." Lexi completed her call with Lange, marking the time. If things went well on Lange's end, they might have their best lead by ten. That meant she needed to do her self-care now.

Lexi went to the bathroom, wet a washcloth, grabbed a bar of hand soap, and returned to the bed. Searching through her backpack, she retrieved a new liner and two fresh socks for her residual limb before digging deeper into the compartment for her prosthetic salve made of beeswax and coconut oil. Several attempts yielded the same disappointing result—it wasn't there. Maybe she'd stuffed it into her overnight bag when she hastily packed for the trip this morning.

After sifting through her luggage, Lexi realized she'd forgotten an essential part of her care as an amputee. Wearing a prosthetic created friction against the residual limb. The liner protected the skin from direct rubbing, and the socks added layers to provide a snugger fit in the socket. Both reduced most of the associated aches and pains. However, the liner collected sweat and moisture, creating a fertile environment for fungus to grow. The salve protected the skin from turning into an itchy mess and kept the skin moisturized. The hotel offered body lotion, but the label said it didn't contain beeswax, the critical ingredient Lexi needed to form a protective barrier over her skin.

Lexi shouted, "Hey, Charlene. Do you have any lotion with beeswax?"

"Sorry, no," came the reply.

Lexi glanced at Croft, hoping he might have a reasonable substitute. He was sitting at the desk in their room, eating his burger and reviewing the folder he'd compiled on the Raven's weapons. "Hey, Nathan—"

He snorted. "Of course not." He flipped a page and looked up at Lexi. "The Raven used British PE4 in New Orleans last year. It was a briefcase bomb, designed to go off when the victim removed a folder from a pocket on the lid."

"That's good to know, but PE4 is plentiful on the dark market. Tracking it won't get us anywhere." Lexi clearly saw the difficulties of chasing the Raven. Other than evilness and ego, he wasn't anything like Tony Belcher. Tony had thrived on creating a robust followership and using people to do his bidding. That was his downfall. The Raven was the opposite. He depended on secrecy. If law enforcement captured a client for whatever reason, he made sure discussing their business arrangements would come with the ultimate price.

The only thing left for Lexi to exploit was his ego. The Raven was so proud of his work he put a piece of himself into every product—a raven's feather. Getting to a client before the Raven knew of their capture was the path to finding him, but that was next to impossible, as Croft had discovered years ago.

"What will?"

"The people who hire him."

"I get that. That's why we're here—to squeeze whoever hired him into giving up where to find the Raven."

"Not where, but how. My gut tells me the Raven is too smart to be easily trapped. We need to find out how the client first contacted him. How did they know how to reach him? Who put them in contact or gave them his number? If we learn that, we'll have a way into his inner circle."

"Maybe then I can stop chasing ghosts," Croft said, "and track something or someone more tangible."

"Exactly."

Lexi unzipped her left pant leg, rolled down the sleeve securing the socket to her thigh, and removed her prosthetic. Instant relief came by removing the socks and liner and finally freeing her skin to breathe the cool air. The sensation was more than soothing. It was liberating. Showering, performing self-care, sleeping, and skin-to-skin intimate moments with Nita were the only times when her leg wasn't encased in neoprene. While on, the liner was the always-present, subtle reminder she was disabled. When it was off, Lexi almost felt like she did before the explosion took her lower leg, but not quite. She was free from the trappings compensating for her defect but not from her defect's underlying limitations. Having one foot always required accommodation.

Lexi's visual inspection of the skin on the nub revealed redness and swelling. But gliding her hand across the surface, she discovered a concerning clamminess. Soap and water would help for the interim, but Lexi wasn't sure how long it would be until she could next doff her prosthetic and clean her leg. This might be her only opportunity to find some proper cream.

She cleaned and dried her stump before donning her prosthetic with a fresh liner and two layers of cotton socks. "I need to find a store that carries the lotion I need." She put on her jacket and snatched the key fob to Nathan's rental car. Unzipping her backpack, she grabbed her mini-flashlight and left her bag on the bed. "I won't be too long."

Lexi walked to the open adjoining door to the other room, knocking on the jamb before poking her head inside. Charlene had gotten up and was plugging in her laptop. "Sorry to bother you, but I need to head to the store. Nathan will stay with you. Is there anything I can get you?"

Charlene looked up, locking gazes with Lexi. Her color had returned, and she moved around more confidently. "No, I'm fine." She stepped toward Lexi with soft eyes. "Thank you for saving my life. I would have never thought to look between the mattresses."

"I'm glad I could help. Until we catch whoever planted the bomb, I suggest you stay low."

"That's going to be a little hard. I'm due in court in the morning for Tilton's trial."

"If we're available, we can drive you. Otherwise, I suggest arranging for a taxi or Uber."

"It's wild to think this town would go this far to keep the status quo."

"When money and power are involved, believe it."

Lexi exited through Charlene's door to the outside, inhaling the cool autumn west Texas air. It reminded her Thanksgiving was right around the corner, but with her mother's death, she wouldn't be in any mood to give thanks. Her father would likely be in a more disagreeable state. Then Christmas, her mother's favorite time of year, would be a month away. The thought of the house not smelling like gingerbread, apples, and cinnamon, and mistletoe and garland not brightening every room brought tears to her eyes. Enough tears that she dialed Nita's number while walking across the parking lot.

"Hi, Lex. How's it going?"

"I miss her, Nita."

A lime green muscle car parked under the gas station's lights across the street caught Lexi's attention. The Dodge Challenger SRT Super Stock was the king of the drag strip for unmodified vehicles. She vaguely remembered seeing a car like it recently, but her mind was too cloudy to recall where. Reaching the rental car, she kept the phone to her ear while shining her flashlight on the car.

"I miss her, too," Nita said.

"What are we going to do for Thanksgiving?" Lexi started her inspection, looking for signs of tampering, but found nothing.

"We should follow your dad's lead, but I was thinking we could go to a movie and fill up on hot dogs, popcorn, and Sno-Caps."

"I would like that." Lexi laid flat on the ground to continue her inspection. After completing one section, a cat darted from underneath, startling her. "Holy shit."

"What was that?"

"A freaking cat. It scared the crap out of me." Lexi shined the light to resume her inspection but couldn't remember the precise spot where she'd left off. *The tank*, she thought. "Maybe we can pick up Dad and go into Denton."

"That's if we don't spend the night before in Ponder."

Lexi shifted to the underbelly at the front of the car. "I've been thinking about that. Maybe we should stay at the house for a while. It's not too far to both our offices."

"That might not be a bad idea," Nita said. "Your dad was lost today. I had to push him to eat."

"That's it. We should pack for a week or two when I get back." Lexi finished her search and climbed to her feet. "Hey, Nita. I gotta go. I forgot to pack my salve, so I'm heading to the store for something."

"If you can't find anything with beeswax, buy diaper paste with zinc. It should help until you get back."

"Will do. I love you, Mrs. Flores."

"I love you, Mrs. Mills."

Lexi slipped her phone into her cargo pocket before stepping back several yards to unlock the driver's door. After the beep, she popped the hood from the inside and checked the engine compartment. Everything looked normal, so she started the engine and turned off the hard rock music. Silence was more palatable at the moment.

She remembered seeing an all-night pharmacy about two miles down the frontage highway road their hotel was on and pulled the sedan from the parking lot to head there. The road was lightly traveled, with no one going in the opposite direction. Only two vehicles were heading toward town with her.

She pressed the gas pedal and accelerated toward the thirty-five miles per hour speed limit. A second later, an electronic beep reminiscent of a car alert sounded. However, this one had a tone not standard in American-made vehicles.

"Shit!" She must have missed something during her check.

Lexi had seconds to react. She jerked the steering wheel toward the center line, where on the other side was a soft grassy shoulder. In a split second, she simultaneously lifted her foot off the gas, unsnapped her seat belt with her right hand, and pulled the handle while pushing the door open. She propped her prosthetic foot against the door and leaned out face up. Tucking her arms close to her chest, she launched herself at a forty-five-degree angle away from the car with as much strength as she could muster, hoping she'd slowed enough to survive the fall. Her back hit the grass first in a forceful thud, knocking the air from her lungs. She rolled, sensing she'd cleared the car.

An explosion. Heat. Pressure. Pain.

Lexi's movement stopped. She remained flat and opened her eyes, fighting the sharp pain in her left arm. Fire engulfed the car. The flames danced, alternating between reaching for the dark sky and hiding among the twisted metal, but they refused to diminish.

A car drove past slowly, but she couldn't hear it over the ringing in her ears. It was lime green. But why didn't it stop?

Another explosion. A bright light. More heat.

The pain became more intense, and Lexi struggled to stay awake, but the pain won.

30

Minutes earlier

When the door closed behind Lexi, Nathan slumped back in his chair. He knew she was an amputee—the entire world did after the Spicewood insurrection—but he'd forgotten, considering how she walked with a near-perfect stride and climbed into trailers with ease, until she took off her prosthetic moments ago. Hell, he walked with more of a limp, and his only excuse was getting old.

He'd never seen that type of injury up close, and it had thrown him for a loop. It was a gruesome reminder of the dangers associated with Lexi's primary job as an explosives expert. If any of a thousand things went wrong, she could lose the other leg or something much more precious—her life. It took strength and determination to return from an injury like hers and more fortitude than he hoped to accumulate in a lifetime to re-qualify for the Special Response Team. But most impressively, it took boundless courage to keep doing the thing that took her leg. Respect barely scratched the surface of the opinion he held of her.

Nathan returned to his review of the information he'd compiled on the Raven. Lexi was right about the path to the Raven's inner circle. It started by reverse engineering how he got onto his clients' radar. He pulled out a case summary sheet and flagged the cases where the police knew or suspected who was the buyer of the Raven's services. There were eight. In the five cases where they didn't know the client, the person had died under suspicious circumstances shortly after using the Raven's services. He circled the three where the police hadn't made an arrest. If the Harrington case was a bust, those suspects would be his and Lexi's starting point.

Nathan heard the squeak of brakes outside their rooms, drawing his full attention. He and Lexi had chosen this hotel because it was off the beaten path with little traffic, making it more difficult for an attacker to blend into the crowd.

He rose to his feet and drew his duty weapon from his holster, pinning it to his thigh before peeking into Charlene's room. She was sitting at her desk, reading from her laptop. "Stay here. I heard a noise." Charlene looked up, acknowledging him with a nervous nod.

Nathan drew back the edge of the curtain closest to the door enough to see the walkway and parking lot with one eye. A minivan had pulled into a parking spot a few doors down, and a woman was unsnapping a sleeping toddler from a car seat. Nathan lowered his antennae and directed his attention to where they had parked their cars across the parking lot. His rental was gone, but Charlene's sedan was still where they'd left it.

Returning his weapon to his holster, he released the curtain and retraced his steps to the adjoining room door. Charlene was alert with a concerned expression. "It was nothing," he told her.

A loud explosion in the distance rocked the area, sparking a queasy feeling in Nathan's stomach. His pulse and respirations doubled at the thought of Lexi becoming the Raven's next victim.

"What was that?" Charlene recoiled.

Instinct told Nathan Lexi was in trouble. He reached for his ankle holster, retrieving a .38 snub-nose revolver. "Take this. Do you know how to handle a gun?" She shook her head. "Just point and pull the trigger. Stay behind the bed and don't let anyone in until I get back."

Nathan dashed outside through her door, drawing his primary weapon on the fly. He kicked it into high gear and ran through the parking lot and onto the frontage road. He stopped in the first traffic lane.

Straight ahead was the gas station. Nothing was out of the ordinary. Nathan looked right but saw nothing but darkness and the distant lights of business. He pivoted left. A virtual knife tore through his gut. Flames had engulfed a vehicle about a quarter mile down the road. He took off toward it, regretting not keeping up with his workout routine since moving to Dallas. Pumping his arms and legs hard, he sucked in more air than he would have if he were in as good of shape as Lexi.

His heart sank when the vehicle's shape came into view. He couldn't be sure, but it resembled his rental car. He ran faster, fearing the worst. His tongue stuck to the roof of his dry mouth, but he forced it loose, shouting, "Lexi!"

Nathan stopped abruptly, close enough for the mangled inferno to radiate searing heat. He raised a bent arm to shield most of his face. "Lexi!" He peeked his eyes past his arm briefly several times to make out the front seat. Flames rolled ferociously through the compartment, making it challenging to discern whether Lexi was inside. He stabbed his hand at the driver's door, which was ajar. The handle was scorching. He manipulated the sleeve of his light jacket to form a protective layer and tried again. In one jerk, the door flew open. The compartment was empty, but where was Lexi?

Nathan frantically scanned the area, starting closest to the wreckage where the fire lit the surrounding area. The further out he went, the more the darkness hindered his ability to make out objects. Then, about thirty yards from the crash, Nathan spotted something on the grassy shoulder. He sprinted to it.

"Thank goodness."

Lexi was lying face down. Her arms were still, bent with her hands beside her head. Her left leg was at an unnatural angle, but he couldn't be sure if it was because the prosthetic was out of alignment or something much worse. The frightening sight knocked the wind from him.

Nathan pressed two fingers against the artery in her neck. He slumped in relief, feeling a solid pulse. He then used both hands to check her legs for obvious breaks, discovering the prosthetic was the culprit for the gruesome-looking injury. He felt dampness, moving on to her arms, realizing it was from blood.

Lexi groaned and recoiled the injured arm. "Nathan." Her voice was weak at first but grew stronger. "There was a bomb." She rolled to the side of her uninjured arm and pushed her torso up.

Nathan helped her to a sitting position. "Is anything broken?"

"I don't think so." Lexi grimaced while pushing up a jacket sleeve. She exposed a deep one-inch gash on her lower left arm and held it out gingerly. "Shrapnel. Everything aches, but that comes with the territory after being in the pressure zone of an explosion. Otherwise, I think I'm okay." She briefly glanced at the wreckage. "I hope you took out insurance on that thing."

"I did, actually." Nathan pointed at her leg. "But I beg to differ about your condition."

"Can you help me get it into place? It requires two hands." Lexi unzipped her pant leg and visually inspected her leg. "The fall twisted the socket on my limb. Just turn it clockwise until I say stop."

"You're sure about this?" At her firm nod, Nathan realigned the prosthetic.

"Can you test to see if the pylon is loose? Just give it a twist. It shouldn't have any give."

One twist gave him the answer. "It's loose."

A siren sounded in the distance.

"No problem. It just needs a tune-up." Lexi leaned back on her bottom and fished a socket tool from a cargo pocket using her uninjured arm. It was too dark for Nathan to see clearly what she was doing, but she rotated the device several times on both ends of the pylon and ankle. Once she returned the tool to her pocket, he helped her to her feet.

"Can you stand on it?"

Lexi tested its stability. "Good as new. I'm lucky my first roll after I hit the ground was to my left side. The socket absorbed most of the force."

Nathan shook his head in amazement. "You're a beast, Mills." Two sets of red strobe lights appeared at the intersection near their hotel.

"Where's Ford?"

A fire truck and rescue vehicle rolled onto the scene.

"In the room with my backup gun."

"You better head back and make sure she's safe," Lexi said.

"I don't want to leave you alone. Whoever did this might try again."

Lexi looked left and right. Several vehicles had stopped, and people from the nearby businesses had come out to gawk. "I'll be fine. There are too many potential witnesses. I'll tell the responding officer what happened, get stitched up, and call in another favor to have the Texas Rangers secure the wreckage and scene."

Nathan shook his head again. "You and your connections."

Nathan Croft doubled back to the hotel to secure Charlene Ford. Firefighters rolled out hoses and doused water on the burning wreckage. Paramedics charged toward Lexi while towing a gurney.

"Were you in the accident? Are you hurt?" one asked.

"Yes and yes." Lexi showed him her arm. "Are you trained to suture on scene?"

He inspected the laceration. "Yes, but I recommend you have a doctor treat you. It looks deep."

Lexi retrieved her credentials and badge from her pocket. "I'm a federal agent on a case. I don't have time tonight. I'd appreciate it if you could patch me up well enough to get through the night."

After more convincing, the paramedics escorted Lexi to their rig. They irrigated her wound and numbed the area. While applying six stitches, a Harrington Sheriff's Department deputy appeared at the open back doors. He didn't look familiar.

"Are you the driver?" he asked.

"Yes." Lexi kept her arm still while the medic continued to treat her wound. "I'm ATF Agent Lexi Mills. This is a federal crime scene."

"Not so fast, Agent Mills. I need to conduct a field sobriety test."

"Do you test every victim of a car bombing?" The paramedic paused briefly and looked at Lexi out of the corner of his eye but said nothing. "I'll be with you as soon as I'm patched up."

The deputy stepped away. A minute later, the paramedic snipped the last stitch. "All done." He glanced at the opening and back at Lexi. "You're the agent looking into the sheriff's accident, right?" Lexi answered with a silent nod. "We were at the scene when Thomas Perez called and asked us to stall. Do you need our help again?"

Lexi let out a loud breath. Finally, she had more people on her side. "I need to make a call to get more help. In the meantime, can you make sure the sheriff's department doesn't get anywhere near the wreckage?"

"With pleasure. We're tired of the stranglehold they have on this town." He exited via the driver's door to not attract the deputy's attention. Lexi then dialed her phone.

"Lexi, I was sorry to hear about your mother. How are you holding up?" Simon Winslow's deep voice was comforting. Talking to a dear friend was reassuring.

"I don't think it's fully sunk in yet." *How could it?* she thought. A day following her mother's death, she was knee-deep in explosives. "I'm calling because I need your help."

"Name it," Simon replied. Lexi explained the events of the evening and provided some background on their investigation. "The governor mentioned the call he made on your behalf last week. I'm happy to help. What do you need?"

"Can you send your nearest patrol to secure the scene and an investigation team to process it? I'll need the wreckage taken to the ATF field office in El Paso while I wrap up things here."

"Boy. When you ask for favors, they're doozies."

"I'm sorry, Simon, but—"

He laughed. "It's fine, Lexi. I'm just busting your chops. I can have a patrol there in fifteen and the investigation team from Midland there in an hour."

"You're a lifesaver, Simon. I owe you one."

"There's no owing among family. Stay safe, Lexi Mills."

31

The plastic shopping bag hanging from Lexi's hand swayed to the motion of her weary stride along the frontage road in the dark. The impact from the fall from the rental car before the explosion had left her limb bruised and sore, but she'd learned to push through minor discomfort eighteen months ago during her training to return to the Special Response Team. If she couldn't handle the pain on the treadmill, she would never make it in the field. Tonight was the ultimate test of her preparation.

The walk to her hotel gave Lexi time to replay her mistake before hopping into the rental car. Thinking of her mother and talking to Nita had split her attention, and that damn cat had made her lose her place during her car sweep. She hadn't become complacent or lazy. If she had, she would have foregone the inspection entirely. But she turned into something more dangerous—distracted. Her job required extreme focus for a reason. A forgotten or poorly executed step often ended in disaster, and tonight was no exception. It had nearly cost Lexi her life. Something had to give, and the solution was staring her in the face. She needed time to grieve for her mother. Until she could focus, she needed to stay in the office or take some time off.

Car headlights illuminated Lexi's path from behind, prompting her to shift deeper onto the shoulder to give the approaching vehicle a wider berth. But the lights didn't pass. Tires crunched the gravel in a constant cadence, telling Lexi the driver was coming for her.

Instinct kicked in. Lexi dropped her bag and, in one swift motion, drew her Glock from her paddle holster, training it on the advancing older sedan. Surprisingly, it stopped. The passenger window was down, and the driver leaned out to shout, "I had a feeling you'd be here. Need a lift, Agent Mills?"

Lexi recognized the voice and face instantly. Usually, the remaining short distance to the hotel wouldn't warrant a ride, but this was an opportunity to gather some intel. "Deputy Perez. Yes. Thanks."

Before opening the passenger door, Lexi picked up her bag and admired the car. It needed a lot of work, but the frame looked in good shape. The particular shade of faded turquoise body paint and white hood stripes, combined with the "302" emblem on the front fender and the original fifteen-inch rally wheels told her Thomas Perez had an impressive classic muscle car.

Lexi slid into the passenger seat. The inside was ratty and needed restoration, but all the original finishing parts were present. "Nice wheels. The Z28 is 290 horsepower of pure bliss."

"You know about cars?"

"You could say that."

"Where are you headed?"

"The hotel farther down the frontage road."

"Got it." Perez signaled and pulled into the traffic lane. "I was home when I heard the call about an explosion and a car in flames over the scanner, so I came out. Amazingly, the call said there were no major injuries. What happened?"

"The same thing that happened to Sheriff Jessup, only this time it was my car. Whoever is doing this knows we're getting close."

"Geez, this is getting crazy." Perez released a nervous sigh, downshifting to pull into the hotel parking lot.

"Over there." Lexi directed him to a spot hidden from the street. "I don't want to put you at risk, but I need to fill you in and ask you some questions. Do you have to be anywhere?"

"No, and by the looks of things, you might need some help."

Once Perez parked, Lexi led him to their adjoining rooms. She knocked twice on the door of her and Croft's room, paused, and knocked three more times in rapid succession—their signal. "It's Lexi."

Croft opened the door with his left hand and held his pistol in his right. "I expected you twenty minutes ago." His words came out accusatory.

Lexi lifted her shopping bag chin high. "I still needed something for my leg but look who I ran into." She stepped past Croft when he moved to one side. Perez followed. "Maybe he can give us some answers."

Perez stopped in mid-stride when he locked stares with Charlene Ford. She rose from her spot on the foot of the bed. "This is a surprise."

"Not when you hear everything that happened tonight," Ford said.

Lexi detailed the explosive she had discovered at the D.A.'s house, forcing Charlene to seek safety with her and Croft. "An hour later, our rental car blows up."

"Geez." Perez shook his head, placing both hands on his hips. "How can I help?"

"I saw a lime green Challenger crawl past my car a minute after the explosion, but it didn't stop. Do you know of anyone in town who drives one?"

A phone chime sounded from the next room. "I have to take that," Ford said before rushing toward her room.

"I've seen one in the department parking lot several times, but I've never seen who drives it."

A memory flashed in Lexi's head. After discovering Derrick Culter's body in his jail cell, Lexi had stepped out the back door to tell Nita the news she wouldn't be coming home that night. During the call, a green Challenger had pulled into the parking lot, and a deputy got out of it and walked past her into the building. "It's Ross. I saw him in the department lot last week with it."

"I knew something was hinky with him when I saw him at the river the night we captured Culter."

"It makes sense. He must be part of the Rat Pack," Croft said.

Lexi's phone buzzed with an incoming call. She dug it from her pocket and swiped the screen. "Agent Lange, I was about to call you. We've had some developments here."

"Here, too," Lange said. "You were right about the Raven's feather, and the techs got a hit on a print on the trigger."

"I'm guessing it belongs to Rusty Ross."

"How did you know?"

"Our rental car was rigged with a bomb tonight, but I escaped in time. His car rolled by like he was checking his handiwork. Now we got him. We just have to find him." Lexi further explained the Texas Rangers were there processing the scene. "When they're done, they'll take the wreckage to El Paso."

"That was quick thinking, Mills," Lange said.

"The last text from the team leader said they should finish within an hour. In the meantime, we'll search for Ross. If we find him, maybe we can hitch a ride to El Paso so we can book him." Finishing the call, Lexi stuffed her phone into her pocket and turned her attention to Perez. "Our rental car went up in flames. I hate to ask, but—"

A loud crash with the distinct sound of breaking glass poured from Charlene's room, and there was a high-pitched, blood-pumping scream.

Croft was closest and dashed inside. Perez followed.

Tires screeched outside while the smell of smoke filled the room, leaving Lexi torn. She had no doubt the room next door was on fire, but the culprit was getting away. She rushed to the adjoining door. Flames had engulfed the bed. The curtain was on fire, and fuel from the Molotov cocktail was ablaze on the carpet. Croft tried to reach Charlene, but the fire trapped her in the corner near the desk.

"Nathan!" Lexi yelled. "A car."

"Go! I've got this!" he shouted, shielding his face with an arm.

"Perez, with me." Lexi darted out the door. Perez followed. Tires screeched again at the edge of the parking lot. An engine roared. Lexi glanced toward it while running toward Perez's Camaro. The vehicle turned east, opposite the crash site where the Texas Rangers had secured the scene. Lexi reached the car first and went to the driver's side, holding out a hand. "Keys."

He hesitated, but there was no time to argue. Lexi was trained at high-speed pursuit and had years of experience testing beefy stock cars on the track. "I'm NASCAR trained. Keys."

Perez slumped his shoulders, tossed them to her, and circled to the passenger side. He hopped in but hadn't closed the door before Lexi had the car in reverse and stomped on the gas pedal. The door swung away from him but slammed shut when Lexi shifted to first gear and peeled out.

Turning right, Lexi spotted taillights speeding away, growing smaller and smaller. Using her prosthetic foot on the clutch, she timed her gear shifts without glancing at the tachometer when the engine reached the optimum whine. The car never shuddered and kept accelerating. The taillights ahead changed and grew larger. She was gaining ground.

Lexi glanced at Perez. He appeared in need of reassurance. His face had turned pale, and he'd braced a palm against the dash with a straight arm.

"Do you know the name Jerry Mills?"

"What Texan doesn't? He's a NASCAR legend."

"He's my dad. I grew up on muscle cars. Your baby will be fine." The taillights turned north. If Lexi remembered the town geography correctly, he was heading toward the oil fields. "But if I have to add a few more dings, we'll restore her."

Lexi prepared for a hard left. She steered to the outermost point on the road, tapped the brakes once, downshifted as she approached the curve, and kept pressure on the gas pedal. She felt both wheels grabbing equally through the turn, confirming her suspicion. This beauty had Positraction. She shouldn't lose a fraction of momentum. Once through the turn, she straightened the wheel, upshifted, and applied more gas. The perfectly executed turn brought out a smile and got her heart pumping. It had been years since she'd put a classic muscle car through its paces.

She'd gained enough distance on the getaway car to make out the distinctive outline of the Dodge Challenger tail end. It was too dark to determine its color, but she'd bet every penny in her bank account it was lime green.

"You really know how to drive." Perez relaxed his death grip on the dash and finally buckled his lap belt.

"He's going to the oil fields, right?"

"Yes. This road runs through them. It ends at the old highway in a T intersection with a stop sign."

"What if I went straight? What's there?" Lexi was still gaining on the

Challenger. Either Ross didn't know how to handle the power or was afraid to.

"A dirt field. That's where the kids do spinouts."

"Perfect. How far?"

"A mile."

Lexi floored the gas pedal, squeezing every last horsepower out of Perez's little baby. "Tell me when I'm a half mile out." She glided the Camaro along the paved country road like it was on skids, continuing to gain ground on Ross. No vibration. No pull on the wheel. This was a beauty worth saving. The maneuver she had in mind would require some bodywork and new tires afterward, but she would do her best to minimize the damage.

Twenty seconds later, they whizzed past a lighted area with retention ponds for the oil field. Perez barked, "Half mile."

Lexi focused. Ross would brake in a few seconds to make his turn. Estimating the distance between their cars, she needed to wait three seconds before reducing her speed to align their vehicles properly. Left would take him west into town, and right would take him east, deeper into the oil fields and across the Harrington River. If he were smart, he'd go into town. Each city block offered a variety of obstacles that could take Lexi out of the chase unexpectedly. But the presence of a fingerprint on the trigger of the bomb that killed Sheriff Jessup told Lexi she wasn't dealing with a smart man. Hence, she lined up, expecting him to turn right. If she guessed wrong, she might miss her one opportunity to catch him.

Brake lights appeared.

Lexi's heart pulsated so hard the pounding in her ears started the countdown, two beats each second.

Thump. Thump.

Ross veered left, making Lexi smile. He wasn't smart.

Thump. Thump.

He rode the brakes, telegraphing his inexperience behind the wheel.

Thump. Thump.

The driver's side front wheel of their Camaro came abreast with the Challenger's passenger side back wheel. Simultaneously, she hit her brakes and drifted the steering wheel left when he started his turn, hitting him.

The Camaro slowed instantly.

Thump. Thump.

The Challenger turned. The front end spun, facing the Camaro, but Lexi didn't panic. If she jerked the wheel, they would flip. She'd seen enough races to know momentum would pull the Challenger away, so Lexi kept a steady grip and steered straight.

Thump. Thump.

She barreled through the T intersection, losing sight of Ross, but she was confident he was still in a high-speed spin.

Thump. Thump.

The terrain got rough. Their headlights wobbled up and down, shining on dirt and desert shrubs.

Thump. Thump.

A berm came into sight. Perez failed to mention the railroad tracks ran across the far end of the dirt field, but they were heading toward the tracks. The raised rails would flip their car with the ease of a toddler with a Tonka truck. Lexi had no choice.

Thump. Thump.

She spun the wheel left, still braking hard. Gravel spit from under the wheels. Momentum took the rear end farther than she expected, turning the Camaro around.

An abrupt stop.

"Shit," Perez repeated between breaths.

Lexi didn't have time to comfort him. She pressed the clutch, shifted to first gear while giving it gas and steering toward Ross's position. Twenty yards down. Forty yards. Sixty. Finally, their headlights illuminated the lime Challenger as it sat on the westbound shoulder. The windows on the driver's side were shattered and jagged along their frames. The car had new body damage, likely caused during a rollover. She parked twenty feet away, so the headlights shined into the cabin.

Lexi and Perez flew from the car, weapons drawn. Her heart was still pounding from the chase, but she stepped lightly. When Ross' silhouette came into view, the hairs on the back of her neck tingled. She had a sense the threat he posed hadn't passed.

32

Three minutes earlier.

Whoever was behind the wheel of that hot rod catching up to Rusty in his Challenger sure knew how to handle it. The closer it got after turning north to go deep into the oil fields, the more he realized he'd made a colossal mistake.

"Shit, shit, shit, shit."

He should never have let Milo drag him into his grand scheme of paving the way to get out of jail and take back what was once his in this town. He should have realized the gravy train was over and been happy with the new car, nice clothes, and the fact he hadn't gotten anyone pregnant. Though, he would have missed the ability to throw enough money around the bar to bring home any woman in town. Despite Milo's frantic grasping at straws, the apparatus to cover things up—the sheriff, district attorney, and district judge—were gone, and Rusty was at the bleeding edge of what remained.

The car chasing him had gained enough ground to make out it was a classic Camaro. It looked like the one the rookie, Perez, had. Rusty had no idea he could drive like a pro. Too bad he would have to let him go after this stunt. The kid kept his head down and did his job without griping or a single citizen complaint. Rusty would make one up if he couldn't find a legitimate reason to send him packing.

The end of the road was rapidly approaching. Though it was dark, Rusty couldn't chance anyone in town spotting his flashy car, so his only chance of shaking Perez was through the oil fields. Maybe Rusty could get him to roll into one of the many runoff ditches, but he chose wrong. The instant he broke to turn right, Perez accelerated and squeezed his Camaro tighter into the turn, forcing Rusty's car into a terrifying spin. He gripped the wheel tight and stiffened his elbows, bracing for the impact of a lifetime.

The wheels screeched.

The world rotated as if he was sitting on a whirly top. Breathing became impossible. His lungs froze like his hands on the wheel.

An unwise counter-steer when the Challenger slowed sent his world upside down. Side windows shattered with glass fragments floating in the air like water droplets in outer space. His surroundings righted quickly, and the glass settled on the floorboards and seats.

The crotch of his pants got warm and wet—he'd pissed himself. The embarrassing mess jolted him from his daze long enough to realize the engine had stopped. He pressed the start button, but nothing happened. He was dead in the water, so he reached for the only lifeline at his disposal, snatching his phone from his pants pocket and hitting speed dial. It rang once, twice, three times. "Answer, dammit." On the fourth ring, the call connected.

"What? It's late."

"It's all gone wrong, Milo. The feds have evidence I planted the bomb. They found the one in Ford's house and escaped the one I put in their car." Rusty panted in short, rapid breaths, sensing the walls closing in when the Camaro zoomed up next to his car. "I'm about to be captured."

"Where are you?"

The Camaro doors flew open. Perez and that ATF Agent Mills lunged out, drawing their weapons. They approached Rusty's Challenger lightly on their feet. "Hands! Show us your hands!" Mills yelled.

"East side of town on the road heading to the northern oil fields. The ATF is here. Get me out of this," Rusty said to Milo in a desperate plea. He turned his head, staring Mills in the eyes while holding the phone to his ear. He sensed a single flinch might cost him his life.

Milo said, "I'll send someone. Just keep your mouth shut."

"Hands! Show us your hands!" Mills repeated her order and stepped forward, pressing the muzzle of her pistol against his temple. "Drop the damn phone."

Rusty complied. Once the phone clinked against the center console, he raised both hands slowly, splaying his fingers to not appear as a threat.

Mills stepped back. "If you're not hurt, get out."

Perez yanked the car door open with a loud creak.

Rusty moved gingerly, keeping his hands in plain sight. He hadn't realized the rollover had left his back sore, but it wasn't as uncomfortable as shimmying out in wet britches. "I'm trying."

Once out, Rusty placed his hands on the roof, realizing his car was totaled. *Dammit*, he thought. He still had forty-two payments.

Out of the corner of his eye, he saw Mills holster her gun before cuffing his hands behind his back. She patted him down but whisked her hand away when she reached his upper pant leg. "Did you piss yourself?"

Rusty had no words for his embarrassment.

"You have the right to remain silent..."

Milo disconnected the call after hearing the ATF agents arrest his dirty-hands guy. Rusty had violated the Raven's one simple condition of service: don't get arrested. The rule had teeth because those in custody made deals in their best interest, and the Raven made sure no one talked about his process.

Milo had three options.

The first was to do nothing and wait for the fallout. But Rusty knew too much about Milo's operation, including hiring Culter to kill the judge. Equally important, Milo lived by one rule: trust no one completely. He couldn't trust Rusty wouldn't talk.

His second option was to rally the other deputies on his payroll to make sure Rusty never left town, but Milo wasn't sure where their loyalties lay.

They might refuse, and Milo would lose his one opportunity to handle this himself.

His final option was to involve the Raven, who had more resources and a longer reach than Milo had ever dreamed of. It was risky, but Milo already suspected the Raven kept an eye on his clients to ensure compliance with his terms. If he told the Raven right away, that might establish trust and provide the opportunity for a second chance.

The path was clear. Milo had to come clean, so he fished out the burner phone from his nightstand. His hands shook as he dialed the only saved number. The call connected.

"Yes, Mr. Tilton. I've been expecting your call."

Milo's throat thickened with fear. His assumption was correct. The Raven had a spy in town. "I have a problem requiring your attention."

"Your man is sloppy, Mr. Tilton. Do you have the staff to take care of it?"

"I'm afraid not."

"Then what do you propose? My rules are clear."

"I need your help."

"Are you sure you want me to clean up your mess? Once I start, I won't stop until it's done."

"I'm sure." Those two words sealed Rusty's death warrant, and, if anything went wrong, Milo's too.

33

"Consider yourself fired, Perez." Rusty Ross squirmed in the backseat of Thomas' lucky lady. His growl was defiant, smug, and unrealistic all rolled into one. It was absurd to think he still had any say in the workings of the Harrington Sheriff's Department or had any way of getting out of this mess.

Perez remained silent from behind the wheel, but Lexi was in no mood for arrogance after being on the receiving end of two failed attempts on her life. She shifted in the front seat to look him in the eye. "No one can help you, Rusty. I have you dead to rights on torching our hotel room and the bomb that killed Sheriff Jessup. And if I rustle up enough surveillance video in the area, I'm sure I can link you to the device in my car and the one I disarmed in the D.A.'s house."

"Whatever you think you have, it won't be enough."

"Maybe not in Harrington under your brand of justice, but once I book you, you'll never set foot in this town again."

"It will never get that far. I want my lawyer."

"You know the routine. The lawyer comes after we book you. Until then, sit back and enjoy the ride unless you want to tell us who's paying you to set those explosives."

Lexi returned her gaze out the windshield when Perez turned into a parking lot, discovering a collection of fire trucks in front of her hotel, dousing the smoldering remains of the fire in Charlene Ford's room. She worked the crank to lower the window to get a better look, letting in the pungent smell of smoke. It appeared the firefighters had contained the fire to Ford's room. Croft was standing near Ford's car in the parking lot, speaking to a firefighter, with an unreadable blank expression. It was impossible to know whether the outcome was positive.

Perez parked clear of the cordon and pulled Ross from the backseat by the elbow. "We'll see who's unemployed by tomorrow."

Lexi snickered and flanked Ross on the other side, gripping him by the arm across the parking lot. Croft spotted her and sprouted a grin, but Charlene was nowhere in sight. Was she dead? Injured?

When she and Perez marched Ross closer, Croft knocked on the back fender of Ford's car three times. The driver's door opened, and Charlene slid out, much to Lexi's relief. She had a bandage on her right hand. The injury reminded Lexi of her own on the forearm. The paramedic's numbing agent had worn off, and the cut had a constant dull ache.

"Here's your fire bomber," Perez said with the bitterness of disdain.

"I'm glad you made it out, Charlene." Lexi gestured toward her bandage. "Are you hurt badly?"

"It's just a minor burn," she replied.

"This one here"—Croft wagged his thumb in Charlene's direction— "insisted on saving her satchel and laptop."

"It has my notes on the Tilton trial that restarts later today. I wasn't about to start from scratch. I'd have to request a postponement, but that bully doesn't deserve to be out on bail one day longer than necessary."

Lexi appreciated Charlene's feistiness in the face of being a target for someone's unfair advantage. Her instincts told her Milo Tilton was pulling the strings, but she couldn't tie him to the killings without proof. Rusty Ross was the only link, but he wasn't talking.

Lexi tugged on Rusty's arm. "We need to get this one booked in El Paso. Our ride should be here soon." She walked him several feet from the group, forced him to sit on the ground, and pointed an index finger at his face as if training a mischievous puppy. "Stay." Returning to Charlene, Lexi lowered her voice. "I'm worried about you until Tilton's trial is over. I arranged for the Texas Rangers to keep two patrols in town until the danger has passed, but I'm afraid that won't be enough to keep you safe."

"I'll stay with her." Perez spoke in an equally hushed tone and redirected his attention to Charlene. "You can stay at my place if it's okay with you, ma'am."

"After tonight, it's more than okay."

"That makes me feel much better about leaving," Lexi said. "But even if you convict Tilton, you're still at risk until every bad actor in the sheriff's department is purged."

"Which is why I have a meeting with the state's attorney general next week to develop a game plan."

"If he needs a little push, let me know. I'll bend the governor's ear." Lexi turned to Croft. "Did our stuff survive the fire?"

"Yes, but everything might smell like a campfire."

"Thank goodness." Lexi wasn't concerned as much with her personal items as she was with the new bomb suit. It had taken Ronald months to get one delivered, and she likely wouldn't get a replacement until next year. After one clearing operation in it, she dreaded the thought of going back to her old, bulky suit.

Soon, a Texas Ranger arrived in an SUV, saying the investigation team was wrapping up at the crash site and would leave for El Paso within a half hour.

"Thanks, Sergeant Gage. It won't be long until we can get our gear." Lexi gestured toward the fire remains. "It's next door."

"It looks like you've had a rough night," Gage said.

"You don't know the half of it." Besides the fire and car bombings, she'd disarmed a pressure plate bomb and was still reeling from her mother's death. The aftermath of either was enough to floor her, but each incident, one after another, fueled her to keep going.

Lexi and Croft waited patiently for the fire department to finish soaking Charlene's old room and issue the all clear before entering their room and retrieving their belongings.

Once packed, Lexi jumped into the front passenger seat of the ranger's SUV, and Croft got into the back with Rusty Ross. Before leaving the lot, Lexi rolled down her window and flagged down Deputy Perez. "I'm sorry about the damage to your Camaro. Do you have my number?" He nodded. "Call me in a few days. You can file a claim with your insurance, and they'll go after the ATF for a settlement, or you can call me. I meant what I said. My dad restores classic muscle cars. I'll convince him to take it on as a project. We'll fix the damage for free, and if you're interested, we can restore her for the cost of the parts."

"I'll certainly call." Perez's beaming smile said his Camaro would have a spot in her father's garage for several months.

Gage headed west toward the crash site, where another Ranger SUV and the wrecker loaded with the charred remains of Croft's mangled rental car were lined up on the shoulder. He slowed and turned on his overhead lights, blocking traffic for the others to pull out and begin their trek to El Paso. Barring any complications, they should reach the ATF evidence yard by sunrise.

The route to El Paso skirted the Davis Mountains to the south. Straight and desolate, it lulled Ross asleep in the first thirty minutes and tested Lexi's ability to fight the monotony of staring at the same taillights for the last hour. The caravan had maintained equal spacing, never varying more than two miles per hour, adding to the tedium. The only respites were the occasional passing headlights of eastbound eighteen-wheelers and the uncomfortable ballistic vest she'd donned before leaving town. Croft had done the same.

A glance toward the backseat confirmed Croft was wide awake with his eyes peeled to the northern horizon and the dark shadows of the distant Guadalupe Mountains. The road behind them was dark, except for the moonlight shimmering off the solid shoulder line of the interstate like the strips of a reflective vest. The mesmerizing sight reminded Lexi of long family road trips when she was a child.

Suddenly, the line disappeared, starting fifty yards back, but it made no sense. Lexi glanced forward. The line was visible and shimmering in the headlights. She snapped her stare out the back window again. The line had disappeared, but this time starting twenty yards back. Something was gaining on them. Fast.

An alarming reality sunk in. "Incoming!"

Gage picked up the mic mounted to the dashboard. "Bogey to our six."

The SUV at the front of the caravan swung into the left lane of the two-lane highway. The wrecker gained speed. Lexi spun her head to the rear again. The bogey gained momentum, lining up its front passenger window with their backseat.

"Get down!" Lexi yelled. She crouched but kept her eyes at window level.

Croft slipped to the floorboard and grabbed at Ross' arm, but Ross threw him off. His voice was groggy. "What the—"

Automatic gunfire from a high-powered rifle erupted, piercing the back compartment. The dull plunking came at a terrifying pace, so fast Lexi couldn't determine how many shots the men had fired or how many weapons they'd used. Rapid shallow breaths threatened to make her dizzy, but she regained enough composure to draw her gun. A red light appeared in Lexi's peripheral through the windshield.

Wheels screeched against the pavement.

A crash. Metal on metal.

The gunfire stopped.

Lexi popped her head up more and shifted her sight behind their car. The driver of the lead SUV had slammed on the brakes and forced the attacking vehicle into its back bumper and tailgate. The damage was catastrophic for both cars, bringing them to a stop.

Gage slammed on the brakes, coming to a skidding halt. A quick forward check confirmed the investigation team's wrecker continued speeding away. It made sense. They were unarmed lab techs. Gage reversed and flew back to the crash, angling the SUV so the headlights shined into the attackers' vehicle when he stopped.

Gage and Lexi burst from the front doors, Croft from the back. Lexi and Croft had to circle their vehicle, while Gage had a straight line of attack. All had their weapons drawn and aimed at the attacking vehicle as they rushed forward. If the attackers survived the crash, they would have far superior firepower over the agents' handguns. Ballistic vests might not defend against their powerful bullets in close quarters.

The roadway was eerily silent as if the grim reaper had arrived to claim his latest victims. The only sounds were the tapping of Lexi's, Croft's, and Gage's feet against the highway. Gage swung around to the driver's side of the Ranger SUV its driver had used as a battering ram to check on him. Lexi and Croft paused, waiting for an answer. Glancing inside it, Lexi noted the airbags had deployed, and the driver had slumped over the wheel. She prayed his sacrifice was not the ultimate one, and the impact had merely dazed him.

Gage pulled the door open and pressed two fingers against the driver's neck. He gave a thumbs-up, signaling the officer was alive. Gage continued to push toward the attackers. Lexi and Croft resumed as well.

The group came up to the rear of the police unit. The impact had crunched the tailgate and bumper and forced them two feet into the back compartment. The attackers' car became clear. It was a new Bronco. Its front end wasn't visible and was somewhere inside the back of the Ranger SUV. The engine compartment was several feet into the front passenger area. The misshapen hood had popped open, and the windshield shattered. A body was protruding face down from it on the passenger side. The head lay at an unnatural angle, suggesting the person's neck likely broke during the crash.

The Bronco's airbags had deployed, shielding some of the car's interior from view and making it difficult in the dark to determine how many people were inside and whether they were conscious.

The driver's head moved. Then his hand.

Gage opened fire. A double tap to the scalp. It was impossible to determine if the driver had a weapon, but it didn't matter in this circumstance. All three officers reasonably feared for their lives.

Lexi was two steps ahead of Croft, so she pushed past the front passenger door and signaled him to remain there. The force of the crash had twisted it into an unusable hunk of metal. Her pulse was speeding as if she was taking a race car for a test drive and had pushed it past two hundred miles per hour. Going that fast always got her heart racing but facing probable death had it thumping so wildly she thought it would burst before she inspected the backseat. Lexi held her weapon with both hands close to her chest and peeked inside, discovering the area was empty.

Every muscle relaxed when Lexi's shoulders slumped in relief. "Clear." She stuck her head in the open front window, confirming the passenger was dead. Scanning the driver, she saw he had an automatic pistol in his right hand. Gage's shot likely saved her and Croft.

She returned to the front of the Ranger SUV with Croft while Gage tended to his injured fellow Ranger. Gage pressed the tactical radio microphone clipped to his lapel. "Dispatch, this is Romeo Eighteen. Officer injured. Major collision with two vehicles. Two DOA. I need rescue and two wreckers at my location."

"Copy Romeo Eighteen. Rolling units."

Gage turned to Lexi and Croft. "Go to the back of my rig. We need to set up flares for a quarter mile."

"I'm on it," Croft said.

Lexi helped Gage ease the injured out of the damaged vehicle once he was awake and talking. He had no apparent broken limbs or ribs, but his face was severely bruised, and he had several bloody lacerations. They walked him to Gage's SUV and guided him to the front passenger seat.

Lexi glanced in the backseat. Ross was still there, slumped in his seat. "Ross, are you okay?"

Ross coughed. His voice was thready. "I'm hit."

"Shit." Lexi scrambled to the other side to open his door. He outweighed her by at least fifty pounds, but she dragged him out of the opening. He groaned when his bottom hit the pavement. She laid him flat.

Though the headlights pointed toward the other vehicles, they provided a dim glow bright enough for Lexi to see dark spots on his clothing. She loosened it to see where the blood was coming from, but blood was everywhere. As far as she could tell, he'd been shot several times on the left side and arm. He was losing blood fast, and his face was getting paler by the second.

Lexi had but one chance to get a declaration. "This is bad, Ross. You're going to die." She grabbed him by the lapel. "Who would do this?"

Ross moaned again, coughing up blood. "Milo. I called him."

"Did he pay you to plant the bombs?"

"Yes." His voice was fading.

"Sheriff Jessup, Charlene Ford, and my rental car?"

"Yes, he wants you all gone."

"And Culter and Scooter? Did you kill them?"

"Yes, Milo told me to." Ross shook and coughed and coughed and shook, forcing Lexi's grip loose.

"The Raven? Did the Raven supply the bombs?" Lexi grabbed Rusty by the lapels again, hoping to cajole one last answer, but his body went limp, his eyes motionless. Lexi pressed two fingers on the side of his neck, checking for a pulse but found only stillness. Rusty Ross was dead.

34

Daylight threatened to break, pushing its first bands of purple and blood orange on the eastern horizon. The coming morning meant Lexi wouldn't make it to Ponder to attend the appointment at the funeral home to put into action the plans her mother had already laid out. It also meant she should let Nita know of the delay. Lexi sent a text asking her to call when she woke.

Meanwhile, she surveyed the contingency of Texas Rangers and state and FBI investigators swarming the highway. The Rangers diverted traffic while the others documented the crime scene under sets of portable lights brightening the area like a stadium. The county coroner had processed Ross' body and moved on to the dead driver. Agent Willie Lange had arrived twenty minutes ago to see the aftermath for herself.

Lexi, Croft, and Lange didn't stray far from the coroner technicians. They were looking for anything that might tell them the attackers' identity since the Bronco they were driving came back stolen from El Paso.

"I have a hit on the prints," the tech said after running the attacker's index fingerprint through the mobile scanner connected wirelessly to a nearby laptop. She rattled off his name and asked Lexi for her email address to send the perp's Texas driver's license record. The name wasn't familiar, but she and Croft would have a decent starting point to find out why they killed Ross and, more importantly, if Milo Tilton had hired them.

Lexi's phone buzzed in her pocket with an incoming call. The caller ID gave birth to a smile. "I gotta take this."

Croft acknowledged with a nod while Lange offered a finger wag.

Lexi stepped away several yards before swiping the call. "Good morning, beautiful."

"You say that because you're not here to smell my morning breath."

"After the day I've had, I'm not smelling like a bed of roses."

"How's the case going?"

"I'm going to be a lot longer than I thought." Lexi kept her explanation vague. Telling Nita she barely survived a car bombing, firebombing, and an ambush with military-grade automatic weapons in one night wouldn't serve any good. That news would have to wait until she returned to Ponder after the danger had passed.

"I figured as much when you texted last night, saying you got a hotel room."

"Can you take Dad to the funeral home later this morning?"

"We already planned on it and talked about stopping for a late breakfast in town."

Lexi harrumphed. Unless he was traveling, he never ate breakfast out. Her mother took particular pride in preparing a hot, hearty meal every morning. She'd always said, "*A good breakfast sets the tone for the day.*"

"I reacted the same way," Nita said. "Your dad has a lot of adjustment ahead of him, and cooking meals will be a big part of it. What if we sign him up for a home delivery program? That way, he's only preparing for one, and he never has to wonder what's for dinner?"

"This is why I love you." Lexi tamped down the emotion threatening to bubble over at the thought of her father eating alone at the kitchen table. From as far back as she remembered, he and her mother ate every meal together when he wasn't on the road with his NASCAR team. Even on days spent in the garage with Gavin, they would break and come inside the house for lunch. Lexi's father was so set in his ways she wasn't sure whether he could make the adjustments.

"Lexi." Croft waved her over. "They found something."

Lexi raised an index finger, asking him to wait one minute. "I gotta go, Nita. I'll text or call when I have a better idea when I might make it home."

"I love you, Lex. You can do this."

"I love you." Lexi stuffed her phone into her cargo pocket and returned to the wreckage where the coroner was working. "What do you have?"

The tech handed her a clear plastic evidence bag. "I found this in the man's breast pocket."

Lexi turned the bag to the unobstructed side opposite the chain of evidence sticker to inspect the contents. The corners of her lips turned slowly upward, forming a satisfied smile. "A raven's feather." She turned to Croft. "We're on the right track."

"This helps prove what Ross told you before he died," Croft said. "Milo Tilton hired Ross to plant the bombs, and the bombs had the Raven's calling card. Tilton must have sent the Raven after Ross. We need to bring Tilton in."

"Tilton is already on trial for murder. We need to do this right," Lange said. "Get an arrest warrant from an AUSA when they open up for business today."

"I can do one better," Lexi said, pulling out her phone. She dialed. The call connected.

"Back to task force hours?" Delanie Scott said. Her chipper voice said she'd already started her day. Her tone turned solemn. "Maxwell told me about your mother. I'm so sorry for your loss, Lexi."

"Thank you, Delanie. It was a shock for all of us." Lexi took a deep, calming breath, forcing herself to focus and not give in to the heartache lurking over her shoulder. "I'm calling because I need your help on the Raven case."

"Of course. What do you need?"

Lexi told her about the previous day's series of events, leaving out her minor injury and how her inattention made her miss the bomb in her car. "With Ross' roadside dying declaration, can you get us an arrest warrant and a search warrant for Tilton's home, office, and vehicles? The evidence we've collected points to the Raven supplying the bombs and the ghost gun in the judge's killing. When we pick up Tilton for murder, we can squeeze him into telling us how to find the Raven."

"When do you need them?"

"We're just under two hours away from Harrington. Can you get it by then?"

"You're lucky I'm sleeping with a federal judge's clerk. Give me a second." Delanie's voice muffled for several words before she returned to the call. "We'll wake Judge Russel in an hour. You'll have them by the time you hit town."

"Thanks, Delanie. I appreciate your help. What's the best deal you're willing to offer him?"

"You tell me. You taught me murderers never walk."

Lexi didn't have to think about her response. Milo Tilton had six bodies at his feet, and he'd tried to kill her and Croft with the present Ross left in their rental car. There was only one option. "Life instead of death."

"Then we're in agreement," Delanie said.

⸻

Milo had a decision to make before finishing breakfast at his kitchen table. His trial resumed in two hours, but the district judge appointed by the governor to replace Judge Cook wasn't on Milo's payroll. And his squeaky-clean record made him unbribable and a wildcard in the trial's outcome. If Milo stayed and got convicted, the Raven might consider his incarceration violating the rule. If he fled, he could pay for a new identity and outrun the Raven and the law.

He sipped his coffee and swallowed the last bit of the scrambled eggs he'd whipped up on the stove, deciding his best chance at survival was running. His lawyer, Jackson Price, would arrive in an hour for court, but Milo would use the time to pack what he needed to embark on a new life.

Four suitcases, he thought. More would be hard to track and might draw suspicion. Milo packed for every season, hoping to survive long enough to break out each variety. Toiletries, medications, wall chargers, and his night-stand tablet rounded out his upstairs packing. After lugging each suitcase to his SUV in the garage in three trips, he brought a leather backpack to his home office for the essentials.

Once Milo removed the floorboards covering the in-ground safe, he emptied its contents. He placed fifty thousand dollars, the last of his emergency cash, the ledgers from his side business at the detention center, and a loaded .38 revolver into the backpack. He couldn't think about leaving without grabbing one last essential, his last bottle of twenty-five-year-old scotch.

Once he'd safely stowed the bottle in the pack with the other items, Milo looked about the room, considering the possessions he'd amassed. The books, paintings, furniture, and cigars were all disposable. Cigars? We'll maybe not them. Milo scooped a handful from the box and added them to his bag, deciding he was ready to disappear.

The doorbell rang. Milo checked the time on his phone. Jackson was a few minutes early.

Red and blue overhead lights had cleared the sparse early morning eastbound highway traffic, creating a clear path to Harrington. Willie Lange made excellent time behind the wheel of the ATF tactical SUV from the El Paso field office. Somehow, she'd found a radio station disc jockey in far west Texas with enough guts to play Captain and Tennille and Barry Manilow back-to-back. Lange was in music heaven. Lexi likened it to hell but abided by the unspoken rule of road trips: the driver chooses the music.

Ten minutes from Harrington, Lexi checked her phone for messages again but still hadn't received anything from Delanie about the arrest warrant. Different scenarios spun in her head, explaining the delay, ranging from falling asleep on the couch waiting for the hour to pass to falling back between the sheets with her latest love interest.

"Come up for air, for heaven's sake," Lexi whispered, still staring at her phone, when a notification popped onto her screen, saying she'd received an email from Delanie. A satisfied grin formed when she read the subject line. "We have the warrants," Lexi announced.

"It's about time." Lange shifted taller in her seat and increased their speed. Tilton was due in court soon, so it was a race to get to him before the proceedings began. "I'm anxious to see this dirtbag in cuffs."

"Me too. I've had too many close calls because of him." Lexi had accepted the dangers associated with the job the first day she'd put on the blast suit, but she was concerned her death might have a devastating impact on Nita and her father. Nita would be heartbroken, but she was young enough to fall in love again. But her father was a different story. He lost his best friend of forty-five years last month and his wife of forty years two days ago. If he lost his only child so close to those deaths, Lexi was sure it would destroy him. He would never rebound, and Nita might find him dead in his bed from an overdose to escape the pain. Lexi needed to stay alive for his sake, which in turn meant Milo Tilton needed to go to prison.

Croft leaned forward from the back, extending his head into the gap between the two front row seats. "I'll flip you two for the back door."

"You must be certain he's going to run," Lange said.

"Aren't you?"

Considering the rapid unfolding of last night's events, Tilton had to sense Lexi and Croft closing in. If the man had any sense, he'd already be in the wind. But if there was a chance he was still in his home, Nathan deserved to put the cuffs on. He'd been hunting the Raven the longest.

"It's yours if you want it," Lexi said.

Passing farms, ranches, and oil fields, they reached the outskirts of Harrington. Lange turned off their overhead lights to not attract attention. Otherwise, a member of the Rat Pack might alert Tilton to their presence. The FBI team from Midland recruited to assist in the search of Tilton's home was standing by at a coffee shop less than a mile from the house. Lexi sent the team leader a text alerting them to meet there in fifteen minutes.

The houses in town were primarily older craftsman-style like Charlene Ford's and modular homes in rows for the oil workers. Then there was Milo Tilton's home. It rivaled any million-dollar home in Dallas and was on a lot big enough to hold a Dallas Cowboys scrimmage game.

Lange pulled into Tilton's circular driveway made of brick pavers in a herringbone pattern. It was a pricey addition, likely paid for from the illegal under-the-table money from the prison labor scheme he'd run for years. A dark Mercedes sedan was parked near the front entrance at the driveway's apex. A man dressed in a high-priced, tailored suit emerged from it when the driver's door opened. He directed his gaze toward Lange's official SUV when she parked behind him. Lexi recognized the man as Tilton's lawyer.

Lexi, Lange, and Croft opened their car doors and exited in an unplanned, synchronized show of force. Jackson Price stepped toward them, pursing his lips tightly, telling her he suspected something was awry. "May I help you, Agent Mills?" Remembering her name suggested Lexi had presented a clear and present threat to his client when they met at the restaurant.

"You're Milo Tilton's lawyer, right?"

"Yes." Price glued his attention to Croft, who took off in a jog toward the back of the house.

Lexi snapped her fingers in front of Price's nose to get his attention. She showed him the images of the arrest and search warrants on her cell phone. "We have warrants for your client's arrest and to search his home and cars. Is he inside?"

"I believe so." Price kept his focus on Lexi's phone, reading the specifics of the documents. His prominent Adam's apple bobbed up and down to a hard swallow.

"Do you have a key to his home?"

"Whether I do is none of your business. It's not my role to help you arrest my client."

"Then I'll need you to step aside until we have him in custody."

Price bowed, waving his hand dramatically. His smugness screamed *shyster*.

Lexi and Lange approached the front door and rang the bell. "Federal agents. Open the door," Lexi yelled. They waited for a thirty-count before ringing again. After the next count, Lexi and Lange drew their duty weapons and prepared to break down the door.

Lexi's phone rang. It was Croft. "Please tell me you have him," she said.

"Yep," Croft replied with a satisfied chuckle. "His suitcase got caught on the sliding glass door rail."

Charlene Ford positioned the tablet at the head of her conference table so all meeting participants could see the screen. "Can you hear me, Ms. Scott?"

"Loud and clear, Ms. Ford. Thank you for the use of your conference room." Delanie was well-dressed and appeared ready to make Milo Tilton wish he'd never crossed paths with this hard-nosed prosecutor in the video call.

"It's a pleasure after the long night I've had," Ford said. "If there's a chance of wrapping up both our cases in one meeting, I'm up for it, but the judge in Tilton's trial issued only an hour postponement."

"That should be plenty of time." Delanie's eyes shifted on the screen. "I see everyone is in place."

Milo Tilton was beside his lawyer across the table, wringing his hands. His pale, clammy complexion made him look as nervous as a first-time expectant father in the waiting room. Lange was standing in a corner to observe the questioning about to begin. Lexi and Croft sat on the same side of the table as Charlene.

"Mr. Price, your client is under arrest for..." Delanie detailed the crimes they suspected him of, starting with the murder for hire of Judge Cook and ending with the attempted murder of Rusty Ross. Lexi had convinced her to not reveal Ross' death until they had Tilton's cooperation. "Ms. Ford and I are prepared to offer your client a chance of escaping a death sentence, including the one associated with murdering his wife."

"I have yet to hear any evidence implicating my client." Jackson Price shifted in his chair. If the motion had been smooth, Lexi would have suspected he had an ace up his sleeve. But the movement was jerky and stiff, telling her he felt cornered.

Lexi slid her phone across the table to Price and Tilton, displaying a picture of Rusty Ross sitting very much alive in a law enforcement SUV with a Texas Ranger guarding him. "As you can see, last night's attack on our transport missed its target." Lexi neglected to clarify she'd taken the picture before the attack and Rusty was currently lying in a morgue. "He's very talkative and in a place where you can't get to him. We know you paid him to do your dirty work. We can tie you to six deaths and the attempts on my life with the car bomb. We know about the Raven. You tell us what we want to know and live the rest of your life in a protective wing of a federal prison. Or you take your chances in a state that puts murderers to death after we've had our swing at you."

The muscles in Tilton's jaw visibly rippled. "I knew I couldn't trust him." His outburst brought him halfway to a confession.

"Then tell me about the Raven," Lexi said.

Price tugged on Tilton's arm, drawing him closer for a private conversation. Between the head shaking and bursting neck veins, Lexi was sure she had him. Price turned his attention to Lexi. "We'll need an assurance of a protective wing."

"You have it," Delanie said. "We'll house him in a supermax, where his only interaction will be with the guards. But he confesses to all counts in writing and provides Agents Mills and Croft everything he knows about the arms dealer known as the Raven."

"Then we have a deal," Price said. "Tell them, Milo."

"I called the Raven with a burner phone..." Tilton detailed his conversations with the Raven, the weapons he provided, the amounts and methods of payment using Swiss accounts, and the meeting location in Carlsbad where he picked up the items.

"How did you contact the Raven when you were in jail?" Lexi asked.

"Rusty brought me the burner."

Lexi slid an evidence bag containing a flip phone Croft had found in the backpack Tilton was carrying when he cuffed him. "This phone?"

"Yes."

"How did you first learn of the Raven and get his number?" Those were the big money questions. The answers could tell Lexi and Croft how to infiltrate the Raven's inner workings.

"Devon Hastings, the first federal inspector assigned to oversee my detention facility. I paid him regularly to not ask questions and to bury complaints into the detainee labor contracts with the local business owners. Years ago, I had a problem with a rancher who threatened to tell the state attorney general about our operation if I didn't cut him in. I told Devon. He told me he knew a guy called the Raven and how to reach him."

"And how was that?"

"Get on Facebook and post in the Motivational Quotes public group. I had to embed the number to a burner phone in the first three paragraphs and hashtag the post with the word 'nevermore.' A man using a blocked number called two days later. He told me to drive to a rest stop on I-10 and sit on a particular bench. A burly man in a dark suit showed up. He took a photo of my driver's license. Before he left, he said they would be in touch if I pass. I guess I did because a week later, the Raven called." Milo went on, describing the type of explosive the Raven had provided to eliminate the problematic rancher.

"Is there anything else?"

"About a month later, the Raven contacted me on the burner phone, asking me to provide him two foreign national detainees from my facility who would be amenable to working with him. I did it in exchange for a future favor, which I cashed in for the ghost gun." Tilton supplied the names.

Lexi slid another evidence bag across the table. It contained his business ledger with names, dates, and amounts of every payoff he'd made to everyone involved in this illegal labor scheme. She tapped an index finger on it. "Every person in this book will try to make a deal. If I later discover you've lied about any of this, your stay in the protective wing will end, and we'll throw you into gen pop."

Tilton's eyes darted, suggesting he was reconsidering his statement, but he remained silent.

Lexi removed the burner phone from the evidence bag and placed it in the center of the table. "Set up a meeting with the Raven."

Lexi's chest filled with excitement when Tilton lifted the phone. If the Raven answered and agreed to meet, she could soon have Kris Faust's killer behind bars.

Tilton dialed, placing the call on speakerphone.

"Yes, Mr. Tilton." The Raven's deep and slow voice hissed on the letter S. Lexi recalled the drawing of the Raven she had on her office wall, reproducing every feature in her head. His voice matched his thin pale face, high cheekbones, long dark stringy hair, and bloodred eyes to a T.

"I need your services again."

"I have other clients who require my attention, Mr. Tilton."

"But I need to take out one more car tonight. Otherwise, everything I've planned will be ruined."

"All right, Mr. Tilton. Come to the park at sunset. I'll text you the exact location after you arrive."

The call disconnected.

Tilton stared at Lexi with a pale, blank expression. "You had better catch him. If you don't, I'm as good as dead."

35

The downward slope of the winding path leading to the viewing level of the migrating bats at Carlsbad Cavern National Park was torture on Lexi's leg after the previous thirty-four hours she'd experienced. The angle of descent placed additional pressure on her residual limb at the bottom of her prosthetic's socket, rubbing the already tender nub in a not so nice way. Each step hurt more than the last, but Lexi wasn't about to give in to the pain when she and Croft could have the Raven in custody within minutes.

Nathan Croft politely slowed his pace to match hers. "You gonna make it, Mills?"

"I'll be fine." Or at least she hoped.

The setting sun invited lower temperatures into the fifties, muting the fragrant smell of the well-kept flora lining the trail. Lexi zipped her jacket higher to the collar, taking care not to hit the microphone hidden underneath it. The small tear on her left sleeve brought back the memory of leaping from the moving rental car seconds before it exploded in flames from a bomb built by the man she and Croft were there to meet. She would take great pleasure in cuffing his hands and reading him his rights.

Lexi recognized two people on the way down as members of the Midland FBI team who had searched Milo Tilton's home and cars earlier in the day. Without knowing the exact meeting location, the park was too big for Lexi, Croft, and Lange to provide containment, so the entire FBI crew of eight agents caravanned and took up positions in the park an hour ago to help take down the Raven.

When Lexi reached the bottom of the hill, she pulled out Milo Tilton's burner phone and typed out a text message to the Raven's number. *Here.* "Now we wait."

"This has been a hell of a few days," Croft said. "I can't remember the last time I've been on the run like this." He locked his stare on the mesmerizing stream of bats swirling from the brush-covered cave, creating a spotted black trail in the darkening sky.

Lexi snorted, recalling the months she'd spent chasing Tony Belcher and the Gatekeepers. Some days seemed like they would never end as she'd crisscrossed the Southwest while chasing leads and staying in front of threats. "The closer we get to the Raven might mean days like these will be commonplace."

"If that's what it takes, then so be it."

The burner phone buzzed with an incoming text message. Lexi read it and said clearly into the tactical microphone hidden under her jacket collar, "Picnic area eight. Teams on the exits, remain in place. The rest converge on area eight slowly. Do not attract attention."

Lange and the FBI agents acknowledged. Lexi and Croft followed the signage along the sparsely lit trail to the appropriate picnic area. They passed two men heading up the hill from the opposite direction. Lexi gave them a close inspection, but neither man resembled the drawing of the Raven.

The trail narrowed after the turnoff. Lexi and Croft drew their duty weapons, holding them at the low ready position. The way was dark without the lights from the main path. The sound of chirping crickets was prevalent in every direction.

The crack of a twig brought Lexi to a stop and sharpened her senses. She focused intently, searching for any clue that might give away the Raven's location. She inhaled, hoping to take in a stray scent of aftershave. She cocked her head, expecting to hear rustling in the shrubs. She squinted to zoom her stare on the shadows in the tree line, waiting to discern the silhouette of the Raven. But she neither saw, heard, nor smelled a single clue.

Croft resumed his slow walk. Lexi followed.

The deeper they went into the picnic area, the darker their surroundings became, giving the advantage to someone who might be already there and hiding. The hairs on the back of Lexi's neck tingled when she realized she was a sitting duck. She and Croft lined up back-to-back in the center of four picnic tables, scanning the brush and trees while keeping their weapons trained on their line of sight.

"I have nothing," Croft said.

"Same." Lexi shifted her visual search from looking for the Raven to looking for his calling card. In the near darkness, the outline of an object protruding from the grated tabletop came into view. Its dark color made it nearly impossible to focus on, so Lexi walked closer. Two steps away, she knew the Raven had been here. His calling card taunted her, saying he was as free as a bird and couldn't be caught.

Lexi snatched the feather by the tip from its perch. "He was here." She pressed her mic. "All teams. Check all adults before letting them leave the park." Lexi turned to Croft. "We need to review the surveillance video."

Jogging up the hill was much kinder to Lexi's tender leg than going down. The ache was more manageable, allowing her to make better time with her muscular legs. However, her fast pace made it difficult for Croft to keep up, so she slowed three-quarters of the way up to match his pace.

"I gotta get in better shape." Croft sucked in air at a rapid pace, but he was underselling himself. A steep hill like this would challenge anyone not at the top of their game. Lexi's only advantage was her ever-present drive to prove her disability wasn't a deficiency.

At the top, the visitor's center lights brightened their path. They went inside and spoke to a security guard in a blue uniform near the entrance. She directed them to an employee-only door past the information desk. The security office was at the end of the brightly lit corridor. Lexi and Croft entered, finding one guard on duty, monitoring the surveillance feeds. The room was outdated with older equipment but neat and orderly.

Lexi held up her badge and credentials. "We're ATF Agents Mills and

Croft. We've tracked a suspect here and are checking every adult exiting the park. We need to check your surveillance recordings for today."

"I'll have to radio my supervisor." Lexi nodded and waited while he retrieved a portable radio from its charger. "Sergeant Banks, this is Officer Moore. I have two ATF agents here. They want to review our security feeds."

"Let them," Banks said over the air. "I'll be right there."

Lexi leaned over the guard's shoulder. "Do you have a camera on picnic area eight?"

"Yes. We have them on every site."

"I need you to bring up the feed and reverse it until I say stop."

"You got it." The guard punched several commands into his keyboard, bringing up the recordings of the area. He reversed the images at triple speed, slowing when Lexi and Croft appeared on the screen.

"Continue," Lexi said. "I want to see who was there before us."

Several minutes of recording time flew past. If not for the occasional rustle of leaves in the wind and a passing rabbit searching for food, the image would have appeared still. When the running timestamp hit twelve minutes before Lexi and Croft had arrived at the site, a man dressed in black emerged from the bushes, walking backward, meaning he'd used that route to leave. He was tall and thin, but his wide-brimmed hat blocked his face. Before leaving, the man had placed the feather where Lexi had found it.

The recording continued to reverse, showing the man had first stood directly in front of the security camera when he arrived. He held up a piece of paper with a typed message, careful not to show his entire face, only his glowing red eyes. The statement read, "You have tapped at my chamber door. I'm coming for you, Agent Mills."

36

Fifty hours after leaving Ponder, Lexi finally turned onto the long gravel road leading up to her parents' house. *Parents*, she thought. She was thirty-five years old, and this was the only home her parents had lived in. It would always be her mother and father's home, though her mother wasn't alive to enjoy it. However, calling it her parents' house would conjure up the painful memory of watching Nita bring her back to life, only to lose her hours later. But referring to it as her father's would, in a way, erase the memory of her mother. She settled on two words: the house. The phrase was safe, simple, and something she could say without falling apart.

The totality of the investigation hit Lexi like a brick wall when the outline of the house appeared. She'd been on the go almost the entire time, inspecting wreckage, clearing pressure bombs, jumping from exploding cars, driving in a high-speed pursuit, dodging bullets in a deadly highway ambush, arresting suspects, and chasing ghosts.

The hour's nap on the plane from Midland wasn't nearly enough sleep, leaving Lexi beyond exhausted. She needed to put something into her stomach, stand under a hot shower for several long minutes, and crawl into bed and into Nita's arms. But comfort would have to wait. When she passed the side of the house, she noticed the left garage door was open, signaling her father was up and tinkering.

234   BRIAN SHEA & STACY LYNN MILLER

After parking under the shade tree, Lexi circled to the back of her SUV to retrieve her bags. The screen door at the back porch creaked, drawing Lexi's attention. While seeing her wife walking out was as soothing as a long, tender kiss, not having her mother there to greet her saddened Lexi. Unless her mother was in the shower, she trekked out the back door every time Lexi wandered over for a visit. Lexi's melancholy settled in her chest and throat at the thought that visits here would never be the same.

While the tailgate rose at a slow, steady pace, Nita approached. Each step closer pumped more energy into Lexi's weary body. They exchanged no words when Nita wrapped her arms around Lexi's torso. Lexi shed no tears when she pulled Nita tight. The rejuvenating embrace made it seem like the two-day barrage of harrowing events had never happened. Almost.

Nita pulled back. Her wrinkled brow meant she was worried. "I have breakfast warming in the oven."

Lexi closed her eyes briefly, sighing at how good a full stomach would feel. "That sounds wonderful, but I want to check on Dad first."

"It will keep until you're ready." Nita grabbed the overnight bag and backpack from the rear compartment of Lexi's SUV. "What about your gear? I'm not sure if I can lift it."

"Thank you, but leave it. I'll take it to the office tomorrow. Before you go inside, I need something." Lexi coaxed Nita to drop the bags, eased her chin up with a hand, and pressed their lips together in a long, gentle kiss. It hadn't the hunger typical between newlyweds, but instead gratitude for Nita's kindness, devotion, and patience. Lexi couldn't have spent the last two days chasing killers and the Raven if Nita wasn't here watching her father. She let the kiss linger without deepening it to stress her point until Nita released a faint moan. "Thank you for being here for Dad."

Nita stroked Lexi's cheek with a finger and offered a closed-mouth smile as her initial reply. "It's called love." She picked up the bags and retreated into the house, leaving Lexi to discover whether her father was still devastated.

Lexi walked gingerly toward the garage, feeling more swelling in her residual limb than she typically experienced following a short flight. It made her leg extra tender, but she was sure once she doffed her prosthetic, showered, and got off her feet, it would return to normal.

The faint sound of country music playing on the radio grew louder when she passed the open-door threshold. The lights over the last bay were on, and the Shelby's hood was up. Her father was near the front bumper, staring into the engine compartment. He'd folded one arm across his prominent belly, propping up the other with its elbow bent while he tapped the side of his face with his fingers. He assumed that posture only when something stumped him.

Lexi considered asking him how he was holding up, but he was never one to talk openly about his emotions. Instead, he spoke of memories and told stories about his entertaining and annoying friends and family members who were gone. The best way to show her love and concern was to join him in his world.

She stepped up to the bumper and joined him in gazing at the engine. The protective mat over the fender and the collection of tools on it and nearby on the polished concrete suggested he'd been there for a while. "What seems to be the problem?"

"A ticking noise started yesterday."

"The oil is fine, so that's not it," Lexi said. "Plugs?"

"They looked dirty, so I changed them, but she still ticks."

"Valves or lifters?"

Her father waved his hand over the collection of loose tools. The valve spring compressor was a dead giveaway that he'd checked and ruled out the valves.

"Ahh. Gaskets?"

"Nope. And before you ask, the pulleys and belts are all new. Gavin and I replaced them months ago."

"Hmm." Lexi rubbed the back of her neck, her tell the mystery had her stumped. Few likely causes remained. "Is the ticking steady? Or does it increase in speed when you rev the engine?"

"It speeds up."

"It could be an exhaust or manifold leak. Is the noise louder on one side of the manifold?"

"No, it's an equal opportunity annoyance."

Lexi snickered. "It could be a rod knock."

Her father snapped his fingers together. "Rod knock. Gavin would have had this diagnosed within an hour. Why didn't I think of it?"

"Because Gavin was meticulous. He tracked down problems by following the anatomy of the subject. You attack problems more willy-nilly."

"Willy-nilly?" He formed fists and placed them on his hips. "I am not willy-nilly." He added a playful wink because every mechanic who ever stepped foot in a Jerry Mills garage knew Gavin was the one who kept the place organized, not him. "Nita said you left Harrington empty-handed. I'm sorry, Peanut."

"This guy is smart and will be hard to catch."

"I have faith in you. If anyone can catch him, it's you."

Lexi yawned, sensing her exhaustion winning. "I'd love to stay and help you, but I need to eat and get a few hours of sleep."

His eyes shifted left and right, and he exhaled a deep, ragged breath. "Are you heading back to Dallas?" It was clear. He wasn't ready to be alone.

"If it's okay with you, Nita and I thought we could stay here for a while."

"I'd like that." Her father sniffled and wiped his nose with a shop rag. "You best not keep Nita waiting. Happy wife, happy life."

"I love you, Dad." Lexi wrapped her arms around his round midsection and pressed her head against his chest. When he threw his arms around her, she expected him to squeeze tight and give her one of his feet-lifting bear hugs. Instead, he quivered. Quiet sobs accompanied pained intakes of air, cutting Lexi to the core. Her father had experienced many setbacks in his life, but he never fell apart and let nothing defeat him. But grief this deep was winning. He needed to know he wasn't alone. "We'll stay until you get sick and tired of us."

The quaking stopped. Her father cleared his throat and released his hold. "You and Nita are family. I'll never tire of you two." He wiped his nose again and returned to the mysterious ticking. "Come back and give your old man a hand when you wake up."

Lexi acknowledged him with a two-finger salute and headed into the house. As promised, Nita had waffles, bacon, and eggs warming in the oven. Doing breakfast right with butter, syrup, and Tabasco sauce seemed time-consuming when Lexi was already fighting to stay awake. She made a breakfast sandwich out of everything and filled a glass with water. Ascending the stairs, she took a bite. Bacon in this house may have been a regular staple, but it was also sacred, something to be savored. But she was too tired and hungry to eat slowly. When she reached the bedroom door, she was on her third bite.

Nita had Lexi's overnight bag open on the bed and held the jacket Lexi had on the night she escaped the car bombing. When the floorboards under Lexi's feet creaked, she looked up and held out the garment. "There's blood. Were you hurt?"

Lexi rolled up the sleeve on her left arm, surprised the temporary stitches the EMT gave her that night had held. "It's just a scratch."

Nita placed the jacket on the suitcase before inspecting Lexi's wound. "A scratch needing six stitches." Worry was in her eyes.

"I'm fine. Can we talk about it later? I'd like to shower and get some sleep."

"I'm holding you to it." Nita gave her a stern look, saying she meant it. "Your night clothes and a change of underwear are in the bathroom."

"Thank you." Lexi kissed her on the forehead and took another large bite of her sandwich before going into the bathroom. The rest of the food would have to wait until she showered.

Removing her prosthetic was relieving but peeling off her clothes and standing beneath the stream of hot, pulsating water was utterly unburdening. Washing away the dirt, sweat, and grime from the last two days marked the end. She could finally put the events behind her and focus on the gem Milo Tilton had laid at her feet—a way into the Raven's world.

Refreshed but still exhausted, Lexi opened the bathroom door, expecting to see her wife sorting through her dirty clothes, but this incredible sight was infinitely better. It made her swallow the last bite of her sandwich nearly whole. Nita was across the room at the dresser where she'd taken over several drawers for her clothes. She'd taken off her jeans, shirt, and bra and was slipping on her night tank top with her arms above her head. Her back was to the door but angled enough to provide a delicious silhouette of a breast.

Each movement was graceful, mesmerizing, and sexy as hell. Averting her eyes was impossible. Nothing could force her stare away. Lexi hoped to surprise her, but the floorboard creaked one step into the room with her prosthetic, announcing her return. Nita craned her neck while letting the tank top slide past her breasts and dangle to her waist.

"Feel better?" Nita asked.

"Much." Lexi let her gaze drift to Nita's most tantalizing parts. Despite being covered, they held her attention in the most carnal way. "If I'd known there was going to be a show, I would have been out faster."

"I thought I would nap with you."

"I would love that." Lexi sat on her side of the bed, doffed her prosthetic, and placed it upright between the bed and the nightstand.

Nita joined Lexi when she slipped under the covers. Instead of lying flat, she sat with her back against the headboard. "Before you sleep, I have something for you."

Lexi shimmied her bottom backward and matched Nita's posture against the wood. Nita silently handed her an unsealed envelope with Lexi's name handwritten on the front. The writing was her mother's.

"What is it?" Lexi asked.

"I found it when I was going through your mother's things by her chair in the living room. I only read the first paragraph, but I think it's what she wanted to give you after the wedding. If you want some privacy, I can wait in the hallway."

She squeezed Nita's hand. "Stay." If this proved half as emotional as Lexi suspected, she would need Nita's steadiness.

Lexi turned the envelope over, looking for more writing, but it was blank. She then ran her fingertips reverently over the front. This might have been the last thing her mother wrote before she died. The pages within represented her inner thoughts on her final day, and the prospect of reading them had Lexi frozen. Once she read them, there would be nothing more to learn from her mother.

Lexi opened the envelope carefully and pulled out a single sheet of stationery. Unfolding it, she remembered why she always liked her mother's penmanship. Every word was like a piece of art with fluid, smooth strokes. This had the same appeal.

The letter had the date of the wedding and started with, *Dear Daughter.*

Lexi drew Nita's hand close to her chest, feeling another wave of grief building. She continued to read.

Today is your wedding day. This is the day I'd prayed for since I first held you in my arms. I wished you the same happiness I shared with your father, a sense of peace that could only be found by walking through life with your true love.

I couldn't be prouder of the woman your father and I give away today. Watching you grow from the daredevil little girl to the sometimes rebellious teenager to a confident, strong woman has been a blessing. You have the grit of a survivor, the patience of a saint, and the humility that comes with being self-assured.

Knowing you have found a partner with those same qualities makes this day even more special. Nita is your perfect match. You both are caring, independent women who complement the other's strengths and forgive the other's weaknesses without judgment. You both are ready for marriage and all it brings.

I give warm wishes to you and Nita as you experience all the joys and face all the sorrows life offers. I have no doubt your love will sparkle, and I am grateful to have a front-row seat to watch your life together unfold.

My love for you is always and forever. Mother.

Blinding tears made it impossible to return the letter to its home in the envelope, but Nita took it. Lexi didn't want to lose sight of her mother's last words to her, but she was sure it was safe. Nita was the keeper of her heart and would care for it as if it were a sacred scroll.

The wave of grief crashed the instant Nita let go of her hand. Lexi felt alone, floating in a sea threatening to lose her in its vastness unless someone latched onto her. Nita quickly returned and held her tight in her arms, keeping her anchored and reaffirming her mother's words. She and Nita were perfect for each other. No matter what life threw at her, Lexi was certain she would get through it because Nita was by her side.

EPILOGUE

Prison had reduced Milo Tilton's world to a seven-foot-by-twelve-foot room made of concrete and metal twenty-three hours a day. Even the stool, desk, and bed—anything of substantial size an inmate could use to incapacitate a guard—were constructed of hard, cold concrete.

The toilet-sink combination unit was a joke. It worked but provided enough water pressure barely sufficient for a Barbie house. The automated cell shower wasn't any better, and he could use it only three times a week. The soap was bland and antiseptic. How he missed the woodsy undertones of his body wash and shampoo.

His only entertainment comprised the books and writing paper he could buy at the commissary and a small black and white television with limited access to educational and recreational shows. His only connections to the world were a small meal slot on the metal door and a three-foot-high by four-inch-wide window, his only way of telling time and whether it was night or day.

A month of incarceration was long enough to get down the routine and know when to expect his meals and one hour of recreation out of his cell. Most days, guards escorted him to the "pit" as he'd heard another prisoner refer to a small windowless gym area resembling an empty swimming pool with a pull-up bar. Once each week, the guards took him to a cage in an outdoor courtyard when the weather cooperated. Each eight-foot-tall pen was big enough for Milo to walk ten paces lengthwise and thirty-one steps in a circle, but walking wasn't the chief attraction. A sixteen-foot-tall grid of wood beams and fencing covered the area, but he still had a clear view of the sky. Today should be his one hour of bliss in the cage.

Like clockwork, the guard removed his breakfast tray from the service slot, prompting Milo to start a half-hour home improvement show on the television. When it ended, he stood near the door, rocking on his heels. One minute later, the solid outer door opened, revealing his three-guard escort through the barred inner door.

"Right on time, fellas.".

"Jacket," one said. Milo grinned, anticipating his hour in the sun.

After putting on his prison-issued peacoat, another guard said in a flat tone, "Hands and feet, inmate." This one was all business, never saying a word beyond instructions. Milo extended his hands before his feet through slots in the bars to receive the handcuffs and ankle shackles. He stepped close to the bars, allowing the guard to attach the belly chain.

Milo had memorized the number of left and right turns to the cages but not the number of steps. Sadly, that would come over time, punctuating his mundane existence. One step outside, he inhaled the cold air. He wasn't sure of his exact location, but the frost on his window in the morning meant he wasn't in a southern or west coast state.

Once inside the cage, Milo sat on the concrete, removed one tennis shoe to use as a pillow, and laid on his back with his knees bent. The guards retreated underneath an overhang and leaned against the wall.

Clouds were out today, blocking the sun, but he wasn't about to complain. The brisk air and natural light were a treat. He watched the billowy bodies slowly roll past overhead, trying to make out what they resembled as he used to do as a kid.

Soon, a dark object floated high overhead, circling like a bird searching for prey. It remained at altitude for several rotations. *Pathetic*, Milo thought. He was jealous of a bird, coming and going wherever it pleased. Those days were over for him, but he took solace in knowing he'd never go hungry and wouldn't end up as another animal's kill like the bird flying with the clouds. He would die a decrepit old man in his concrete cage.

The bird completed another circle before going into a nosedive. It had found something to feast on. At least Milo's feathered friend would have a full belly today. His little buddy continued to dive and gain speed. Gunshots rang out from outside the courtyard. Milo assumed the guard snipers were taking potshots at the hawk, or whatever breed of bird was barreling toward the ground, but they missed.

Then.

The bird struck the fence wire overhead at high speed, spraying liquid inside the cage and soaking Milo. He spat and blinked away the gasoline-smelling liquid. In an instant, Milo realized he should have known he wouldn't be safe, even here. He was the prey. He raised his hands over his head, shaking like a newborn baby right out of the womb. Two words slipped past Milo's lips before the bird exploded in a fiery ball. "The Raven."

Returning to Midland was the best decision Jackson Price had made in years. He was starting over but not from scratch. Thanks to Thatcher, his law school roommate, one of the town's most prestigious firms hired him. He was bottom rung among the associates, but it was better than unemployment. His hourly rate was comparable to what he charged in Harrington, but this job didn't come with the perks he earned while working for Milo Tilton. Milo had paid enough under the table to force Jackson into cooking his books and making the IRS think he had twice the clients. That kind of money was hard to hide. Living without it meant radical adjustments to his lifestyle until he could claw his way up to a partnership, but thankfully his buddy would carry him for a while, especially on Saturdays, to rub elbows with the partners.

Jackson pulled into an unmarked parking space near the back of the Midland Golf and Racquet Club parking lot. Management had reserved the spaces in the first three rows for their VIPs and gold and platinum members who paid extra for a close parking spot. He was several years away from affording one of those status symbols.

After popping open his trunk, Jackson shouldered his golf bag and slogged it to the racks in front of the clubhouse like a caddie right out of high school. He spotted the two partners with whom he and Thatcher were slated to tee off within thirty minutes near the row of fresh carts but not Thatcher. He was likely inside the pro shop signing for the cart he and Jackson were supposed to share.

Jackson went inside, discovering Thatcher at the counter. He stepped beside him. "Morning, Hef. Thanks for inviting me today."

"No problem, Jackson. You can be my guest until you get your membership sorted out." Thatcher accepted the cart key and walked with Jackson toward the door. "Oh, and cool it with the nickname. The new partners are wound a little tight."

"So they might frown on you running through women like Hugh Hefner at the Playboy Mansion." Jackson placed a hand on Thatcher's shoulder, recalling the memory of the parade of women that went through their dorm room and him occasionally enjoying the sloppy seconds. "No problem, buddy. Your history is safe with me."

They loaded their clubs into the cart and joined the partners on the driving range. The introductions were brief, but one partner inspected him with a critical eye. "I understand you had a practice in Harrington and represented Milo Tilton at his murder trial."

"Yes, I did on both counts."

"I wouldn't call pleading guilty for life in prison a win." The partner was fishing. Milo's trial was headline news after the courtroom murder. While the pleading in federal court was closed to the public, the one in county court for the murder of his wife was not. On the surface, the change in plea looked like a complete collapse in defense, which it was, but not for the reason the partner might have suspected.

"Considering what my client faced, he chose the path of least resistance, and I couldn't disagree with his decision."

The partner harrumphed, took his driver from his bag, and proceeded to an open bay on the range.

Following their warm-up, Jackson joined Thatcher at their cart and prepared for the round by digging out three fresh golf balls from the main pouch of his bag and marking them with the dollar sign symbol. It was a childish play on his last name, but he'd used the mark for decades and wasn't about to change things up.

While driving up to the first tee, Thatcher glanced at Jackson. "These two play loose with the rules."

"At ten dollars a hole for skins, it better not be too loose." Jackson shook his head, hoping to reel in a little extra cash today.

At the tee box, the partners took honors by hitting first. Both their balls were in play but not before narrowly escaping danger. One bounced out of a fairway bunker, while the other hit a tree about 150 yards out and kicked sideways. Thatcher hit away, his ball landing about two-thirty out on the left side of the fairway.

"Nice shot, Thatcher." Jackson winked. It was odd not calling him Hef on the course.

While the others waited at the back of the tee box, leaning on their drivers, Jackson stuck his long tee in the ground one foot behind the markers. He placed a ball on top with the dollar sign pointing straight up. Using his driver was the strongest part of his game. He could hit it long and straight. After three practice swings, Jackson lined up with the ball even with his left armpit.

"Now, for the money swing." A forty-dollar pot was riding on every hole. Jackson had to make each drive off the tee count. He pulled the club back. Reaching the apex of his backswing, Jackson clutched for the downswing. He pivoted his hips, adding extra power for distance, noting he'd lined up his swing perfectly for impact.

The club hit the ball.

A bright flash.

An explosion rocked the first tee, sending a beautiful plume of smoke into the air visible from the outdoor patio of the clubhouse bar. Pandemonium erupted among the staff and patrons, but a satisfied grin formed on the face of the Raven's tablemate as he watched the tendrils evaporate.

"Thank you, my friend," Robert said. "This was a treat."

"I thought you should get to see the results of your labor. Your work is getting more ingenious by the day." The Raven pulled out two twenty-dollar bills to pay for their drinks and laid them on the table. "Come, Robert. You will love the next project I have for you."

"Is it for that pesky Lexi Mills?" Robert's eyes narrowed, accenting his half-cocked grin. His protective nature was in full swing, a trait the Raven had appreciated since their boarding school days.

"She will have to wait. This is much bigger."

Remote
Lexi Mills Book 5

The Raven is back. And this time, he's not playing games.

The aide of a powerful U.S. Senator is killed in a mysterious car crash in a remote part of the Tahoe National Forest. Twelve hours later and fifty miles away, ATF Agent Lexi Mills is called away from her honeymoon to defuse a bomb in an active bank robbery where a sniper's bullet nearly takes her out. Clues found at both scenes point to one person—the Raven.

Lexi and her partner, Nathan Croft, are on the hunt for the notorious criminal mastermind who has eluded them for months. Their efforts uncover a sinister plot involving the Raven and a controversial high-tech weapons project. A conspiracy that reaches the highest echelons of power in the federal government.

With the president threatening to kill the experimental project, increasingly desperate attempts to defy him are resulting in a rising body count. Peeling back layers of deceit, Lexi realizes the unholy alliance has its sights set on something that could bring the country to its knees: their next target is the president.

Now the hunter has become the prey, and the Raven is closing in. One wrong step could be Lexi's last. Mills and Croft must risk everything to stop an assassination.

When lives are at stake, no matter how remote the chance of success, Lexi Mills refuses to back down.

Get your copy today at
severnriverbooks.com/series/lexi-mills

ABOUT BRIAN SHEA

Brian Shea has spent most of his adult life in service to his country and local community. He honorably served as an officer in the U.S. Navy. In his civilian life, he reached the rank of Detective and accrued over eleven years of law enforcement experience between Texas and Connecticut. Somewhere in the mix he spent five years as a fifth-grade school teacher. Brian's myriad of life experience is woven into the tapestry of each character's design. He resides in New England and is blessed with an amazing wife and three beautiful daughters.

Sign up for the reader list at
severnriverbooks.com/series/lexi-mills

ABOUT STACY LYNN MILLER

A late bloomer, Stacy Lynn Miller took up writing after retiring from the Air Force. Her twenty years of toting a gun and police badge, tinkering with computers, and sleuthing for clues as an investigator form the foundation of her Lexi Mills thriller series, as well as her Manhattan Sloane novels. She is visually impaired, a proud stroke survivor, mother of two, tech nerd, chocolate lover, and terrible golfer with a hole-in-one. When you can't find her writing, she'll be golfing or drinking wine (sometimes both) with friends and family in Northern California.

Sign up for the reader list at
severnriverbooks.com/series/lexi-mills

Printed in the United States
by Baker & Taylor Publisher Services